THE BOOK OF
LESTER

ANDREW THURBER

"Dreams can be shattered or restored with one choice."

All scripture quotations are taken from the New International Bible, Copyright © 1973, 1978, 1984, 2011 by Biblica.

This novel is a work of fiction. Names, characters, places and incidents are either the product of the author's imagination or are used fictitiously. It is the intent of the author and publisher that all events, locales, organizations, and persons portrayed herein be viewed as fictitious.

Cover by Chase Hancock

And I say, "THANK YOU!"

Who knew a story could be birthed out of a single wide
trailer on a model home lot, thank you Jesus for giving me
a story and the strength to finish it.

Thank you coffee, plus espresso for inspiring me and
giving me the extra focus and energy that I required on
those days I needed the boost.

Many thanks to my wife for being the first one to drudge
through the 125,000 word paragraph and all of the love and
support you have always given me.

Thank you to all of my editors, Christina Miller for having
the patience to teach me how to write and Domingo Cruz
for helping me polish it up and reading it over and over and
over again.

And, of coarse, a special thanks to my dad who was the
first one to introduce the world of books to me.

Prologue

Block the pain, Les, block the pain. Les's lungs burned, but he had to keep reaching farther and farther, faster and faster. His muscles strained as pain tore through them. He could see the wall. He had to have that record. He had to. This is why he sacrificed. His body ached, but his goal was in view: the far edge of the pool.

Water whooshed by his ear. He forced his head down despite the desperate urge to come up for air. His chest expanded to capacity. His throat felt as though a thousand bees had stung all at once. He stretched out his hand, grazing the wall with his fingertips. Flinging his head out of the water to gasp for air, he snatched a glimpse of the time clock.

Six thirty-three?

He smashed the top of his blaring alarm. Wincing, Les grabbed his right shoulder as he rolled onto his back. He stared at the ceiling, unmoving. The weekend of boozing had caught up to him. His brain felt as though someone had taken a blowtorch to it. This is why he dragged his thirty-year-old carcass to his mentally drowning job: to enjoy forty-eight hours of freedom. Back to the prison yard, back to the chains that encased him, loathing over a desk for four hundred and eighty minutes a day. Only to be paroled into society for one hundred and seventy-two thousand seconds. The start of an endless cycle of wasted time had begun.

I hate Mondays.

CHAPTER ONE

==

"Late again!" Lester John slammed the door of his 2002 Honda Civic. He grimaced as he clutched his right shoulder. "Tylenol, why do you mock me with your suckiness?"

Lester jogged toward the front doors. With every step his hangover blossomed like a flower in season.

He reached the Air Parts entrance doors just as Jerry Humberger arrived and grabbed the handle.

"Hey, dude, why can't you wait up?" Jerry puffed, catching his breath.

"How did you park so fast?" Lester eyed Jerry's curly, blond mess. "Don't you ever comb your hair?"

"Dude, if I say, 'Hey, wait up,' and you wave, then I think you're going to wait for me."

Lester pushed open the heavy steel door. "I'm late again and I don't want to get written up. I already have to listen to Miss Copeland's psycho-babble, so I'm kind of in a hurry."

"I just wanted to tell you, man . . ." Jerry paused as they passed through security. He eyed the guards as though he was carrying a concealed weapon. "Just wanted to tell you about this sick party I got planned for this weekend. It includes a hotel room, lots of tequila, and . . . that's all I got so far."

Lester rolled his eyes. "Sounds great."

"And I have a very important announcement to make." Jerry grabbed Lester's arm and made him wince. "Seriously, bro, this is the invention of the century. I'll explain it to you at lunch."

Again? Les turned toward his department.

"Wait, wait, let me paint a picture for you. Your electricity is turned off and you want to smoke some weed, but you can't find your weed because you can't turn the lights on. Unless . . . pause for dramatic effect . . . your weed glows in the dark. I have just created glow-in-the-dark weed. Pot smokers will never lose their weed in the dark again!" Jerry took a bow with his arms open and a huge smile on his face as the imaginary crowd roared.

"Great, Jer." Les didn't try to hide the sarcasm in his voice. "You have now made me nine minutes late because you had to tell me about your stupid invention that allows potheads to not pay their electric bill, but still get high. You have now just wasted nine minutes of my life and given me my fourth write-up this month. Thank you and good-bye."

Les flung open the auditing room door, and there stood Miss Copeland. A mountain of a woman, she brushed imaginary lint from her tailored suit as she blocked his way to his station. The streaks of gray in her pulled-back hair ran parallel to the pinstripes in her black pants, and she held her spine as straight as a West Point cadet.

Would she listen to another lame excuse for his lateness, or would he be annihilated?

"Mr. John, please come to my office after you punch in." Her refining-school politeness cut through Lester as always.

Entering her office was like walking into a hospital room: not a speck of dust anywhere. No pictures of family or friends. Even her screen saver was professional: "Air Parts, the Company You Can Count On."

"Have a seat, Lester," Miss Copeland said in her stern but polite voice. "I'm concerned about you. I can handle the occasional tardiness, but this is the fourth time this month, and we have two more weeks to go."

A prick of discomfort started to press against the back of his eyes. "I'm fine."

"You don't look fine. Honestly, you look pathetic. Your clothes are wrinkled. Your shirt is un-tucked, and if I am not mistaken, those where the same clothes you wore to work on Friday. Did you just pick them off your floor this morning?"

Lester cleared his throat. But no words would form.

"Let me ask you something," Miss Copeland leaned back in her chair. "Are you satisfied with your life?"

Whoa! Didn't expect that. Lester was all prepared for the corporate babble speech. *For every ten minutes an employees is late over the course of a year, he costs the company thousands of dollars. . . .* blah, blah, blah. But was he satisfied with his life? Sweat beaded on his forehead.

"What kind of question is that?" He stared back into her eyes. She was waiting for an answer.

"I don't know. Maybe." Lester shrugged.

"Maybe? What's satisfying about it?"

Miss Copeland was playing a mind war, and his mind was soaked in rum right now. *For the love, just write me up already!* "To be blunt, I don't think about my life. I do what I have to do."

Miss Copeland crossed her arms. She was not backing down. "Think about it now."

Lester scratched his forehead. "Don't I have to get back to work?"

"That can wait. Answer the question. Are you, Lester John, satisfied with your life?"

Lester tapped his bitten-off nails on the bottom of the chair that got more uncomfortable by the second. "Um . . . sometimes."

"Sometimes?" Miss Copeland squinted for a second then took a drink from her coffee mug. She leaned back in her chair with a look of complete emotional control, gazing into his eyes the way a mother would look at her child right before a spanking. "When you finish your work for the day, do you feel a sense of accomplishment?"

Lester did everything he could to prevent himself from being overtaken with hilarity. Of course he didn't have a sense of accomplishment. He counted resistors and screws for a living. The temperature in the room rose twenty degrees. The plain, white walls of the office seemed to move closer and closer. Any moment now they would engulf him in a sea of plaster. "Are you firing me?"

"No, but if you continue to show up late, you're going to leave me with no choice."

Lester exhaled as the room's temperature fell twenty degrees. His mother would kill him if he got fired from this job.

"I ran into your mother's friend, Nancy, last week in shipping. She said you used to train for the Olympics. Is this true?" Her tone was underlined with disbelief.

Les dropped his gaze to the neat stack of files on her desk. The manila folder on top had his name printed on it in black marker. He nodded.

"What happened?"

Lester smashed his eyelids together. He swore to himself that if he hadn't, his eyeballs would have toppled to the floor. "Don't want to talk about it."

An awkward silence hung in the air for a few brief moments. "I understand."

Miss Copeland reached into her top drawer and pulled out a pair of black plastic reading glasses. She slid them on, then she opened the folder. "I've been going through your files. You have a communication degree from Penn State, but you've been working as an auditor here at Air Parts for the past four years."

Miss Copeland drew her attention from the folder back to Lester as she peered over the rims of her glasses. "Why are you not using your degree?"

"You wouldn't understand."

"Try me." Miss Copeland took off her glasses, put the tip of the arm in the corner of her mouth, and let the glasses dangle.

Lester rubbed his hands over the armrest, clinching his jaw, his nostrils flaring. "Look, I know what you're trying to do. Just drop it. You say you understand, but you don't. You've never seen the world from my eyes. Have you ever loved something or someone so much that nothing else mattered as long as you could love that one thing?"

Miss Copeland visibly swallowed.

"Exactly. When it's ripped from your heart, nothing can replace it. Nothing. So you go on, living in the moment, living from one event to another. Hoping, wishing to revitalize a glimpse of your past life only to be miserably disappointed time and time again." Lester wiped his nose. "There is no pot of gold at the end of the rainbow, just a bunch of leprechauns flipping you the bird."

Lester gave her a smile filled with bitterness. "You will never understand."

Miss Copeland laid her glasses on her desk. "You have fifty-five hours of sick time. If you don't use them, you lose them." She pressed her forefinger against her lips. "Work until lunch today and then take the rest of the week off. Next Monday, I want you here in my office at seven o'clock sharp with answers to my questions. Take this week to do some self-reflection, find out if counting screws is something you want to continue doing. Find some meaning to your life. Find that pot of gold."

She must be kidding. "Okay. I will."

She pointed her finger. "Don't waste this week drinking and playing video games. Take it seriously. I also saw in your file that you were a member of Phi Kappa Sigma and listed winning the Madden Challenge under your career goals."

"I'll take it seriously."

Lester stood to leave. How could she blast winning the Madden Challenge? The winner gets 100K and the right to tell his boss to go to hell.

"One more thing." Miss Copeland detained him with a sharp glance. "Keep this between us. I don't want everyone knowing that I gave you a week off for being tardy."

CHAPTER TWO

===

Lester closed the office door and leaned against it. What had just happened? Did he just show up to work late and get rewarded a free vacation? What a bunch of psycho-crap Miss Copeland tried to pull with all those ridiculous questions. Lester couldn't wait to tell Jerry. Maybe they could start the weekend party early, say, tonight. This was going to be a great week!

On his way to his locker, Lester pulled out his Ipod. When he reached locker number fourteen, he stowed his backpack, sent a quick text to Jerry, and strolled to his audit station. It was seven thirty-four, and the first portion of his day had already ticked away.

Living for ten o'clock.

The first of the three fifteen-minute mandatory breaks began with everyone filing like cattle out to the courtyard. The smokers sat together in one corner, inhaling each other's second-hand smoke. The few who didn't smoke headed straight for the vending machines to inject their bodies with caffeine and sugar.

"My mid-morning caffeine and sugar fix never tasted better, now that I won't have to see this place for six more days." Lester sipped his soda.

Suzy Nelson grazed the back of Les's right arm on her way to the vending machine. "Have I ever told you how attracted I am to guys over six-four?"

Les's body went limp as he tilted his head to the sky. "Every day since you started working here."

"How tall are you again?" She wiggled her blonde eyebrows.

"For the one hundred and sixty-fourth time. Six

five."

"Hmm, imagine that. What are the odds of a girl like me and a guy like you?" She paused, turning her head slightly then looking over her shoulder, trying to be sexy. Suzy flounced directly in front of Lester, shaking her hips and upper body in an over-exasperated manner as her short blond hair and black highlights bounced with every step. She looked like one of those obnoxious sign holders trying to get you into their store. She wore her jeans way too tight and—her makeup? Les wanted to rub a wet washcloth all over her face just to see what was underneath.

Suzy turned her attention away from Les for a few seconds as she unwrapped her candy bar. "I saw you go into Miss Copeland's office this morning. Did you get written up again?"

Suzy's annoying little-girl voice grated against Lester's nerves.

"You were late again. What, is that, like, six or seven times this month?" Suzy moved closer to Les, chewing on her candy bar, small pieces of chocolate falling out the sides of her mouth. Les held his soda out in front of him to keep her from getting too close.

"Four, and I was just making sure Miss Copeland knew I was starting my vacation at lunch today." Les sipped his soda while keeping his eye on Suzy.

"I didn't see your name on the vacation board this morning."

Crushing the urge to dump his soda all over her head, he placed his can on the nearby table. "Why don't you—"

"Hey dude! And pretty lady."

Suzie quickly turned her head in delight.

Jerry. Thank God.

Suzy batted her eyes. "Do you really think I look pretty today?"

"Like a fox."

Suzy giggled. Lester clinched down on his molars as his jaw bone tightened.

"So Jerry, when are you going to take me out?"

"Sorry, I don't take girls out on dates. I gotta handle some business with my boy Les, but I'll catch you later."

"You're such a flake, Jerry. Insensitive, corn flake. 'Catch you later?'" Suzy mumbled. "You won't be able to catch me later. I'll probably already be caught." Her face reddened under all that makeup. She glanced around, but no one seemed to have overheard. Then she ran off, no doubt to eavesdrop on someone else's conversation.

"Les-meister, I got your text. What's up?"

"Don't tell anyone. It's a secret."

"It's sealed in the vault, dude." Jerry threw away an imaginary key.

"Instead of writing me up for being late again, which was your fault, Miss Copeland told me to take the week off to find answers to two questions. So I was thinking about this weekend—"

"Whoa, big fella. What are the questions?"

"Who cares?"

"Dude, what are the questions? Maybe I can help you answer them." Jerry raised his hand, palm up, emphasizing his most serious voice.

"You've never helped me answer a question before in your whole entire life. Back to the weekend party plans—"

Jerry tapped Les's nose. "As soon as you give me those questions."

"You're driving me nuts. 'Am I satisfied with my life?' and 'Do I find a sense of whatever from my job?' or something."

"Dude." Jerry's eyes grew wide. "Just what I had inspected."

"Inspected? Are you high?"

"No, man, this is serial stuff. The hunter has set the trap for the prey."

"Why can't I ever have a normal conversation with you?"

"Listen, man, you're going to do nothing but play video games and drink beer all week, then you're gonna par-tay with your boy this weekend and get totally trashed. You will be driving to work on Monday with a major hangover and no answer to those questions. You're screwed, man, totally screwed."

The smile Les mustered up must have looked cheesy. "Thank you, Dalai Lama, but I'll be fine."

"That's your problem, man. You don't ever listen with your eyes."

He had to be high. "On that note, I'll see you at halftime."

"At the Mystery Machine?"

"Mystery Machine at noon." Lester turned back toward his department.

"Hey, Suz, you need a ride home tonight?" Jerry's voice cut through the buzz of the crowd.

"Did I ever tell you how much I like guys with curly blond hair?"

Les shook his head. That guy will never learn.

###

Ten eighteen.

Lester joined the herd of employees trudging back into the auditing room. Miss Copeland stood at the door, her eyes speaking her silent mantra to everyone coming in late from break: *You have fifteen minutes for break. That is more than enough time to do everything you need to do.*

At his station, Lester logged in to his computer and scanned the list of orders he needed to pull. Only an hour and forty minutes to go before Les-meister's week of fun begins.

This is going to be a great week. He zoned out into his computer screen and Ipod music.

A few strokes of the keyboard and, voila, the last order of the week. It was eleven forty-five, too late to start on a new order but too early to clock out. He pretended to do something important on the screen.

The last fifteen minutes dragged on and on while Les willed the little clock at the corner of the computer screen to go faster. When someone tapped his shoulder, he jolted as if he had been electrocuted. He spun to the right. "Miss Copeland."

"Come with me, Lester."

He felt as if he was in high school again, taking the long walk to the principal's office. Nervousness wheezed inside of him, just like the time he and Jerry had poured out all the water bottles in the science lab hamster cages and replaced them with vodka. It was well worth the three-day expelling to watch those hamsters try to run on their little metal wheels, crashing their faces into the sides of the wheel and flipping over onto their backs. It was classic.

Her silence made his anxiety worse. Had she

changed her mind? Would she make him work the rest of the day, or worse, the rest of the week?

"Have a seat, Lester. I saw you come in late from break."

I knew it! That Jerry always makes me late. Why didn't I tell him to shut up and walk away? I swear, if–

"How can you guarantee me that you are going to take my questions seriously?" Without missing a beat, she continued. "How will I know you're not going to waste this week in a drunken stupor, zoning out in video-game land, thinking of some uninspiring answer to my questions on your way to work on Monday?"

What, is this lady in my head? I bet she has electronic bugs in the courtyard.

Miss Copeland opened her top middle drawer and pulled out a small, brown leather book that read "Gideon" on the front.

Lester's back stiffened. Was she going to make him do a book report? Are there CliffsNotes for this "Gideon" book?

"Don't get so nervous. I'm not going to make you read the whole thing. I do want you to promise me that you will pick it up and read it a couple of times during the week. Whenever it strikes you, open the book to any page and start reading."

This couldn't get weirder. Pick up this little book, open it to any page and start reading it in the middle of the story—it sounded like something Jerry would do.

"Someone gave me this book when I was about your age. It helped me put things into perspective."

"How will you know if I read it?"

"I'll know by the answers to the questions I gave you." Miss Copeland held out the book.

Lester grasped the book's corner between his thumb and forefinger. The sooner this strange conversation was over, the better. "Is that it?"

"You're free to go, and remember, I'll know by your answers."

Lester turned to leave, then stopped in the doorway. "What if I read this whole book and I still can't answer the questions?"

She shot him an I've-been-through-this-before smile. "As I said, I will know by your answers."

This office was no place to waste a single second of his week off. "See you Monday."

Les strode to his locker, not bothering to hide the annoyance he knew must show on his face. He grabbed his backpack and tossed the book and IPod inside.

"Lousy supervisor." Jerry was right—it's a trap.

But how could Jerry be right? This vacation was already starting off weird. First, he has to answer questions, now he has to read a book. What was this, anyway, high school? Plus Jerry had been right so far.

Maybe Jerry was right about other things too. What about listening through the eyes? Les shook his head. The guy got lucky. Les glanced at his watch: twelve-twelve. So much for meeting Jerry at noon.

Les hustled through the parking lot toward his Civic, glancing up at the sky. Perfect Pennsylvania weather. Sixty-five degrees with a light breeze. What a great day to be out on the lake with a buddy, a fishing pole in hand, the quiet of the water, and enough beer to sink a small ocean liner. In the last row, he spotted Jerry's van, Rastafarian music blaring, parked on the grass right behind the giant "Air Parts" sign. Two big skid marks defaced the grass behind Jerry's back wheels. Les slid the van's side door

18

open.

"Dude! When the music is a play-en, go a-way-en!"

"Suzy?" Les raised his brows. "Jerry, you told me to meet you here at halftime."

"That, my friend, was twelve minutes ago."

"What are you guys doing?" Les poked his head in the van door.

"Just chilling, man, bumping some beats, munching on a homemade sandwich Suzy made."

"Jerry said he'd give me a ride home if I would give him part of my sandwich, so we decided to come out here and hang. Why don't you join us, Les?"

One quick look from Jerry was all it took. Fine, he could have her. "I gotta get going. I have a lot to do today. I'm off to start my vacation!"

"Later, dude. I'll call you tomorrow." The side door to the Volkswagen Euro van slammed shut.

Talk about uncomfortable. Why was Jerry hooking up with Suzy? Now Les wouldn't see him all week because he'll be too busy mooching off Suzy, trading rides home for who-knows-what. Then he'll turn up again in a couple of weeks, after Suzy realizes what a moocher he is. Just like the previous hundred times.

I need more friends.

CHAPTER THREE

==

Was he satisfied with his life? A sense of loneliness draped over Les like a blanket of depression thrown unexpectedly on his head. His thoughts drifted as he sat in his parked car. He brushed his fingers over the passenger seat, where an old cigarette burn was all that was left of Pam. Her last words to him still echoed in his mind.

All you care about is hanging out with your loser friends, playing video games, and seeing who can drink the most beer. I need a man with goals, and I don't mean the goal of someday being the judge of a wet t-shirt contest. I want to have a family. I want a future. I need more than a radio jock who makes nineteen grand a year. I deserve better. Thanks for wasting six years of my life, jerk.

Had he improved himself at all? Pam dumped him because of his lack of goals and "going nowhere-ness," as she used to say. Had anything changed?

She was finally getting over feeling guilty about the accident. She put up with so much, and it was just a matter of time. She was right then, and she's right now. He needed to change, but what did he need to change into?

He shook his head and ran his left hand down his face as he came back to reality. Before the inevitable depression could set in, he started his car and sped away from the factory.

"I hate that place."

Les pulled into the local video store with one mission: two good movies and a video game that will keep him busy all week. "I accept!" Les yanked the keys out of the ignition and twirled them around and around on his index finger as if he were a gun slinger. As he reached the video store door, he gracefully turned to shoot his imaginary foe that turned on his car alarm.

Inside the store, Les sifted through the movies until he found a new release he hadn't seen. He picked it up and turned it over to read the back, then he caught a glimpse of movement from the corner of his eye.

"That's a good movie. You should get it."

Les turned in the direction of the scintillating voice. As he looked into her eyes, he was lost in a sea of emerald. A swarm of butterflies released into his stomach. His pulse accelerated at an alarming rate, and his gaze fixed on her. Her hair was straight black and hung around her shoulders as loose strands dangled in her face, and her tanned skin— flawless. Her beauty mesmerized him into some kind of trance as everything else faded to black.

Wait a minute. Her lips are moving. She's talking to me! Say something, Les! Say something!

"Ah, thanks."

"It's funny, you look similar to one of the actors. You have the same chin dimple, but don't thank me yet. Wait until you watch it."

"Then I guess I'll retract that thanks until another time, or until we meet again." *Where did that come from? That was actually kind of James Bond-ish.*

"How about until we meet again?" The goddess extended her hand.

Her hand fit perfectly into his. Her perfume made his stomach do a triple somersault.

"My name is Lila."

"And I'm . . ." *brain freeze* . . . "Uh, John."

"Are you sure?"

I am an idiot. "Lester John. John is my last name. I have two first names. I mean John is my real last name,

21

but—" He took a deep breath. "Never mind. Just call me Les." Lester promptly flung his left hand up as though surrendering to some invisible evil cupid who was purposely destroying his conversation.

"I hope you enjoy the movie."

She was so hot, so gorgeous, that she made the whole world dissolve. He scrambled in his mind for a way to tell her, for something awesome to say. He had to say something, anything, before she walked out of his life forever.

"It was nice . . . it was . . . " Lila's perfect smile calmed his nerves. "It was very nice meeting you, Lila. Do you hang out around here?"

"My girlfriends and I go to happy hour over at Eazy Eddie's on Wednesdays. You should stop in some time and let me know what you thought of the movie."

Les would stop by Africa if that's where she hung out. "Yeah, I just might do that."

She could be an Arabian princess. As she walked away, her image burned into his memory, from her big plush lips to the beauty mark perfectly placed next to them. Everything about her was perfect.

Needing to act cool, Les loitered by the movies until Lila checked out. When she had left, he sprinted to the window and watched her get into a black Mercedes SUV.

"Beautiful and rich. What a combo."

Ten minutes later, Les pulled up to the gated community. He pressed a few numbers on the security keypad, and the gate inched its way open. Les stopped in his parking spot, then eased out of the Civic with his backpack and video store bag. With every step toward his condo, he replayed the moments with Lila. He imagined the things he should have said and her reactions if he would have said them. He drew a deep breath. Anxiety hit him like a punch in his chest.

What's wrong with me?

Inside the condo, Les threw his bags on the table and headed for the fridge. He opened it and grabbed a can of his favorite beer. Just the sound of opening it got him excited.

"That's good, really good. One down, seventy-one more to go."

Three cases of beer in a week? Les chuckled and swigged his beer. He flopped onto the couch, propped up his feet, and turned on ESPN. "Now this is the life. If I could only find a way to do this for fifty-one more weeks."

Six beers later, the theme music from *Rocky* blasted him out of a sound sleep. Les took a quick look at the caller ID but didn't recognize the number. "Yeah, hello."

"Were you sleeping?"

"Who is this?" Les wiped drool from his chin.

"This is Miss Copeland. It sounds like I just woke you up from a nap."

Fully awake now, Les scrambled for an answer. "No, I was out of breath from working out. It just sounded like I was yawning."

"So were you productive with the rest of your day?"

What was she, his mother? "Yeah, I got a lot done around the house today. Even did a little shopping."

"That's good to hear. I just wanted to remind you to be at my office at seven o'clock sharp on Monday morning."

"Yes, ma'am, I'll be there."

"Don't waste this opportunity to do some self-reflection."

Les punched the "end" button and threw his phone against the couch cushion. "What's wrong with that woman? Is she going to call me every day and make sure I am self-reflecting?"

This was a disaster. If he stopped answering his phone, she might just fire him, assuming he was messing around. She should have told him all the rules attached to this vacation so he could have declined it.

He stumbled to the fridge and grabbed another beer, then glanced at the kitchen clock. Pinching the bridge of his nose, he tried to focus on the little green numbers. Five fifteen. Time to order pizza. He called Jerry's number. It rang a couple of times, then the voice mail picked up. "You called me, dude. You know what to do."

"Hey, I'm going to order pizza. Do you want in on it? Call me before six, or you're on your own."

Les grabbed his game, "Fable," from the table and inserted it into his Xbox 360. He quickly became lost in a make-believe world called Albion. He became an orphan boy who realizes his dream of becoming a hero by drawing power from both good and evil deeds.

The *Rocky* song blared again, bringing Les out of his current state of mind. He didn't recognize the number but answered the phone anyway.

A woman's high-pitched, overly-excited voice answered. "Hi, my name is Cheryl. I'm looking for a guy named Jerry. We met a couple of weeks ago at Planet Zone, and he gave me this number."

"I'll let him know you called."

"If he doesn't remember me, tell him I'm the girl with the gorgeous brown eyes. His brown-eyed girl, you know, like the song."

"Yeah, I get it." Les continued playing his game.

"What's your name?"

"Hero, and I'm right in the middle of something."

"Hero?"

Les hung up the phone and turned his full attention back to the world of Albion. When he heard the rumble of his stomach, he looked down at his watch.

Nine twenty-four. Time flies when you're a hero.

CHAPTER FOUR

==

"Man, I got a headache." Les rolled over to check his alarm clock. Twelve twenty-eight. "I don't even remember going to sleep last night."

Fully clothed in yesterday's outfit minus the shoes, he dragged himself into the bathroom. "I feel awful."

Les grabbed a towel from the linen closet and draped it over his shoulder, then he turned on the water, letting it run until steam filled the bathroom. He peeled off his day-old clothes and fell into the shower. The hot water felt good on his hangover as he soaped up.

The night seemed such a blur. How many beers did he have? Les rinsed then stepped out of the shower.

After drying off, he put on a pair of old sweat pants and his college fraternity intramural football t-shirt. In the living room, he found an open pizza box with two leftover pieces. A half-eaten piece lay on his coffee table with all the cheese scraped off. Empty beer cans sat all over the floor, and when he reached the kitchen, he found a half can of beer spilled over on the counter, dripping on the floor tile.

He turned his back on the kitchen mess and slogged to his television. The video game was on pause, so he shut it off. Les stooped to pick up the empty beer cans, then he grabbed the pizza box and carried it to the kitchen.

He made a quick count of the beer cans. Nine . . . ten and a half. His head still aching, he spied the shot glass and bottle of tequila next to the sink. Ten and a half beers and a mystery number of shots. That explains why he didn't remember going to bed. Not a bad start to the week.

The odors of stale beer and leftover pizza

overpowered the room. Les grabbed the air freshener from underneath the sink. He sprayed the air, masking the stench.

He dumped the empty cans, then crammed the half-eaten slice of pizza into his mouth as he grabbed his phone. One missed call. He hit the voicemail button.

"Dude, you suck. Wake your butt out of bed, man. I'm guessing you're not answering your phone because you're either mad at me for not chipping in for pizza, or you're just passed out and can't hear your phone. I'm calling to try and wake you up from sleeping in. Catch you later, bum."

Jerry. What a clown. Les hit the delete button. An acute agony spread across the top of his head as if his hangover was summoning a headache monster to crawl about his skull, picking at his brain like a guitar string. He was drawn to the kitchen like a cripple to his crutch. Two quick shots of tequila burned their way down his throat and into his belly. Fazed for a moment, he watched the empty shot glass. The taste of hot sour plums still tingled his taste buds.

Empty and sour.
That about sums up the past ten years of my life.

His hand moved involuntarily toward the bottle. Numbness spread across the spots of torment in his mind. When the shot glass was filled, he spilled a few drops on the counter. He hit it, and in one swoop, the liquor disappeared. The anguish deadened, leaving behind a slight discomfort. He poured and repeated the process one more time. He gazed again at the empty shot glass.
Empty and sour.

27

"Means I'll be good for an hour."

Les seized the video store bag, breaking into song.

"Oh sweet Lila. Sweet Lila. I wish that when you gave me your hand, I would have been your man. Pulling you close to me. Then you would see. Into my eyes to be, a sweet kiss, a sweet kiss of bliss." Les's voice cracked as he took "bliss" to the next octave.

She probably would have bolted out of the video store, crashing head first into the window just to escape. Les shuffled to the kitchen and over to the fridge. He peered into the refrigerator. "Let's see, I could have a piece of cheese for lunch, or a beer to chase away the tequila."

This "doing nothing" stuff was great. He inserted Lila's movie into the DVD player. He nestled down on his couch, armed with a couple of beers and a few slices of cheese.

"I hope this isn't a piece of crap." He hit the "play" button.

Two hours and fifteen minutes later, the credits rolled, followed by sappy-sounding music. "What a waste of two hours. That was totally a chick flick, unrealistic and crappy."

But the dilemma was that Lila knew it was a chick flick, and Les, as a single guy, liked nothing more than comedies with no plot and movies in which everyone gets shot or blown up.

Maybe Lila was testing him, as Jerry said, the hunter setting a trap for the prey. If he was honest and told Lila how he felt about this movie, she'd think he was insensitive and not boyfriend material. On the other hand, if he told her that it moved him to the point of tears, she'd think he's too sensitive, not strong enough to protect her, and also not boyfriend material.

Les stood and paced the living room. He needed a game plan. He used to lie to Pam all the time about her weight and how she looked pretty without makeup. Maybe he could lie his way through this one too. Then again, what if Lila was prepared for him to lie and hated the movie and its terrible acting herself?

He turned on his Xbox and tried to escape his thoughts of Lila and his mind-blowing dilemma.

Two hours later, the *Rocky* song cut through his zone. Les picked up the phone and checked the caller ID. "Jerry."

"What up, broth-a from anoth-a moth-a?" Jerry's voice took on a too-casual tone. "Dude, you are not going to believe this. I gave Suzy a ride home from work yesterday, then one thing led to another, and she's making me pancakes for breakfast. So now things are really awkward. She wanted my cell number and I gave her yours so just wanted to give you a heads up."

"What's wrong with you? Why would you sleep with Suzy?"

"Dude, I never said I slept with her. I just said she made me pancakes in the morning." Jerry's surfer-dude laugh drifted through the phone. "Whoa, man, you totally took me out of context. When I dropped her off, I hinted that it would be nice to have some breakfast waiting when I picked her up in the morning. So this morning she waved me in and made me some pancakes, and man, were they good."

Les tapped his phone against his forehead. "What's the problem?"

"Now Suzy thinks I am her little ride buddy. That's just too much commitment for me, man."

"So you gave her my phone number so she can call

me for rides? Thanks, Jer." The frustration in Les's tone didn't compare to the anger that drove him to change the subject. "Where are you? Can you come over for a while?"

"I'm busy right now, driving around looking for trouble. How about eight?"

Anything to get off the phone. "Fine."

Les dropped the phone. Why did he feel so lonely? This week was supposed to be so much fun, but he was bored out of his mind, and it was only Tuesday.

Back to the world of Albion.

At eleven thirty-four, Les's phone rang. Groggy and half passed out on the couch with Xbox controller in hand, he checked the ID. Jerry.

Les punched the "ignore" button. One minute later, his phone rang again, and a minute after that. Jerry was persistent enough to keep this up all night, so Les answered. "What?"

"Dude, I'm so sorry I didn't call you or show up or whatever, but I met these two smoking-hot chicks in the skate shop, and we ended up going out for drinks, and now I'm calling you."

"Thanks for the invite, jerk." At his boiling point, Les raised his voice. "You know what? You can be a real selfish you-know-what sometimes. Always thinking about yourself. Giving out my phone number so I have to deal with all your psycho-chicks. I've had enough. Don't ever give my number to another girl, you hear me?"

Les's hand shook, and his whole body trembled with his anger.

"Dude, I'm sorry. I thought you were cool with it."

"Well, I'm not! I'm done with this conversation, and I'm done with you!"

As Les hung up the phone, the adrenaline rushed

through his veins. His head throbbed. What was going on? First his job, now his best friend. What next?

Les rubbed his eyes then pried them open to stare at the ceiling fan that was making an annoying clicking sound. A sharp pain split through his head. The throbbing that had started last night continued this morning as if someone had hit him over the head with a metal chair.

He turned over to look at his alarm clock. One twelve p.m. Wow, he had slept a long time. He tried to roll out of bed, but the knife-like vexation stopped him. Maybe he had been hit by a chair. He felt for bumps on his head but found none.

His second attempt to get out of bed was a success but agonizing. Dehydrated from all the alcohol, he shuffled his way to the kitchen. He grabbed a glass from the cabinet, turned on the water, and filled the glass to the brim. He drank the water then filled the glass again and reached for a handful of Tylenol. "These stupid things never work." The pills went down quick and easy. He passed by the half-empty bottle of tequila. He then reversed his tracks and snagged the bottle along with the shot glass.

Les then sat at the small two-person table with his head completely leaned back. Taking deep breaths through his nose and exhaling out his mouth, he set his head forward between both his hands, rubbing his temples. The tall, skinny bottle tinted in amber taunted him. He spun the bottle's cap then flung it off. It bounced across the table. He grabbed the neck of the bottle and took a swig. His head jerked to the side as his body shuddered.

"What am I doing to myself?" He stared at the

bottle of alcohol that warmed his hand. The liquid swished back and forth in a hypnotic manner as the crown of his head pulsated.

I am on a slippery slope to suicide, eroding my insides.

Bitterness overwhelmed him as the image appeared of his dad storming out the front door with a suitcase in hand. It was forever engraved in his memory. As a fourteen-year-old, he'd sobbed in his mother's arms. He could still hear the slam of that old wooden door.

What was happening to him? Why these random thoughts of his parents? He set the tequila on the table as it seemed to stir the hangover monster. He could almost see the pain as it immediately increased as he set the bottle on the table. Jagged thorns raked through the inner lobes of his brain. He reached for the alcohol, but instead of grasping it, he knocked it backward.

Everything moved in slow motion as the bottle wobbled then fell and rolled across the table. Then it crashed onto the tile floor and broke into a thousand pieces.

Les collapsed to the floor and brushed shards of glass away from a puddle so he could suck up some of the liquor. A piece of glass cut into his hand. Blood dripped into the wreckage. The shock from the cut and the vision of blood made him pull back and view himself in the distorted mirror made from tequila and glass.

What had he become? A raging animal with no self-control or discipline. What happened to the once-fine-tuned world-class athlete? His floor now resembled his life: broken and scattered in a hundred different directions.

Blood ran down his wrist as he gazed at a larger

piece of broken glass. One quick slash of his wrist would be easier to suffer through than the turmoil he was dealing with in his thoughts right now. A single tear formed at the corner of his eye. He had never thought of suicide before, but at this moment it seemed like the better of the two options. His hand dragged across the floor, then he picked up a large shard of glass. Another tear formed in the corner of his eye and dripped onto his shirt.

The doorbell rang.

The sudden sound jolted him out of his seated position and off the floor.

It rang again. Les scrambled to his feet, disoriented. He wiped his eyes and opened the front door.

"Hello. Are you Charlie?" A middle-aged man with a Roto-Rooter jumpsuit stood at the door.

"You have the wrong unit."

"Hmm." Mr. Roto-Rooter checked his clipboard and flipped a few pages. "Is this unit seven?"

"No, this is unit fourteen."

"Sorry for disturbing you, sir."

Les closed the door, stepped into the kitchen, and ran cold water over his sliced hand and face. He splashed his face several times then dabbed it with paper towels. His left eye began to twitch. He rubbed both of his eyes, and when he opened them, his attention was drawn to his book bag lying on the table. He stepped over the mess and opened the bag. Les pulled out Miss Copeland's little brown book. How could this book help him?

As he flipped it open, Miss Copeland's words came back to him. *I will know by your answers.*

Lester opened the book to the table of contents. Skimming the titles, he noticed they were mostly men's names. One particular name jumped out: John. His last name.

Did one of his ancestors write this chapter? Les opened the book to the John section and turned to chapter fourteen—his age when his dad left. As he touched the book, he sensed a strange connection between his memories and the book. Les read, "Do not let your hearts be troubled. Trust in God; trust also in me."

God? Trust God? His thoughts of God were barren. His god abandoned him when he was fourteen.

Les continued to read, "Jesus answered, 'I am the way and the truth and the life. No one comes to the Father except through me.'"

Who is Jesus? "I know him as a cuss word."

Les read on. "'I tell you the truth, anyone who has faith in me will do what I have been doing. He will do even greater things than these, because I am going to the Father. And I will do whatever you ask in my name, so that the Son may bring glory to the Father. You may ask me for anything in my name, and I will do it.'"

Les dropped the small book onto the table and closed his eyes. "'You may ask me for anything in my name, and I will do it.'"

Is this Jesus some kind of a genie? Les rubbed his head. He could think much better if he didn't have this tormenting headache. He pressed his palms on each side of his head, hoping the pressure would make the pounding stop. The pain worsened as though someone was lacerating the inside of his skull with a dull knife.

Les took a deep breath. "Jesus, if you are some kind of genie with power, take my headache away."

Les drew in another breath and exhaled. With his head down, he forced open his eyes and pried his hands from his head. He looked to the right then to the left. His headache was gone.

He sat back in the chair, running his left hand through his hair. What just happened? He jumped up, knocking back his chair onto the floor. Still no headache.

Does this Jesus have genie-like powers? Does anyone else know about this Jesus-genie? Is this why Miss Copeland wanted him to read this magic book—to find out about this genie named Jesus who works miracles with his father?

Les lost his father when he was fourteen. Maybe Jesus lost his father too. *What have I stumbled upon? Could this be magic or maybe just a freakish coincidence of the Tylenol kicking in at that very moment? Could this Jesus actually have the power to grant wishes?*

Jesus did just grant Les's headache request. But why does Jesus talk so much about his father? If you have seen the son, you have seen the father? Les didn't want to be anything like his father.

He flipped to the second and third pages of the book and scanned them. "Holy Bible, the New Testament."

So this is a Bible. His mother had brought one home one time after hanging out with a girlfriend she attended church with. She had never asked Les to read it, and he was never curious. Les could remember only a handful of times when he had ever stepped foot in a church. After the divorce, his mom occasionally went to a Saturday night church service with her girlfriend. She'd mentioned a couple years later that God helped her deal with the divorce and move on with her life. Les felt as though she was using God and church as a crutch to make herself feel better, but never did he think the Bible was a book of magic.

Does she know what kind of power this book has in it? He had to find out more about what this genie could do.

35

He opened the book again and started reading from the beginning of the John section.

    Two hours later, Lester finished the last word in John and closed the book. He sat in silence, trying to comprehend the words he'd just read. "Jesus was crucified even though he did so many good things. Maybe it's not a good thing to have genie power."

CHAPTER FIVE

==

The *Rocky* song cut through the air of Les's condo, giving him a little startle. Les picked up the phone. Jerry. He hesitated then answered.

"Hey, man, just wanted to give you a call and apologize for acting like a pothead yesterday." Jerry's voice sounded surprisingly quiet and humble.

"I'm sorry too. I over-reacted yesterday. I wasn't having the best of days, and I lashed out at you."

"Dude, it's totally cool. I want to make it up to you and take you out tonight. I'm on my way."

Jerry showed up as Les got out of the shower.

"Honey, I'm home."

"I'll be out in a second."

"Take your time, Leslie."

Jerry and his not-funny joke. Just because Les took more than ten minutes in the bathroom to get ready, Jerry didn't have to insult him. So he wanted to shave and put gel in his hair. Nothing wrong with that. Jerry could use a few grooming tips himself.

"Hey, Leslie, make sure you smell good, because your condo smells like an armpit."

Jerry always knew how to get under Les's skin. "Maybe you should put on some cologne so everyone who walks by doesn't get high."

Jerry's infectious laugh pealed through the apartment. Les couldn't help smiling as he checked himself out to make sure he was perfectly groomed. Stylish jeans with holes in them, white button-down, short-sleeved shirt, Steve Madden loafers, clean-shaven face with short sideburns and gelled, spiky brown hair.

Jerry was lounging sideways on the love seat with his legs dangling over the arm. "You clean up pretty nice there, Cinderella. I didn't know we were going to the prom."

Les buttoned the second-to-last button on his shirt. "Hey, I have felt like a bum the last couple of days, cooped up in this place. It feels good to clean up and get out."

"Where do you want to go?"

"It's Wednesday right. Ever heard of a place called Eazy Eddie's?"

"Yeah, I've gone there a couple of times, but the crowd is kind of snooty. A lot of the corporate stiffs hang out in there after work, complaining about their portfolios." Jerry's voice held no excitement.

Les grabbed his keys and cell phone from the table. "Good, because that's where we're going."

"Why there?" Now Jerry's voice turned whiny.

"Because you blew me off yesterday, so I get to pick." Les turned and pointed at his best friend.

Jerry leaped up from the couch with both hands raised. "You're punishing me?"

"Shut up, Jer. It's going to be fun: you, me, some hot chick I met a couple of days ago, and her friends." The expression on Jerry's face went from zero to sixty in under a second.

"Why didn't you say that in the first place?" Jerry tried to tap dance on the living room carpet.

Les smiled. "Calm down, stop doing your happy dance, and let's go."

Fifteen minutes later, the smell of greasy fried food in Eazy Eddie's reminded Les that he hadn't eaten very well the last couple of days. "Let's sit in the bar section so we don't have to wait."

Jerry ordered a pitcher of draft beer for the two of them, then they ordered twenty-five hot wings and a basket of fries to split.

"This feels good." Les sipped his beer.

"What feels good?" Jerry scrunched his eyebrows.

"You, me, drinking some beers, scoping for chicks."

"Are you getting all sentimental on me, Leslie? Would you like a hug?" Jerry spread his arms wide and pouted his lips, making kissing sounds.

"Shut up, jerk." Les slapped Jerry's arms away. "I was trying to say that it's been a while since we've been able to do this. Since I bought the condo and we live separate, we don't hang as much, that's all."

Jerry took a packet of Splenda out of the plastic holder and placed it on the table like you would a paper football. "Make a field goal."

Les, unenthusiastic, held his hands together and formed a goal.

"If I make this, I get first pick of the girls." Jerry flicked the packet before Les could reply. The yellow packet swirled through Les's fingers and smacked against his chest.

"Yes! Score. So when are these hot chicks of yours supposed to show up?" Jerry rubbed his hands together.

Les picked the yellow packet off of his lap and nonchalantly threw it at Jerry. "I don't know for sure that they'll be here. I met this girl in the video store, and she said that she and her friends come here sometimes on Wednesdays."

A look of horror slid across Jerry's face as though he'd just seen someone get hit by a car. He flicked aside the packet. "That's it? No phone number, no e-mail address? Just 'video-store girl' and 'sometimes on Wednesdays?'"

Arrogance spread across his face. "You have a lot to learn, my young panda-dung."

Les clinched his fist and banged it against the table. "Do you deliberately say things wrong to get under my skin? I don't ever remember you having a relationship that lasted more than thirty seconds, and I am not the one who uses someone else's phone number as a screening process. Also, for your information, it's padawan, not panda-dung."

Jerry took a swig of beer with a smirk of mischief. "Chill out, dude. We can call you the Jedi master of women if you want. I didn't know it meant so much to you, O king of the Star Wars geeks." He leaned back in his chair with a glance of triumph.

Les paused for a moment to gather his thoughts and to take a bite of a chicken wing. "Okay, I'm sorry. It's just that I like this girl, and I want her to show up."

"Have another beer and wing and cross your fingers. I'm just saying, dude, if you don't get the digits, it's hard to track them down." Jerry dipped a wing into some blue cheese. "If not, I can call the two ravishing foxes from the skater shop."

"Sounds like a plan." Les picked up another wing and turned it in his hand, searching his mind for a way to ask the question burning in his heart. He tossed the wing onto his plate. "Have you ever read the Holy Bible?"

"Twice."

Les popped his head back, stunned. "Why haven't you ever mentioned it?"

"Didn't think you cared." Jerry shrugged his shoulder.

Astonishment seared through Les's intelligence. How could his best friend keep this insight about a book of obvious divine secrets from him? "Have you ever read the section of John where it talks about God having a son named Jesus who basically has genie powers?"

Jerry sneered loudly with chicken still in his mouth and made Les feel senseless. "Genie powers? Where did you get that?"

"Bible John." What was he laughing at, anyway? Les wasn't brainless. This wasn't a figment of his imagination. He felt more alive today reading John then he had in months. It's not wrong to want to believe in something outside of your own reality. It was his right to believe whatever he wanted. "It also says that we can have these same powers as Jesus, even greater. It's kind of like Star Wars and the force—the more you believe, the greater your power will be."

Les sat on the edge of his chair. Did Jerry understand his new passion regarding this subject?

Jerry leaned in closer and narrowed his eyes. "Dude, you do know that Star Wars is not real, and the Bible has never been proven to be more than a collection of old stories, don't you? You've been cooped up in that condo of yours too long."

Les wiped his mouth with a napkin then waved it in front of Jerry to pull his attention from one of the waitresses. "Let's do a hypothetical."

"I hate hypotheticals." Jerry's face showed a strong lack of empathy.

"You believe God is real and Jesus is his son. What if this Jesus guy actually did the things he said he did and is everything he claims to be? What if the Bible has magical secrets to empower us to do great things if we believe in Jesus' power?"

"And what if Chewbacca and Yoda came walking through that door? All you're giving me is a bunch of what-ifs and hypothetical ideas."

Les rested his elbows on the high-top table so he could use his hand to help him illustrate his next point. "Do you remember when Luke's X-Wing sinks and Yoda raises it from the murky water? Luke doesn't believe it, and Yoda says, 'That is why you fail.' Luke tried to use the Force to raise the X-Wing, but he couldn't because he lacked faith in the Force. In the Bible John, Jesus repeatedly talks about believing in him and that he has been sent by the father and if we have faith as small as a mustard seed, we can move mountains, just like Yoda when he moved the X-wing."

Jerry covered his face with his hands and bent backward, making babbling sounds. He gradually turned his hands out the same way you would play peek-a-boo. "Dude, I'm supposed to be the weird and off-beat one. Now you just ran by me with your Star Wars Bible theory."

Les leaned back in his chair, determined not to let Jerry's mocking faze him. "It sounds weird, but for some reason it makes sense to me in that way. This morning, I woke up with a terrible hangover and one of the worst headaches I ever had. I was sitting at my kitchen table and asked this Jesus with genie-like power to take the pain away. Dude, I kid you not. Seconds later, I didn't have a hangover or a headache any more."

"You're tripping me out, bro. Can we talk about something else?"

Les, fired up, clasped his hands together and tilted forward. "Haven't you ever wanted to believe that there is another force out there, greater than ourselves, a source of power that can turn ordinary men into heroes? What if there really is a force-like power that can be ours for the taking if we believe in it?"

Jerry reclined, resting his hands behind his head.

Les could tell he was bothered by their conversation as a look of pity saddled onto his face.

"And what if you get bit by a spider and get spider powers? This is a ridiculous conversation. Can we drop it?"

"Fine." As he surveyed the door, Les lifted his mug of beer and took a long drink. Why hadn't Lila shown up?

"It looks like neither your ladies nor Chewbacca are showing up tonight." Jerry finished his beer. "You want to get going?"

They meandered to Jerry's van. Inside, he turned on some alternative music. Les watched the houses and the people pass by. Why was Jerry being so mean? Were they finally growing apart? Was this the end of their friendship? As the van rolled up to the gate, Jerry turned down the volume. "I don't feel too well after all those wings. I think I'll go home and crash. Tomorrow's a work day."

Lester jumped out of the van and closed the door behind him. He peered through the rolled-down window. "We'll talk tomorrow. Thanks for dinner."

"Hey brah, do yourself a favor. Stop reading the Bible." Jerry put the van in gear and drove off with Lester still standing on the pavement.

Les hadn't felt this confused since the day Dad left. Had Les stumbled upon something that few people knew about, or was he going crazy? How could Jerry say he read Bible John yet know nothing about Jesus and his genie-like power?

The only thing Les knew for sure was that he'd had a headache today, and now it was gone.

As Jerry drove out through the gate, the twist of

guilt in his gut made him regret having lied to his long-time friend. What was happening to Les? Why does he think the Bible can give him magical powers? Is he losing his mind, being cooped up the last couple of days?

I should hang out with him more. I miss that.

Within minutes, Jerry pulled into parking spot 34A. He hopped out of the van and ambled to his door. He labored to open it, nudging it with his shoulder and finally getting it open enough to slip his body through.

"Probably should do laundry." He picked up the dirty clothes that were behind the door and placed them on the kitchen counter. From across the room, he noticed a rip in the tin foil that was plastered on his windows. Of all the things he didn't need, sun penetrating his man-palace was at the top of the list.

Jerry plopped down on his black pleather sofa, stretched out his back and arms, and gave a big yawning yell. He then snatched his pipe from the coffee table and scraped out the resin that was left from yesterday's smoke session. He grabbed an old gaming magazine and his half-ounce bag of weed, laid them on his lap, and poured out the marijuana. First he separated the seeds and stems from the marijuana, then he packed his pipe. He reached for his lighter and tried to make it light. When nothing happened, he shook it a few times then threw it onto the coffee table. The lighter bounced and fell to the floor.

With pipe in hand, Jerry walked to the kitchen, looking for matches. He checked his junk drawer with one hand while holding his pipe upright with the other.

"Nothing!" What else could he use? Paper? He snatched a fast-food napkin from the counter and rolled it up. He switched on the stove and lit the napkin then held it over his pipe and sucked in. The flame touched the marijuana inside the pipe and glowed orange.

The napkin crumbled, and a searing pain rushed over his fingers. With a shout, Jerry flung the napkin into the sink. "Oh, snap!" Running his hand under the water, he took another puff from the pipe with his other hand. The smoke from the napkin filled the kitchen, but the smoke alarms remained silent since Jerry didn't keep batteries in them.

Examining his hand under the water, he found a small burn. No big deal. He dried his hand with a tattered dishtowel, then he shut off the water and stove.

He puffed on the pipe and let the smoke stay in his lungs for thirty seconds before he started to cough. Jerry was ready for another puff when a knock on the door startled him. He froze but still took another toke.

More knocking. "Jerry, are you home?"

Jerry ran to the bathroom, taking another hit from the pipe. He set it on the counter while grabbing the air freshener. He sprayed the living room, kitchen, and his clothes before looking through the peephole.

Old man Al? What was he doing up at this hour, looking pathetic and old, propping himself up with a wooden cane?

Jerry cracked the door and leaned toward the opening. "What's up?"

"I helped to can peaches at my grandson's house today. They gave me a bunch to take home, but they're too heavy for me. Could you help an old man?"

"Let me get some shoes on." With a huff, Jerry grabbed some flip flops from his room. *Guess I can do this for the old man. He's never asked for help before.*

Jerry stomped to Mr. Al's 1973 Chevrolet Caprice Estate station wagon with the wood paneling on the side.

The car was unlocked, and Jerry grabbed the box of peaches from the back seat. He placed the box on the ground while he locked the doors.

Why was Mr. Al up so late canning peaches? That's so random.

In the hallway across from Jerry's apartment, Mr. Al held the door open for Jerry. "Leave them on the counter there, and I'll put them away later. I'm so glad you were still awake. How about a glass of warm milk and honey? Soda pop?"

Soda pop? "Sure, what have you got?"

"Let's see, I don't drink much soda pop anymore. Here's a Tab."

"They still make that? It'll work."

As Mr. Al prepared the soda, Jerry inspected the apartment. No TV? Just bookcases stuffed with notebooks and old leather-covered books and tons of dust. How depressing. What does he do all day? Jerry roamed toward the rocking chair in the corner. In it sat a worn-out, black-covered book. Its title was so faded, he could barely make it out: Holy Bible.

"Here you go, son." Mr. Al had a friendly, old-man voice. He handed Jerry his drink. "Sorry the place is such a mess. I haven't had company in quite a long time. Have a seat on the sofa."

Jerry cautiously shifted over to the stained love seat and sat down. Mr. Al sat in his rocking chair with the Holy Bible on his lap and sipped from a steaming cup. "When I was your age, I was fighting in World War II. How old are you? Twenty five, twenty six?"

"Thirty." How was he going to get out of here? Would Old Man Al fall asleep in a few minutes? It had to be way past his bedtime.

"When I was ten years younger than you, I was in the trenches at Normandy," Mr. Al continued. "I don't talk about my time during the war very often, but I feel like I need to tell you something tonight."

Jerry swallowed back a yawn. Would this conversation ever end, or would he have to endure it until his high was shot?

"When I was in France in 1944, I was running to help my wounded buddy when I was shot from behind. They got my right knee. I dropped like a stone. I still remember the way the mud tasted when I fell face-first into the muck."

Old man Al rocked back and forth as his face unfolded the moment. "Lieutenant Larkin was hiding in a nearby shed and saw me go down. He ran out and shot two German soldiers who were coming up behind me to finish me off. The lieutenant dragged me toward the shed. When we were about twenty yards away, an assault of bullets came at us from the roof of the building across the street. Two bullets hit Lieutenant Larkin in the chest, and I got it in the hand and foot." Mr. Al held up his hand to exhibit his scar.

"You were shot three times?" Jerry's tone was curious.

"That wasn't the end." Mr. Al stopped rocking and slanted his chair forward. "I had to crawl twenty yards to the shed while I bled out of three holes in my body. Shots fired all around me, and I was waiting for one to hit my skull so I could give up. I made it inside the building and lay there on the cold concrete, contemplating death."

Jerry wiped the sweat from his hands onto his shorts. The jarring image of Mr. Al lying helpless implanted tenderness into Jerry's impeded mind.

47

"I thought it would be easy to give up and let myself bleed to death, and I thought about how much I wanted to get away from this horrible place surrounded by horrible people. Then the sounds of war quieted. The only thing I could think about was the Lord's Prayer that I learned as a young lad. I recited it out loud: Our Father which art in heaven, hallowed be thy name. Thy kingdom come, Thy will be done in earth, as it is in heaven. Give us this day our daily bread. And forgive us our debts, as we forgive our debtors. And lead us not into temptation, but deliver us from evil: For thine is the kingdom, and the power, and the glory, forever. Amen."

Jerry snapped his eyebrows together.

"As soon as I said 'amen,' a medic named Gabe was on top of me, yelling, wanting to know where I was hit. He started patching up my wounds, and that's all I remember until I awoke in the infirmary two days later. I was sent home shortly after learning that everyone else in my platoon was killed the same day I was brought in." Mr. Al leaned back in his rocking chair, blinking tears from his eyes, and sipped from his cup.

Jerry followed suit and took a sip of soda. He smacked his lips together. How long does Tab syrup last before expiring?

The creaking of Mr. Al's rocking chair stopped. "For years I wondered why God spared my life. I've seen some horrendous things that no man should ever have to see. I've done things that no man should ever have to do. But they happened and I have had to accept them for what they are."

Mr. Al gazed at Jerry with his old blue eyes that had seen so much suffering but had so much love inside them and so many tears glassing over them. "In moments like

48

this, I know why God kept me alive."

Jerry's throat turned dry as his palms started to sweat again. He took a quick drink of the stale-tasting soda.

Mr. Al placed his cup on an old wooden TV tray and turned his focus toward Jerry. Waiting for his full attention, he pointed his crooked finger at him. His face became somber and his eyes sincere. "I can't let you leave tonight without asking you a question. Are you satisfied with your life?"

"No way, brah, this is crazy. You're freaking me out."

"I know my question is a little forward, but I need to know."

"If I don't have an answer, are you going to give me a Bible and tell me to read it to help me answer that question?"

The wrinkles on Mr. Al's face drew back with astonishment. "Yes, but first I was going to tell you about Jesus."

"Okay, I am officially freaked out of my mind, and with that I say good night." Jerry stood and set his glass on the table next to the love seat.

Mr. Al exerted himself as he struggled to get out of the rocking chair. Jerry paced by him, and Mr. Al touched the center of his back and whispered several jumbled words under his breath as Jerry passed by. "I'm sorry if I scared you with my war stories. I felt as if I needed to tell you."

Jerry whirled to face the old man with his bloodshot eyes. "It wasn't your war stories that freaked me out. It was that question about whether or not I am satisfied with my life and the whole Jesus thing. I don't need your Bible and I don't need your fictional Jesus. I need to go."

Mr. Al closed his eyes and raised both hands,

mumbling and whispering again. Jerry slowly backed out of the room. He tried with all of his willpower to unglue his eyes from the old man. He turned the door handle, and the squeaking noise pierced his nerves. Mr. Al opened his eyes and smiled.

"I'll see you soon."

CHAPTER SIX

==

     Les scuffed his way through his front door and caught sight of the empty movie case on the kitchen table. It brought back the bittersweet memory of his Arabic princess, Lila. Why hadn't she been there tonight? He reached for the one thing that always gave him comfort: beer.

     After a long swig, he wiped his mouth with his sleeve. Drinking alone again. He sat at the kitchen table and set his can on the movie case. Next to it lay the little brown book that had turned his mind upside down and his friend against him. Why was Jerry so freaked out about this book? Les took another pull from the can and settled it on the movie case again.

     "I need to get to the bottom of this." Les grabbed a notebook and pen from the kitchen drawer, seated himself again, and flipped through the notebook until he found a blank page. He drew a deep breath. "Okay, Jesus, make me a Jedi disciple. If I want to become a master, I must understand where the master gets his power. Belief was the root of power used in the Force. A Jedi's strength flows from the Force."

     He paused, taking a few chews on the end of his pen. If he was going to pull an all-nighter, he needed to switch beverages. He pitched the beer can in the sink and started a pot of coffee. When it was finished, he poured himself a cup and picked up the little New Testament again. It seemed so small in his hand, but the very essence of life radiated from inside it.

     Les turned the pages to the Book of John and started to write down all of Jesus' miracles and all the passages about faith and believing. "Their faith in him" rang loud in Lester's head.

"A disciple's strength flows from Jesus. Jesus is a force that combines with belief to make miracles. This in turn will allow me to do greater works than he did."

Lester slouched back in his chair with his hands on his head. Jesus wasn't a genie, but the force behind the power of the miracles. His disciples become like Jedis, having been taught by the Jedi master. That way, they can still use the force after Jesus dies.

He paged through his notes, struggling to understand. At the end, Jesus showed up like Obi-Wan Kenobi in a spiritual form to help guide other Jedis, or disciples in this case, into the Jedi faith or Jesus faith. But how can a student do greater things than the master?

Les paused to chew on the end of his pen again.

"He can't unless the same master works through the student to create these greater events." Les stood and sprinted to the kitchen. He searched for something that would hold a large amount of water. As he rummaged through his cupboards and pantry, he sensed a great energy and excitement in the room, igniting a passion to see the power of Jesus at work.

He opened his fridge and emptied what was left of a gallon jug of milk. He rinsed it out and then filled it with tap water from the kitchen sink. Les gripped the jug with both hands and cleared his throat. "Jesus, I make you my master! Let me work through your force and turn this jug of tap water into wine."

Les stepped back from the jug and watched it, waiting for it to turn red, purple, or some kind of color. Nothing happened. Five minutes went by, then ten. Still nothing.

He scratched his head, exhaustion setting in. Three thirty-four in the morning, and his four cups of coffee had worn off.

The next morning, Jerry smacked the annoying alarm clock for the second time. This would be a good day to call in sick. On second thought, he'd better save those sick days for hangovers.

He swung his legs over the side of the bed and muddled to the bathroom. Still in yesterday's underwear, he did a quick mirror check, splashed some cold water on his face, and plucked a few nose hairs. He could get by one more day without shaving.

As he reached for his toothbrush, he knocked aside his pipe to reveal a black burn spot on his bathroom counter. "All because of crusty old Al."

Minutes later, dressed in his work uniform of a white collared shirt and khaki pants, Jerry grabbed his keys from the kitchen counter and swung open the front door. In the apartment across the hall, two paramedics strapped Mr. Al to a gurney.

The site of an IV line taped to Mr. Al's left arm and the pallor of his skin sent a shock through Jerry. How could this have happened? He was fine last night. . . .

As the paramedics wheeled Mr. Al into the hall, Jerry dashed to them and grabbed the stocky female worker by the arm. "Is he going to be all right?"

"Too early to tell."

They loaded the motionless, wrinkled man into the ambulance. The sirens screamed as they drove off and left Jerry standing in a state of shock in his doorway, mouth open. What did he say to that old man last night? Did he have anything to do with what happened? Could he have prevented it?

Jerry drifted into the old man's apartment. He glanced around the living room and saw a notebook on top of the old, faded Holy Bible. The notebook looked just as old as the Bible, maybe older. Jerry picked up the notebook and flipped through a couple of fragile, dry pages that almost disintegrated as they turned. The only thing on each page was a list of names with lines drawn through them. There must have been hundreds, maybe thousands of names in this notebook—all crossed out.

This is really weird stuff. He flipped a few more pages, then to the back of the notebook. The last page was filled with names that weren't crossed out. On the last line, he read, "Jerry from across the hall in apartment thirty-four." Chills ran down Jerry's body. He dropped the book. What was up with this guy? This was getting freakier by the minute.

I've got to get out of here. Jerry bolted toward the door, his panic increasing with each step.

Wait, what if this guy dies? Jerry backtracked and grabbed the notebook. He tore out the last page and headed for the door. In the hall, he looked both ways then returned to his apartment. He rushed to the kitchen sink, poured a glass of water, and guzzled it. By this time it was ten till seven, and Jerry was going to be late for work again. But how do you dash off to work when your neighbor is deathly ill—and you were the last person he'd spoken to?

His brain shouldn't feel this burnt out from coffee.

Les let the shower's hot water stream over his face as he thought of his antics the night before. How could he have thought he could do miracles like Jesus and turn water into wine? Jer was right, the Bible is nothing more than a collection of old fables. He must have thought I was going crazy last night with all my talk about Jesus being a genie and Star Wars and the Bible. His headache yesterday must have been nothing more than a coincidence of timing and Tylenol.

Oh well, the Force is still with me. Les made the sound of a light saber striking an invisible foe. He was ready for a fun-filled day. On Monday, he'd tell Miss Copeland the truth: he had read the Bible, and it was a nice story just like Star Wars.

Well, not just like Star Wars. Star Wars was much more entertaining, but good nonetheless.

He'd tell her that he was satisfied with a life of mediocrity and counting spare parts for a living. Yep, that's what he'd tell her Monday morning. He couldn't wait to see Miss Copeland's face when he gives her Bible back to her and explains to her that it doesn't work.

But how did it change her life so much? Poor old single woman, confused by a silly storybook. Maybe he can set her straight on Monday.

Les grabbed his towel from the shower rod, a new sense of power and enlightenment surrounding him. He felt good, really good, that his life was back on track and he was complacent with his life—in a good way. He rubbed his head with the towel then wrapped it around his waist.

An image of Lila danced in his head as he dressed for the day. Now that would make his life complete, a hot little Arabic princess. That was what he was missing in life. Maybe that's what he'll tell Miss Copeland.

55

Les stepped through the doorway of his master suite into the living area, amazed how quickly his place becomes a mess. Candy wrappers on the floor, a beer can, coffee mug and a bunch of papers, some crinkled up, some with a few scribbles, and others filled with words.

"What a waste of time." He passed the paper explosion and spotted the jug of tap water. He shook his head. What was he thinking? He opened the fridge and surveyed the contents, but nothing looked appealing. He drifted from the fridge, letting the door close itself.

He chose a strawberry Pop-Tart with sprinkles, and as he ate it facing the water jug, his chest and head heated up. That stupid jug. He never wanted to see it again. He felt as if burning coals would burst out of his chest any second if he didn't dump out that jug of water.

He threw the rest of his Pop-Tart onto the counter and made his move. He grabbed the jug and tipped it upside down. The water poured into the sink, but instead of clear liquid, a red substance flowed out.

Lying sideways in the sink, the jug's outside was clear. That red fluid continued to pour out. Les grabbed the jug and lifted it to eye level to examine it closer. He spun the jug around and carefully arranged it on the counter. Then he reached for a clear glass from the cabinet and poured some of the liquid into it.

The red substance filled the bottom of the glass, enough for a good-sized swig. The liquid was clean and bright and begged Les to taste it. He raised the glass and swirled the substance, then he lifted the glass to his nose. The aroma was intoxicating and filled his senses with a tropical array of fruit. Les slowly tipped the glass to his mouth.

He swished the substance around in his cheeks, and

his taste buds celebrated the perfect blend of fruit. When he swallowed, a warm, comforting feeling swept through his body. His tongue buzzed with the passion that had just passed through. That four letter word rang in his head: *wine*.

This was nothing like the cheap, boxed stuff Les had in college. After several minutes, he still tasted the sweetness of the wine lingering in his senses. The smell and the taste were so intoxicating and vibrant just from one sip, he wanted to lift the jug and drink and not stop until it was gone.

Then a thought pounded through his head like a cadence: *you turned water into wine, just like Jesus.*

He shook his head. How could he have turned water into wine? Just minutes ago, he doubted the mere existence of God and had come to a conclusion that the Bible was nothing but a collection of old stories.

Les stood in front of the plastic jug and glass of wine, his thoughts jumbled. His proof stared him dead in the face. He had tasted and consumed this wine that was once tap water. He had asked and believed with his whole heart that Jesus could do greater works through him, and he had.

Les dropped to the kitchen floor with his back against the dishwasher and his knees pulled up to his chest. Once again, he wept. His whole body shook uncontrollably, and his abs clenched together, giving him a pain in his stomach.

Then he heard a voice he had never heard. It soothed from inside his body.

Believe.

CHAPTER SEVEN

==

Having cleared a day off with his supervisor, Jerry pulled a chair into his closet, climbed on the chair, and stood so his face was flush with the back corner. An old computer sat there, with wires running everywhere down the back of the closet, all connecting to a circuit strip.

Jerry had modified this large model to suit his purposes, and it took up a lot of room in the closet. He rummaged through some clothes to find the keyboard and plugged it into the hard drive. The computer was already on, and with a few key strokes, the screen came to life. He punched in several codes and heard the noise of the hard drive thinking. Then a tray on the side of the computer monitor popped open.

Sitting on a tray were five eight-inch-long, florescent-colored marijuana buds illuminating the dark closet. The glow-in-the-dark weed was very sticky and difficult to pull apart. The stench of the bud was so potent, he had to pull his face away for a few seconds until his senses could adjust.

Controlling the light, water, fertilizer, and temperature, Jerry had created the perfect marijuana-growing atmosphere inside his computer. Never before had anyone gone to this extreme to collide these two worlds. His creation was superweed marijuana, perfectly grown in liquid PCP, combined with a flourescent-green protein plasmid from a substance that came from jellyfish and made it glow.

Jerry had been working on this secret for years until he spilled the beans to Les the other day at work. Les didn't understand the significance of Jerry's accomplishment, but he would this weekend when he tried it for the first time. It was the perfectly cultivated super-plant, using hydroponics. He wouldn't tell Les about the PCP or the protein plasmid until after he smoked it.

Jerry gazed at the work of art like a proud new father who just saw his baby for the first time. All great scientists must try out their products before unleashing them to the public. What better time than now?

He needed to escape reality for a moment, get his mind off the old man from across the hall. A few strokes of the keyboard, and the glow-in-the-dark marijuana plant went back inside its domain. Jerry stepped down from his chair with the sticky glowing substance between his forefinger and thumb. The weed felt as sticky as fly paper. He couldn't get it off his fingers.

Breaking it up to smoke it was even more of a challenge. He decided that he needed to document his findings and write about his experience like a true scientist. He went to his room to look for a notebook but couldn't find anything except the envelope his electric bill had come in.

"Good enough. I'll just transfer the findings over to a notebook later today."

On the top of the envelope, he wrote the date and "Trial One: Smoked from Bong." He grabbed his three-foot, all-yellow glass bong from under his kitchen sink, filled the base with water, and carried it to the coffee table. He anxiously situated the broken-up marijuana in the end of the stem, then he inserted the carburetor in its hole. Deep breath . . . exhale, deep breath . . . exhale.

"Trial one, engage." His new lighter hit the florescent substance and ignited instantly as Jerry inhaled through the mouthpiece. The smoke filtered through the water and up the pipe. Jerry inhaled until the entire pipe was filled with thick, grey smoke. Then he pulled his lips from the mouthpiece and exhaled while covering the top of the bong with his hand.

A few deep breaths and Jerry was ready. He fastened his mouth back on the mouthpiece and released the carburetor, creating a shotgun effect. He inhaled the pipe full of smoke all at once, then he held the smoke in his lungs as long as possible until his breath ran out and the coughing started. His eyes watered, and he cleared his throat and sat back on the couch.

Jerry felt as if he were sitting on a cloud and the whole world had just been put in slow motion. He blinked then waved his hand in front of his face, but his vision blurred. He stared at the ceiling, not at all concerned about his blurred eyesight.

After a few minutes, a fly landed on his nose, drawing his eyes to cross and making him laugh as drool started to form on the left corner of his mouth. It started with a slow chuckle, then he let out a hearty laugh as if someone had told him a hilarious joke, then he laughed as though someone was tickling him all over. After a few minutes of this laugh cycle, he stopped and his eyes cleared.

"Whoa, I'm really stoned! Man, I should not feel this good!" He stood and pranced around the room, rubbing his arms. The feeling was incredible: not a care in the world, as if he had entered a bubble of happiness. Only one thing bothered him, and that was the guilt he felt for feeling so good.

Why did he feel guilty for feeling so great? Here he was in his man-palace, incredibly high, feeling the best he had ever felt in his life, and he felt guilty about it. Trying to dismiss the thought, he grabbed his keys to the van and took off on a munchie run. As he opened his front door to the outside world, the air had never smelled cleaner. He was skipping on clouds. Every step he took, he felt good to be alive.

"This is going to be a great day!" He climbed into his van and rolled down the windows, then he cranked Bob Marley. As he drove, he felt as though he was in a giant video game and he had only one life to live and he'd better not crash or his game would be over.

Jerry pulled in at the corner gas station and wandered inside. Playing invisible bongos as he bounced around the store, he tried to read the labels to decide what to buy. The words all seemed to run together like a bowl of alphabet soup. He grabbed a pack of two glazed donuts, a sixteen-ounce orange juice, a pack of watermelon Bubblelicious bubble gum, a tube of toothpaste, and a two-dollar scratch-off "win for life" ticket.

Hands completely full, Jerry dropped the items onto the counter. The wrinkled cashier with smoke-stained teeth, whose name tag read "Gretchen," asked in a deep, raspy voice, "Will that be all, hon?"

Jerry looked up from his wallet and froze as he caught her gaze. The whites of her eyes were yellow along with her skin tone and she reeked of alcohol and cigarettes. "What's the matter, son, have you never seen a playboy bunny?"

Her laugh was quickly followed by several mucus-filled coughs. What could Jerry say? He handed her a twenty. She reached for the money with a hand that looked like a claw with long, yellow nails. "You're one of those shy boys, aren't you? That's okay. Shy boys like to get messed up too."

She gave another disturbing laugh and cough. Jerry looked around the store to see if anyone else was around. No one was.

How could there be no one else in the store, no other employees or customers anywhere? Gretchen handed Jerry his scratch-off. When she went to give him his change, she dropped all of it on the floor inside her station. "I'm such a klutz."

Jerry rolled his eyes. He had both of his hands full with the bags, so he set the bags on the counter as he waited for his change.

Gretchen popped up from behind the counter and grabbed Jerry by the shirt. She pulled him in close to her face, her eyes burning with insanity. Her breath stunk of rotten eggs and tar.

Jerry's body stiffened, and he couldn't move. Then he went limp and stood motionless, staring into those eyes.

Her skin looked like old leather with six hairy moles protruding from her face. "Today I make you my son, a son the whole world can be proud of. Eat, drink, and be merry. Resist authority, indulge in everything, kill or be killed. Today I make you my son, because today you will kill!"

Jerry tried with all his might to pull away, but he could not. Her eyes burned with hatred, and her whitish blond hair slithered like baby snakes. She ran one claw through his hair while she held the back of his neck with the other. She stuck her tongue out and thrust it from side to side, dripping saliva all over the counter.

Gretchen slapped his forehead with such force that he crashed to the ground. He shook his head and scrambled to his feet then burst through the gas station door. Wildly sprinting toward his van, he heard her wicked, raspy laughter from inside the store.

He shot into the driver's seat and sat there for a moment with the keys in the ignition. Then he realized he forgot his stuff. His heart raced at an alarming rate as anger filled his whole body.

"Revenge, take revenge," a voice inside his head was saying. The voice grew louder. "Revenge. Take revenge."

He proceeded past the second row of seats to the back of his van and found a long tire wrench that was curved at the end.

"Revenge. Take revenge!" The voice now sounded as if it came from somewhere in the van.

Jerry slid open the side door and jumped out. He stalked toward the store, every thought focused on taking the wrench to that grotesque woman's head. He slapped the long wrench against his hand a couple of times as he closed in on the store. His heart pounded and blood surged to his face. He was going to kill this old hag with one swipe of his wrench and put her out of her misery.

As he opened the door, it gave a faint tone to signal that someone was entering. The element of surprise was gone, but all he needed was one good swing. It happened within a blink of an eye, although everything seemed in slow motion.

Her eyes burned into his, mocking the sight of him. "You're pathetic!"

Then it happened. In his anger and rage, he spoke no words, but let his actions speak. The wrench crashed into the side of Gretchen's head with such impact that Jerry felt the sting of the vibration in his hands.

Gretchen made no attempt to move. Blood splattered the counter.

Jerry felt a release from his soul. He finally felt free.

His vision blurred. He blinked twice then saw behind the counter a teenaged boy with dark, messy hair and several piercings.

"What's with the tire wrench, bro? Are you okay? Do you have a flat?" The boy, about eighteen years old, slouched over the counter.

Jerry squinted, surveying the store as his vision cleared. The room spun, and he leaned against the counter to steady himself. Where was the grotesque cashier he had just killed? Where were the items he bought? Where did this kid come from?

Jerry stumbled to the door and grabbed the handle. He pushed the door open with his left hand, keeping the wrench in his right. In the parking lot, he crashed to the ground and landed on his left side. His vision blurred again, and he could barely make out the form of his mustard-yellow van just fifteen feet from him.

He crawled to the van with the tire wrench still in hand. The comments and stares of the people passing him didn't matter. Their words were nothing more than noise to him.

Was this just a bad nightmare, and would he wake up any second? He crawled faster—one arm, one leg, one arm, one leg. Faster—one arm, one leg, now with his head down, one arm, one leg—faster—

Searing pain raced through the top of his head. Cursing, he looked up. He'd cracked his head on the side of the van door. He rubbed his head and, moaning, he climbed through the open door and collapsed onto the floor. As he lay there on his back, eyes closed, he tried to digest everything that just happened.

Then his mind and body whirled as if he'd just

stepped off one of those spinning carnival rides. He was going to vomit. Hot sweat poured down the sides of his face, and his whole body shivered. The carpet under him, touching his skin, making him want to scratch all over.

Should he take off all his clothes and burn them with his cigarette lighter? Should he scratch his skin with a knife?

Where did these crazy thoughts come from? Did he just imagine killing a cashier named Gretchen? Or is this the most realistic nightmare he has ever had?

Jerry opened his eyes. His van spun like the tin-cup ride at the fair. The musty smell of his van carpet seeped into his nostrils as sweat continued to pour down his face. Bile came up in his throat. He grabbed the van door and shoved it open just in time.

His vomit spilled all over the pavement and splashed up onto the blue Ford Explorer parked next to him. His throat burned and his stomach churned. Tears flowed out the corners of his eyes as a migraine-like headache crashed into his skull. There he was, on his knees in the corner gas station parking lot, with puke on his shirt and tears running down his face. He was in too much pain to be embarrassed.

Footsteps pounded near Jerry's head. "Hey, jerk, what do you think you're doing? You had to puke all over my rims? Just because you can't hold your liquor doesn't mean I have to pay for it, you little puking punk."

Jerry knelt there, emotionless.

The large, bald, white-supremacy-looking dude's face turned red, and a vein stood out in his neck. "Boy, you answer me when I speak to you!"

When Jerry didn't respond, the man reached to grab him by the back of the shirt collar, cursing.

With the speed and power of a trained weapons specialist, Jerry struck the man in the Adam's apple with the tire wrench. Jerry's vision cleared as the large man dropped to the pavement, gasping for air, both hands around his neck.

Trembling, he glanced at the tire wrench in his hand, then back at the man. Jerry rushed to the driver's seat, turned the ignition, and backed out of the parking spot with the sliding door open and the man lying on the ground. The squeal of tires and the smell of burnt rubber filled the air as the van barreled down the road.

What had he done? First the old man, then the old witch-woman cashier, now this. He gripped his stirring wheel tightly. Should he go back to see if that man was okay?

What if I killed him? I don't want to go to jail. I won't survive in jail. Maybe it wasn't real, like the old cashier woman wasn't real. Maybe he was going to wake up in his apartment any second now.

Minutes later, Jerry pulled into his spot at his apartment complex. It was real, it had happened, and that fact hit him in the stomach as hard as he had hit the man with the tire wrench. His hands quivered as he turned off his ignition.

Why did he do it? How did he react so quickly? Did anyone see him? The thought of his face all over the store video crushed every hope of getting away. The man, if still alive, would report his description or his van, and the authorities would soon find him. If the man was dead, then the surveillance cameras would reveal his identity.

The man could be dead. The words rang hollow in his soul. He was a murderer. He woke up this morning as a normal, working-class man with every intention of going to work and having a normal Thursday. How could things have gone so bad?

Would he spend the rest of his life in prison? Tears rolled down Jerry's face. He could run, but they would eventually find him. He should be a man and face the consequences and go back to the gas station. He should face the authorities and tell them everything. Or he could stay here and wait for the police to come and get him.

No suggestion sounded good to him as he tapped his fingers on his steering wheel, staring out his windshield.

CHAPTER EIGHT

==

Lester's face was wet with tears as he struggled to pull his trembling body to a standing position. Something had released from his body. He felt different, new.

He rotated his shoulders. The pain he had lived with the last nine years of his life was gone. He lifted his arm straight up in the air and stretched, something he hadn't been able to do since his swimming days. No pain.

Uncontrollable laughter flowed from his mouth. Les bent doubled, tears and laughter mingling.

After several waves of laughter and an aching, sore stomach, he settled in a kitchen chair. A deep breath of exhaustion exhaled from his lips as his senses tingled from whatever just happened. He blinked hard and rubbed his eyes. Then he leaned back in his chair and stretched his shoulder again. No pain.

The tingling sensation left, so he stepped back into the kitchen to re-examine the jug. No doubt Jesus had made himself real. No doubt Jesus' name carried power. But why Les?

Had this ever happened to anyone else? Had anyone other than Jesus ever turned water into wine?

What do I do with this jug of wine that healed me? Les sat back down at his kitchen table and turned his attention to his notebook. He flipped through the many written pages, looking for some kind of formula he might have written down that had triggered this reaction.

The words "faith" and "believe" kept coming across his notes, highlighted in florescent green. He also found several references to Star Wars and one whole page dedicated to why Star Wars was the key to understanding the Bible. At the top of the page, he had written, "The Holy Force."

The first line read, "Force: a powerful life-force that fills the cosmos and can be used for harm or good."

Second line: "Holy Spirit: a power that is given through the name of Jesus and used only for good, which would implement the good side of the force."

Third line: "Dark side of the force: used to do harm and evil—could cross-reference with the Bible's Satan."

The start of line four: "Jesus and God act as Jedi masters, the good side of the force. Satan acts as the Sith Lord, trying to tempt mankind to come to the dark side. Both work within the force, one using light and the other darkness."

Les tipped back in his chair and collected a deep breath. "My brain hurts."

He ran his hands back and forth through his hair. What would he do with this power?

His phone rang. Jerry. Les hit the receive button. "What's up?"

Les heard nothing but the sound of short panting. Then it would stop. Then it would start again. "Jerry, are you there?"

The phone disconnected, so Les hit Jerry's name and called, but the phone went straight to voicemail. He tried again with no luck. He set his phone on the counter as a sense of urgency swept through his mind. Trouble?

Les grabbed his keys and was out the door, headed toward Jerry's apartment complex. Les called the factory to see if Jerry was at work. The conversation lasted about thirty seconds before he knew Jerry was in danger.

###

Lynn Li, R.N., wished her shift was over at St. Bernard's Hospital's ICU. Six hours had passed since Eugene Allen's admission, and she had six more to go. She entered Mr. Allen's vital signs in her portable computer. Why was Dr. Sheepstone so adamant about her making rounds on this patient every twenty minutes? He was no worse than any other vent patient on the unit.

Lynn checked the vent's calibrations, entered a few notes, and left the room to find some coffee. In the break room, she caught a glimpse of the half-empty pot, the red light still on. She grabbed a Styrofoam cup from the cupboard and filled it up to about half an inch from the top, then she sprinkled in creamer and sugar substitute.

She headed back to the nurses' station, picked up Mr. Allen's chart, and turned to the patient information section. His face sheet told her that Eugene Abraham Allen was born in 1923, age eighty-five. He served in the United States Navy from 1941 to 1948, received a Purple Heart during WWII, and was a 1952 graduate of Berean Bible College.

Lynn finished her coffee and checked her watch. She grabbed her clipboard and headed for the bathroom.

As she washed her hands, Robin darted through the bathroom door in a blaze, smashing open one of the stalls and not bothering to latch it behind her. "Ah, I thought my bladder was going to explode this time."

"Why do you wait so long? You know you can damage your kidneys."

The sound of the toilet flushing and a sigh of relief harmoniously sang as Robin stepped out from the stall. "Tell that to Dr. S. He has me so busy, I have to schedule my pee."

Robin stood next to Lynn to wash her hands and splash water on her face. Lynn handed her some paper towels.

"Yeah, I know what you mean, but you still need to make sure you take care of yourself. I read a study in Women's Health that said nurses are some of the unhealthiest people. The article stated they interviewed one hundred nurses, and seventy three of them said they put so much effort into taking care of other people, they don't have enough energy left over to worry about themselves."

"Interesting. Can you get me that article? I would like to blow it up and tape it on Dr. Sheepstone's office door."

The two girls laughed as they exited the bathroom.

"X-ray is here to do a portable on my patient. Can you help me roll him over?"

Lynn examined her watch. "Sure, I have a few minutes. I hear you just got engaged."

"Praise the Lord for having mercy on my soul. I got me a man to get on his knee!" Robin held out her left hand as a solid carat diamond shimmered in the light.

Lynn gently took Robin's hand, fighting the jealousy that swelled in her mind. "Wow, you are so lucky."

"Wait a minute." Robin said, pulling her hand away. "What is an exotic Asian diva like yourself doing still single?"

Lynn stopped outside Robin's patient's door. She looked down at the floor, her bottom lip quivering. "I am a loser magnet."

Robin faced Lynn and tipped her chin up. "I waited ten long years for Marcus. I had to endure several disastrous relationships before him, but it was worth it to watch him slide this ring on my finger." Robin gazed down at her ring. Then turned her attention back to Lynn. "You're a good catch. Don't let anyone tell you otherwise. You are young, skinny, and have a great career. Don't settle. He will come."

"I'm twenty-eight. That's not young." Lynn dropped her head back toward the floor.

"Hold the phone. Hold the phone." Robin jerked her head to the side, pointing her finger at Lynn. "Girl, I am thirty-five years young. You're young. Better yet, you look young."

Robin opened the door to the patient's room. "Hey, Royce."

The alarm on Lynn's watch went off to signify her twenty-minute check-up duty. "I'm sorry, Robin. I have to get back."

"That's all right. We'll catch up later."

Lynn headed to the nurses' station and grabbed Eugene Allen's chart. She turned to the social worker's assessment on her clipboard. Eugene Allen had been the pastor of Creekside Assembly from 1952 until 1982. He had been a missionary to Guatemala, had founded the Zion Orphanage for Children of Guatemala and served as its president until 1998. From 1998 to present, he worked as a counter clerk at Little Al's Peach Farm.

Counter clerk at a peach farm? How random was that? Why was an eighty-year-old man still working?

Inside, she traversed over to the old man. What a life of selfless dedication this man lived. He probably had helped so many people. Was he satisfied with the way he lived his life now that he was on the brink of death?

She reached out and took the old man's hand. Immediately her fingers tingled. Why hadn't she realized before that she had been living every day for herself and no one else? Was this why she was still alone? Here lay a man who had dedicated his life to helping people by giving himself for his country, pastoring a church for thirty years, and starting a orphanage in Guatemala. Eugene Allen probably never knew the feeling of having a savings account or a 401K.

Tears rolled down Lynn's cheeks. She brushed them away. Why was she crying? Why did she feel so much emotion while touching this man?

She grabbed one of the rolling stools and pulled it close to the bed. Sitting there now with both of her hands around his right hand, she knew she needed to talk to this man, needed to find out why he had dedicated his life to these causes. "Don't you dare die on me before we can talk, you promise?"

Lynn stood and situated his hand tenderly on the bed. She took a deep breath and wiped her face with both hands. "Okay, get composed. Stop being emotional. You're a professional."

She went through the drill of checking the machine and charting on her rolling computer. When she was finished, she gazed at the motionless man, and for some reason, she knew he could tell her something that would comfort her.

He looked so peaceful lying in that hospital bed, even with a tube coming out of his mouth and IVs hooked to his veins. A glow surrounded him.

"I'll be back." Lynn saved her notes in the computer, unplugged it, and rolled it out of the room.

CHAPTER NINE

===

The drive was a blur, the red lights Les had driven through were a blur, the horns honking were faint and sounded far away. What was going on with Jerry? Maybe he was okay, but if so, why did Les have such an overwhelming urge to find him?

The tires screeched as he rounded the bend through the apartment complex entrance. Les slowed the Honda, not wanting to bottom out his car over the speed bumps. He caught sight of the mustard-yellow van, and his anxiety eased a little.

He parked two spots down from the Euro van. Les trooped toward the apartment as a man on a mission, but when he glanced back, there was Jerry in his van, both of his hands on the steering wheel, staring blankly ahead.

Les faithfully plodded over to the van and waved, keeping his eyes focused on Jerry. Les approached the driver's side of the van and rapped on the window. "Are you okay?"

He sat still as a wax statue, his hair soaked. Les tried the door, but it was locked. He banged on the window. "Jerry—"

Jerry haltingly deviated his neck like an owl, turning toward the window. His stare was cold and hollow. It sent chills down Les' back. Something was different about Jerry's eyes. . . .

Cursing, Jerry opened the door. Along with him came a putrid smell of rotting fruit. His face was pale, and his filthy shirt and pants were ripped and splattered with dirt and throw-up. He was bleeding through his jeans in a couple of places.

Les tentatively stepped toward his friend, waving his hand in front of his nose. "What happened to you?"

Jerry blinked hard, wiped his eyes, and eased down out of the van. "My throat burns. I need some water. I feel like I'm going to die."

"Let me help you."

"Don't need your help, just need some water. Can't you see I'm having a bad day? I'll tell you about it when we get inside."

Les followed closely behind as Jerry staggered up the walk. In the hallway, Jerry unlocked the door and swung it open.

The stench drifting out of the apartment almost knocked Les over. He scrunched his face. "Whoa! It smells like a musty marijuana factory in here."

Jerry stuck his head underneath the kitchen faucet, letting the water pour all over his face and into his mouth. Drinking and slobbering all over the place and spilling water everywhere, he attacked the faucet like some kind of raging animal.

"Dude, what happened to you?"

Jerry shifted his attention toward Les and wiped his mouth with the front of his shirt. "You wanna get high?"

"I want you to tell me why you look like you just got mugged."

"What do you care? You think I'm a terrible, selfish friend who thinks only of himself. Don't bother to apologize. I could care less. Right now, I need to get high."

"Jerry, I'm your best friend." Les followed Jerry to the closet, where he stood on a chair and rummaged around an old computer on the top shelf. What was the guy searching for? He looked as if he needed to go to the hospital, and in his condition, he had no business climbing on the furniture. "Get down off that chair."

"Abracadabra!" Jerry popped his head down, holding out a florescent marijuana bud in his hand. "This is what I was telling you about the other day. Isn't she beautiful?"

Jerry held the bud in his hand, feasting his eyes on it like a hungry animal about to devour his meal.

"You're scaring me, man. You're acting really weird right now."

"What's so weird?"

"Dude, I have never seen you like this before. What's going on?"

Jerry tilted his head to the side and raised his eyebrows. Despite his brash expression, fear lurked behind his hollowed eyes. "I'll tell you if you get high with me."

He crossed over into the living room and sat on the couch. With eagerness in his eyes, he broke the marijuana into smaller portions.

Les stood directly across from him with the coffee table separating them. What had happened to make him act this way? What had filled him with this anger and craziness?

"Do you remember when we were in seventh grade and I stole some of my mom's stash and we got high behind that corner gas station?" Jerry didn't look up as beads of sweat dropped to the coffee table. He kept working the marijuana buds as a skilled craftsperson. "We became brothers at that moment, bonded forever by a supernatural experience. We've always been there for each other. Who was there for you during your teenage years, growing up without a father? Who was there for you when Pam ruined your Olympic dream? Who was there for you when Pam left you? Who left all his friends and moved with you to a completely new place, not knowing anyone? Who has always been there to comfort you, no matter what?"

Jerry's voice grew louder and more aggressive. His eyes turned bloodshot red as he raised his head and licked the paper joint, pressing it together. "I'll answer for you. It was your closest friends: alcohol, marijuana and good old Jer."

Jerry held out the joint. "I need you to smoke with me now. If this is our last time to smoke together, then let's strengthen our bond one last time. I can't tell you what happened today unless you get high with me."

Les stood confounded at the perfectly rolled joint, his mind teetering. His index finger and thumb grasped the doobie. "Where's the lighter?"

"Yes! Wait until you smoke this stuff. It's the best high ever."

"Let's do this." Jerry tossed the lighter to Les then marched to his surround-sound stereo. He put in *The Best of the Doors* and turned up the volume as "Riders on the Storm" started to play.

The room went cold and Les trembled with a nervous shake. He took a few puffs and coughed with a force that made his chest hurt.

"Give me that, you lightweight!" Jerry grabbed the joint from Les's hands as he was still coughing. "Can't handle the good stuff, can ya, Leslie?"

"It's been a while. Give me a break." Les bent over with his hands on his knees.

Jerry took several deep tokes then handed it back.

Les puffed, trying to hold in the smoke as long as possible, but he coughed after every puff.

"Love Me Two Times" was playing as Les dropped the roach clip into the ash tray. "Man, I am so stoned already."

"I told you this stuff is good."

They sat back on the couch, eyes closed, listening to Jimmy Morrison take their minds on a ride. Jerry turned to Les. "Hey, man, thanks for getting high with me. I had a really bad day."

"So are you going to tell me about it or what?"

Jimmie Morrison belted out the chorus to "Break On Through to the Other Side." A sharp pain shot through Lester's shoulder as if someone took a needle and stuck it in. He grabbed his shoulder and rubbed hard, groaning in pain.

"The old shoulder bothering you?"

"It felt a lot better today than it ever had."

"Do you ever think about killing that wench, Pam?" Jerry blurted out.

There was definitely something different about Jerry's eyes. "Are you nuts?"

"Some people don't deserve to live because of the things they've done."

"I don't blame Pam for my injury anymore. Yeah, she was driving and crashed into a tree, but I can't live my life blaming her."

"Whatever, she screwed you over and you know it."

"What good is it to hold a grudge?"

"You can find great power in bitterness, and revenge smells sweet as a rose." Jerry got up and paced the living room. His face looked contorted and his crooked smile seemed evil. "How do you feel? You feel incredible, right? It's the best feeling in the world."

Jerry's laugh was not his own infectious, surfer-dude laugh, but the high-pitched laugh of mischief.

"No, my shoulder hurts and I think it's from the

weed."

"Shut up! It's not from the weed, this weed is the greatest thing you've ever experienced."

Les's head pounded now. Everything in the room was in slow motion and blurry.

Jerry sprawled on the couch with his back on the armrest and his body facing Lester. "Okay, I'm ready to tell you what happened today."

Les wiped his eyes and tried to focus on Jerry, but all he could think about was how dark and cold the room felt. The tin foil on the windows kept out all the natural light, and the three candles on the coffee table gave little illumination. What else was going to happen in this room? A trickle of sweat rolled down Les's neck.

"It all started last night with old man Al across the hall."

As Jerry told his story, Les had a hard time paying attention. His mind kept wandering back to Pam as he thought of different ways he could hurt her. Where were these thoughts coming from?

Jerry's voice was nothing more than a muffled sound that kept sucking Les down into a pit of images of himself and Pam. In his mind, he watched himself smash a beer bottle over her head.

"Hey, you're zoning out on me." Jerry grabbed his arm and shook it.

"Sorry. Keep going." Les blinked hard a few times and worked to concentrate on Jerry.

"Do you remember getting high behind that corner gas station?"

"Off Third Street?"

"Yeah, I stopped in there to pick up a few things instead of going to the hospital."

Hospital? Les must have missed that part as he was drifting off.

"I went up to the counter to pay for my stuff, and this nasty-looking cashier woman named Gretchen started hitting on me. Then she grabbed me by the shirt and called me her son and slapped me on the forehead. I went flying across the store. Then I ran out to my van and got a tire wrench. I slapped it upside her head, killing her for sure."

Les felt his mouth drop open. He must have misunderstood. Jerry would never . . .

His heart rate picked up then. Too much. He tried to swallow, but there was nothing there to swallow. Drool dripped down the side of Jerry's mouth as he talked.

What was happening to them . . .?

Footsteps, two pairs of them, approached the door. Then a knock came, jolting Les out of his semi-dazed state. Another knock, then another rap—not a hard knock or a bang, but an annoying, constant rapping.

They both sat unable to make a move or a sound. Jimmy Morrison continued to belt out the words to his distorted song. Whoever was out there couldn't miss the loud music.

"Maybe it's someone here to complain about the noise." Les sunk down on the couch.

Another knock, then a muffled, old-man voice. "Jerry, are you home? It's me, Mr. Al."

Jerry sluggishly rose from the couch, drifted to the door, and pressed his ear against it.

"It's Mr. Al, your neighbor. I need your help."

Jerry's eye was aligned with the peephole. "It sounds and appears to be Mr. Al, my neighbor who is in the hospital."

Les was stuck to the couch in a drug-induced

bubble. His brain was having trouble sending messages to the rest of his body.

I can't move. I'm going to be stuck here forever. How am I going to eat? I'm going to die of starvation on this couch. Wait a minute. I think I can move. Move your right hand.

Les focused in on his right hand. The sound of static echoed in the room.

"Hold on." Jerry unlatched the lock. Instead of opening the door, he snatched his hand back from the knob. "It's cold—so cold, it almost burned my hand."

He flung his hand around in the air for a moment then wrapped the end of his t-shirt around the knob and turned it. He opened the door, and his body sailed backward as if hit in the chest with some extreme force.

"Jerry—" Les sprang up from the couch and crossed the room to the entry. An old gas-station cashier with a name tag reading "Gretchen" stood in the doorway, laughing. A large, Arian-supremacy-looking dude crossed his arms and stared with his ice-blue eyes.

Les tried to swallow the lump in his throat. The fear in the room was tangible.

"Aren't you going to invite your mother in?" Gretchen peered down at Jerry and laughed again, her voice raspy. "I see you have recruited a friend. Well done, my son, well done. Now invite us in."

Jerry lay sprawled out on the floor, still except for the twitch in his legs. Les tried to focus on the two objects in the doorway, but his eyes couldn't adjust to their peculiar aura.

Gotta get out. It would have to be through a window. Les scrambled for the bedroom, but instead of moving toward the back of the apartment, his body moved forward, in slow motion, toward the door. With each step, his pulse raced faster.

Gretchen's eyes seemed to burn through his soul. "My name is Gretchen, and I am Jerry's real mother."

Les stopped as he reached Jerry's head. His eyes were open, and foam bubbled from both corners of his mouth. What was wrong with him? Les grabbed him under the arms, pulled him up to a sitting position, and leaned him against the kitchen cupboard. When he had Jerry propped up, Les shook uncontrollably as if he was in a snow storm with no coat.

The two intruding guests stood in the doorway, gazing at them with wicked eyes. "Let us in so we can help." Gretchen's manner turned smooth, polite.

Les studied the nasty-looking woman. Was she really Jerry's mother? Why did she ask for permission to enter the apartment? Could Les do anything to help Jerry? The chill in his body made concentration nearly impossible.

The Arian pushed Gretchen out of the way and leaned into the apartment with his arm outstretched, pointing at Les. "Let us inside or we will kill your friend."

The man's voice screeched through Les's brain and awoke him from his fear-induced trance.

Shut the door. Shut the door. Another voice spoke from inside Les's body.

Les reacted out of a natural survival instinct, like a tiger springing on its prey. His senses heightened as he sprung toward the door. With a rapid fire he slammed it shut.

"I command you to let us in!" the two said in unison.

The door vibrated from the banging as it got louder. *Use the Holy Force and command them to leave in*

Jesus' name. The voice inside spoke to Les again, strong and direct but also soft as a whisper.

Les cleared his throat and leaned closer, both hands bracing the door. "I command you to leave in Jesus' name!"

A loud bang on the door made Les jerk back. His ears rang as if someone had plucked a tuning fork inside his head. He stumbled backward a few steps and grabbed the kitchen counter to regain his balance.

His vision then cleared. He rubbed his eyes and the ringing stopped in his head and ears. Instantly he felt uncontrollably sick. He threw up on the kitchen floor and on Jerry's pants. It came out with no warning, spewing out of his mouth and onto the vinyl floor.

When his stomach was empty, Les stepped over the puke and turned the kitchen faucet on. He let the water run into his mouth and down his face and head. His pulse slowed to normal, but his body felt overheated as if he'd run a marathon. He felt dehydrated, so he gargled the water and spit it out in the sink and then drank some water.

Jerry made weird gargling sounds himself. Foam ran down the front of his face, giving him a helpless, sick appearance. His eyes had sunken in and were surrounded by large black circles. His face had turned pale, along with his lips.

Was he dying? The thought hit Les like a bat across the chest. He scrambled toward his friend. He didn't know anything about first aid. He felt for Jerry's pulse in his wrist. Nothing. He laid his head on Jerry's chest and heard a faint heartbeat.

Les grabbed his friend and slung him over his shoulder. Pain shot through the right side of Les's body, but he pushed on. He snatched his keys and opened the door.

Then the thought of Gretchen and the Arian

pounded his mind. It was too late. He had already stepped through the doorway, out into the hall. The sickness returned. He braced himself to be hit. Nothing. He quickly closed the door and aimed for his Civic. The sunlight stopped him for a moment, and he had to wait for his eyes to adjust.

Nearing exhaustion, he delicately laid Jerry in the passenger side seat and buckled him in. Les surged into the car, turned the key, and slammed into reverse. The tires squealed as he jammed it into first.

As he drove, his vision doubled. Two roads, two stops signs, two steering wheels. A sinus-like headache emerged as a dull, deep, throbbing pain pressed on the front of his face. Les forcefully squeezed shut his eyes over and over again, trying to re-focus. He stopped the car at the entrance of the apartment complex. What should he do? He was in no condition to drive, but if he didn't get Jerry to the hospital, he could die. Then again, if he continued to drive, there was a good chance he would get them both killed on the way to the hospital, not to mention drug testing if he had a wreck.

Give him the wine. The strong, whispering voice rose up inside Les again

He gripped the steering wheel and closed his eyes for a moment. "Jesus, I'm sorry I smoked that weed. I'll never do it again if you please just get me home."

He opened his eyes. Two girls rode their bikes into the apartment entrance in front of him. Les shook his head and compressed the bridge of his nose. He looked again and there was only one girl. Suzy. She must have ridden her bike over after work to visit Jerry.

Les slammed the car into neutral and ran out after her, sweat pouring down his face. "Suzy, we need your help!"

Suzy immediately hit the brakes. "What do you need? You look awful."

"It's a long story, but I'm in no condition to drive and Jerry is sick. I need to get him to my place. Can you drive a stick?"

"I never have, but it can't be that hard, right? What should I do with my bike?"

"Wait here. I'll put it in Jerry's apartment." He wheeled it inside. When he came back out to the car, Suzy had the driver-side door open, and her face had paled.

"What happened to him? He looks dead."

"He's not dead, we just need to get him to my house."

"I think we should take him to the hospital."

"Look, I'm not going to stand here and argue with you. Please, just take us to my condo, and everything will be okay." Les leaned in, lifted Jerry's limp body, and gently positioned him in the back seat. Then he climbed into the front passenger seat. "This is what we're going to do. I'll shift and you drive. Every time I shift, you have to put in the clutch."

"My hands are sweating."

"Do what I say and you'll be fine. Take off the brake and put the clutch in. I'll put it in first."

Suzy sluggishly fixed one foot on the gas and the other on the clutch. The blue Civic crept towards the entrance.

"This is the hard part."

"Don't say that! You're making me nervous."

"Ease your foot off the clutch and hit the gas at the same time as I put the car in first." The car lurched forward, came to a screeching halt, and stalled.

"I can't do this. There's too much pressure!"

"Calm down. You can do it, just concentrate. Turn off the key, press the clutch all the way down, and start the car."

It started then quickly stalled as Suzy took her foot off the clutch. "I can't!"

"Calm down, that was my fault. I should have put it in neutral."

"I can barely drive a normal car, let alone a stick. Please don't make me do this." She reached for the door handle.

"Look, if you don't help me get Jerry to my condo, he could die. That would make you an accomplice to a murder. As I see it, you have no choice."

Suzy took a deep breath and gripped the steering wheel with both hands. "Fine."

"Put in the clutch and turn the key. Pretend we're going for a Sunday drive." The car started and Les put it into first gear. "Now slowly take your foot off the clutch and hit the accelerator at the same time." The car lurched forward. "Hit the gas!"

The car spit dirt up from its back tires as it sped forward in first gear. "Now hit the clutch again." Les shifted the car into second. The blue Civic scooted closer to the entrance of the apartment complex. "Let's just speed out of here so we don't have to go into first again."

Suzy nodded and slammed the clutch in as Les shifted to third. The street was clear. The Civic sped away from Westwood Apartments.

The ten-minute ride to Les's condo seemed to take hours with Suzy stalling at every light and Les coaching her through while other cars honked their horns.

Les's head poured sweat again. He turned on the air

conditioner, full blast, and stuck his face directly in front of the vent. The constant starting and stopping didn't help matters, either.

The Civic finally made it to its destination, and Les clicked the button for his gate to open. The car came to a stalling halt in Les's parking space.

Suzy rested her forehead on the steering wheel.

"Help me get him out." Les climbed out of the car and was hit by a flash of sunlight that forced him to stop and gain his composure. Whatever he and Jerry had smoked was not just weed, he knew that for sure. He struggled against letting his mind go into a deep hole of darkness. It had been a constant fight to stay conscious since he'd smoked that joint.

"Les! What are you doing?" Suzy yelled, tugging on Jerry's arm.

Les jogged himself out of his daze. They carried Jerry out of the car, Les taking his upper body and Suzy with his legs. When he opened the door to his condo, the scent of the wine still permeated the room. It smelled so refreshing, he knew he had made the right decision. They carried Jerry to the couch and set down his motionless body.

When he was settled, Les marched into the kitchen. He pulled the cap off the old milk jug, and the sweet, intoxicating aroma hit him. He stopped for a few seconds as he could already feel his mind clearing. He poured the wine-like substance into the glass just as he had done before. He swirled it around and exhaled deeply then ingested the aroma through his nostrils. The passion from the smell almost knocked him over.

His confidence soared. Jerry needed to drink this wine.

Les paced into the living room, carrying the glass of wine.

Suzy's body jarred backward as her forehead scrunched down and her cheek bones raised along with the corners of her mouth.

"What are you doing? Have you gone insane?" She flung both hands down against her thighs.

"Help me wake up Jerry so we can get him to drink this."

Suzy scanned the glass. Her eyes bulged. "I've been doing pretty good here, Les. I haven't completely melted down."

She stopped to let out a few curse words as she pointed at the glass. "What the heck is that?"

"Help me pull him into the guest bathroom."

The two of them dragged Jerry to the tub and sat him in it. Suzy held onto his arms to keep him from falling over. Les stripped Jerry of his clothes, leaving him in his underwear, then he turned on the cold water and plugged the tub with a stopper.

"Just hold him." Les hustled back into the kitchen, poured himself a shot of the wine, and downed it. Instantly, a burst of energy pumped through his veins, and strength surged through his entire body as the darkness left his soul. His mind cleansed, he could finally think straight again. It was as if the weed had fogged up his vision, and the wine was cold air blowing on it as on a windshield, clearing it so he could see again.

He grabbed the ice container from the refrigerator and lugged it into the bathroom. He dumped the whole thing into the tub with Jerry and the cold water. When the tub was full, Les snatched the detachable head from the shower, held it three feet from Jerry's face, and turned it on.

Jerry didn't move for about twenty seconds, then his eyelids flickered. Les dropped the shower head. Jerry's body flinched, shocked by the cold water.

Les then grabbed the wine glass, and Suzy tipped Jerry's head back. Les trickled the wine into Jerry's mouth until it was gone.

After the last drop was poured, Jerry popped opened his eyes. "Why am I so cold? Why am I sitting in your bathtub in my underwear? Suzy? This is awkward."

Jerry's eyes were clear, no longer glazed over. Les's old friend was back.

"You gave us a scare. We thought we were going to lose you." Les ruffled the top of Jerry's head.

"What are you talking about?" Jerry's eyes followed Les's hand as he removed it from his hair.

He thinks this is a joke.

"Don't you remember?" Disbelief riddled Suzy's face.

"Okay, you got me. Can I get a towel?" Jerry stood, dripping water in the tub. "I'm freezing."

"Sorry. Here's a towel, and I'll get you some clean clothes. Go ahead and take a shower, and we'll talk when you get out."

Wordlessly, Suzy wandered into the living room as Les went to get Jerry some dry clothes. When Les came in and sat with her on the couch, she looked as dazed as Lester had felt after smoking that weed. "You okay?"

"Did that—that red substance heal Jerry?"

"It sure did."

"But that's impossible. What is it, some kind of voodoo-magic healing tonic?"

"It's not voodoo, but it is some kind of healing tonic." Les faced Suzy directly. "If I tell you, you have to promise you won't think I'm crazy and that you won't blab it to the whole world."

"Les, I just saw a man who I thought was going to die from some kind of overdose, and he was miraculously healed. I think at the very least I deserve an explanation."

"What are you guys talking about?" Jerry bounced into the living room while toweling off his curly blond hair.

"Who's hungry?" Les jumped to his feet.

Jerry draped the towel over his head and raised his hands. "I could eat."

Suzy crossed her arms and gave Les "the look."

Les signaled with his hand to stop her. "I'll pay for yours, Suzy, how does that sound?"

"Fine, but you're going to tell me what's up with that stuff." Suzy narrowed her eyes.

With his towel still draped over his head and held together at his neck, Jerry shifted two inches from Les's face. "Looks like you're paying for me too, sweet cheeks." Jerry slapped Les on the butt. "I don't have my wallet."

CHAPTER TEN

==

Les blasted the car radio to discourage any conversation. *How am I going to explain this to them? How am I going to keep Suzy from telling everyone?* The three of them rode to the music of Fall of Envy, not saying a word until they pulled into the Applebee's parking lot.

"Way to make a girl feel special." Suzy grumbled. "You help save someone's life, and they take you to Applebee's." Suzy pivoted to face Les as he slid the key out of the ignition.

"They've added a lot of new stuff to the menu." Les said as he unbuckled his seat belt.

Suzy draped her leopard-spotted purse over her right shoulder as she paced out in front of them.

"Whatever. I don't know what your problem is. I love me some Applebee's." Jerry broke into song and dance. "I want my baby back, baby back, baby back ribs. I want my baby back, baby back, baby back ribs."

"That's Chili's, moron." Suzy rolled her eyes.

"Testy, aren't we, little Suzy Q? You need to relax," Jerry said in his outgoing surfer voice.

"Look, I am really annoyed at you and your friend right now, so you can just chill."

"Where is this 'tude coming from, Suzy-bell?"

Suzy whirled around in front of the double doors of the restaurant with both of her hands on her hips, eyes locked on Jerry. "How can you not remember?"

Both boys strolled past her. Each one flung a door open.

"Age before beauty." Jerry bowed, holding the door open.

"I am so glad I helped save your life." Suzy spun and scuffed the top of Jerry's head with her purse as she entered the restaurant.

The conversation stopped as the three of them were seated in a booth back toward the kitchen. The booth seats were green and pink leather. The wood panels on the wall stopped at eye level. The rest of the restaurant was covered with cow and chicken wallpaper, with antiques scattered about on shelves and hooks.

Suzy picked up her menu. "This place is such a drag."

"Can I get you something to drink?"

Les looked up from his menu. "Water with lemon, please."

"I'll have a cerrr-VEZA, cerrr-VEZA. That, my server friend, means 'beer' in Spanish. Beeee-rrr. B-e-e-r." Jerry spoke as if the server was deaf.

Why is Jerry being so annoying?

"Draft beer for you then, sir." The server turned his attention toward Suzy.

She peered over her menu as she examined Jerry from across the table. "Did someone slip you a Red Bull?"

"Man, I feel alive!" Jerry pinched Les's hand.

"Ouch." Les retracted his hand. *Jerry is acting so bipolar. One moment he is almost dead; the next, he is obnoxiously alive.*

"I'll also have water with lemon, thank you." Suzy placed her menu on the table.

"I feel like I could run a marathon. I can take deep breaths like I never could before. I have so much energy! Yeah!" Jerry flexed both biceps.

"What's the last thing you remember from today?" Les poked Suzy in the arm to get her attention.

"Everything gets kind of foggy after they took my neighbor to the hospital. I wanted to go there to see if he's all right, but then I woke up in your shower in my underwear." Jerry paused for a second as he lowered his brow and bit his bottom lip. "Now that I think about it, that was a little weird." Jerry's words flowed fast. He nodded with every syllable.

"Ya think?" Suzy's mouth followed her eyes as they both drew wide open.

The waiter brought their drinks to the table. Suzy ordered a salad, and Lester asked for a grilled chicken sandwich with fries.

"And for you, sir?" The waiter raised his brows in Jerry's direction.

"How many push-ups do you think I can do?" Jerry's eyes shifted from Les to Suzy then back to waiter. He ran his hand over his chin. "How about this? If I can do sixty push-ups in a minute, my meal is free; but if I can't, I pay you." Jerry pointed at the waiter then reclined back with both of his hands resting on the back of his head.

The waiter cleared his throat, looking at Les and Suzy for help.

"I'll have my baby back, baby back ribs," Jerry sang out.

"Fries?" The waiter scribbled on his note pad.

"Yepper doodle." Jerry shook his head like a hyperactive child. "After this, we should go to the gym and rep some out."

"So you don't remember lying in the back of Lester's car looking half-dead?" Suzy squeezed her lemon into her glass.

"Nope, why?" Jerry lifted his glass and chugged his beer as it dribbled out the sides of his mouth.

Les touched Suzy's hand and nodded. "Jerry, you had me smoke some pretty strong stuff."

Shock riddled Jerry's face as he emerged from his hyperactive state. "You smoked my superweed?" Jerry banged his beer on the table, sliding a fork to the floor.

"We smoked whatever you have growing in your closet. It could have triggered your memory loss." Les's chin quivered.

"Now that you mention it, I vaguely remember smoking my superweed this morning after hearing about old man Al."

Suzy shook her head as she squeezed a second lemon slice into her water. "I never heard of anyone blacking out from smoking marijuana."

Jerry scratched the back of his head. "It's not exactly just marijuana."

You have got to be kidding me. Les's forehead dropped onto the table. "What does that mean?"

"Every great chef has secrets he will take with him to the grave."

"What was in the weed?" Les raised his voice as he gazed up.

"Chill out, dude, it's perfectly safe and organic."

Suzy leaned forward with both hands on the table. "Organic? Please, there was nothing organic about what I saw today."

Les's head got hot, and the room started to move under his feet. "You almost overdosed."

"You were in real bad shape until Les gave you this red magic tonic stuff that completely healed your body and woke you up out of your drug-induced coma. That's why you were in the bathtub."

Suzy had finally said it. Les didn't want to interrupt

her, so he just let her say it.

Jerry hesitated. "Okay, let's say I did almost O.D. today and forgot everything that happened. What is this stuff that healed me?"

"I'm not sure, but it's a healing tonic all right, and it's the best-tasting wine you'll ever have in your life." How could Les describe this Jesus-created wine without totally freaking them out?

The waiter brought their food then, and Suzy excused herself to wash her hands. "No talking about anything until I get back, okay?"

When she had left the table, Jerry leaned over to Les. "Dude, what is going on with you and this magic healing tonic?"

"Dude, what is up with you and this killer superweed?"

Jerry blinked and gazed into the distance. "We have a lot to talk about tonight."

"Sandwiches from breakroom vending machines are depressing and gross." Lynn threw down her ham and Swiss and bit into her vending-machine apple instead. Juice ran down her chin. She wiped her mouth with her napkin and rested her forehead on the edge of the table as she chewed and stared at the floor.

"You okay?" Anne, another ICU nurse, swung open the door and let it slam shut.

Lynn snapped her head up. "Great as I can be on no sleep."

Anne poured herself a cup of coffee. "You working a double?"

"Yeah, and I packed only one meal, so I am having a romantic vending-machine supper." Lynn spun the apple in her hand, measuring where she should take her next bite.

"Did you just get those red highlights in your hair?"

Lynn brushed her hand through her hair. "Yeah. I cut three inches off too. It's called a bob cut and it cost me two hundred bucks, but I have to stay trendy. I'm not getting any younger."

Anne's mouth twisted into a wry smile. "I gave up being trendy long ago. I have three kids. After each child was born, my needs became less important. Now if I can find a good pair of sweatpants, I'm happy."

Lynn poured coffee and dumped several packets of sweetener into it. "Do you like being a nurse?"

"Do you mean do I like working a full-time job with barely any time to breathe, then go home to a messy house and three full-time kids?" Anne stirred her coffee with a red stir stick. "And a husband who loves football and beer more than me. This job pays for our life. Do I enjoy it? That isn't a relevant question for my situation, because I have no choice." Anne pulled her scrunchie from her dirty-blond hair with hints of premature gray, then smoothed it into a ponytail.

"No choice? You always have a choice." Lynn bit into her apple.

"When you have a mortgage you can't afford and credit cards that never go away and three kids to feed, you have no choice." Anne started to take bigger breaths as she rested her back against the wall.

Lynn wiped her chin. "Yes, but you made the decision to buy that house and use your credit cards. You wanted to have kids. Those are all premeditated decisions that you made. No one forced you to do any of them."

96

Lynn plainly had struck a sore spot. Anne placed her coffee cup down and rested both hands on the table as she leaned toward Lynn. "Let me tell you something, honey. You don't know squat about life. You and your two-hundred-dollar haircuts and manicured nails. There is more to life than looking cute so some boy will want to date you. I love my kids and my husband. I wouldn't trade them for the world. So until you get some life experience, don't give people advice."

"I wasn't trying to give you—"

Anne rushed out of the break room and let the door slam.

Note to self: don't talk to Anne about her miserable life. Maybe I don't need to get married.

Lynn's watch beeped then. Break's over, time for a check-up.

The chair screeched as she heaved herself up and proceeded to the door. She tossed her apple and the rest of her sandwich into the garbage on her way out. As she exited the break room, a high-pitched voice rang out from around the corner, then fast footsteps. A sick feeling struck Lynn in the stomach as she hurried down the hall.

Something inside her already knew where everyone was going. As she reached the end of the hall, two nurses ran into Mr. Allen's room. Lynn's mind froze for a second, then she recovered and dashed to her patient's room. She flung open the door.

The heart monitor sounded one solid, high-pitched wave, the sound every health-care professional dreads to hear.

"No pulse, no respiration." A dark-skinned male nurse named Tommie picked up the bedside phone and dialed the operator. "Code blue, room 2015. Code blue, room 2015."

Anne dashed in, pushing the crash cart, and behind her rushed the supervisor with a portable computer for charting the code. Lynn inflated the back-board device on the bed, giving herself a firm surface for performing chest compressions.

Anne ripped the ambu-bag from the crash cart and pitched it at Tommie. He tore open its plastic bag, tilted back Mr. Allen's head, and fixed the plastic, triangular mask over the patient's mouth and nose.

After two rescue breaths through the ambu-bag, Lynn positioned her hands on Mr. Allen's chest and started chest compressions, counting out loud to keep their rhythm. "One and two and three and four . . ."

Dr. Mancini's high-pitched voice sounded through her adrenaline rush as he charged through the door. "Give me a milligram of epinephrine."

Lynn shut out the sounds around her, concentrating on the exhausting task of pumping blood through her patient's body. "Fifteen and sixteen and seventeen and eighteen . . ."

She focused on her hands, clasped together and fighting for Mr. Allen's life. Tears started to tighten her throat as always during a code. Her pulse racing, she forced her throat to relax, even as the rest of her muscles screamed in agony.

"Defib. Everybody back."

Tommie tossed the ambu-bag onto the bed and grabbed both her arms. Lynn swallowed and let him pull her away. She raised her hands and backed away from the bed. "Clear."

"Clear." Tommie held his hands high.

Dr. Mancini positioned the paddles. "Give it to me,

one, two, three, clear!"

Within moments, the wailing monitor transitioned to a soothing beat as steady as a metronome.

"Somebody call Dr. Sheepstone." Dr. Mancini stood with hands on hips, watching the overbed monitor.

Lynn's legs felt too wobbly to hold her up, but she pushed past the crash cart and strode to the nurses' station. She flopped down on a rolling chair and snatched the phone receiver. She dialed "9" for an outside line, then the number on the top page of her notes.

The phone rang once. "Dr. Sheepstone."

"It's Lynn from the hospital. Eugene Allen went into cardiac arrest."

"How is he now?"

"We defibbed, and he's in normal sinus rhythm now. Dr. Mancini attended the code."

"I'll be right there."

Lynn hung up, her heart rate returning to normal. Poor Mr. Allen. The chances of an eighty-five-year-old man surviving sudden cardiac arrest were slim.

Dr. Mancini appeared from Mr. Allen's room. "You're the nurse assigned to this old man, right? Get cardiac enzymes stat so we can see how much damage he has. Although it's probably a moot point. I give him about a five percent chance to last through the night."

Five minutes later, Dr. Sheepstone jogged down the hall wearing eyeglasses, jeans, and a black polo shirt. She had never seen him in street clothes before. Tonight he bore an amazing resemblance to Richard Gere.

Dr. Sheepstone slowed to a walk as he approached Lynn. A rush shot through her chest as he heartbeat increased again at the sight of this handsome man. Was she developing a crush? He was in tremendous shape, his biceps bursting through his sleeves. How old was he, anyway?

Lynn's face warmed uncomfortably as the only images forming in her mind were from *Pretty Woman*. "He had, I mean he went into cardiac arrest. Dr. Mancini said he had a lot of damage and will probably die tonight."

"We'll see about that." Dr. Sheepstone quickly washed his hands. He opened the door to Mr. Allen's room, and Lynn followed. Anne threw the last scraps of medication packaging into the trash and pushed the crash cart out.

Dr. Sheepstone ran his right hand through his hair and anchored his hand on his head for a few seconds while studying Eugene Allen. He took a few steps closer so he was positioned at the end of the bed, directly in front of the patient.

He went into his analyzing position: right hand over his mouth, right arm resting in front of his body and left hand holding his elbow. "Eugene, it's not your time. You still have work to do."

Dr. Sheepstone took two steps toward Lynn so he was standing about a foot in front of her. He placed his hands on her arms and looked deep into her eyes as though speaking to her soul. "This man will not die tonight. His purpose has not been finished. I need you to guard him tonight and make sure his recovery is uninhibited."

"How can you tell that he'll live?"

"Some things don't need an explanation. You just have to believe." Dr. Sheepstone released Lynn's arms and strode over to Eugene Allen's bed "A great man lies in this bed."

"Do you know him?"

"Can't you feel the peace flowing over his body?"

100

Lynn jarred her chin forward to examine the body. "I felt that earlier, when I took his hand to comfort him."

Dr. Sheepstone looked at her with compassion in his eyes and smiled. "Stay with him."

Lynn nodded and then looked at the floor. As before, tears welled up in her eyes.

Dr. Sheepstone draped his arm across her shoulders, and she embraced it back. "It's going to be okay. You just have to believe. Get ready for a long night." Lynn held the embrace a few seconds.

Dr. Sheepstone pulled a syringe from his shirt pocket and ripped off the packing. He attached a large-gauge needle to the syringe, then he reached into his jeans pocket and brought out a small vial filled with bright red liquid. He rotated the vial, mixing the contents, and popped the top.

Lynn stepped next to Dr. Sheepstone. "Excuse me, doctor, what is that?"

Dr. Sheepstone halted to give Lynn his attention. "It's a special medicine."

When he had cleaned the vial's top with an alcohol sponge, he drew up three milliliters of the red substance, filling the syringe.

Lynn stepped in front of the doctor. "What kind of medicine, and where did you get it?"

Dr. Sheepstone gazed down. "It's an unusual concoction. An herbal remedy that helps repair destroyed tissue and organs." Dr. Sheepstone tried to side-step past Lynn, but she blocked his way.

She dipped her head. "And where did you get it?"

Dr. Sheepstone smirked. "Where every good doctor gets medicine. Mexico."

"What's it called?" Lynn crossed her arms.

101

Dr. Sheepstone paused for a second, pressing his lips together. "I like to call it nectar."
He advanced past her, shut off the IV pump, and closed the tubing's stopcock. Then he lifted the IV bag from its hook. He swabbed the second port with alcohol then slowly injected the red substance. It filled the bag and gave it a bright red tint, almost like food coloring would.

He then reached into his other pocket and pulled out a clear substance in the same-sized vial. When he injected the IV with the colorless liquid, it shot through the bag, making the fluid somewhat clear again. He flipped the bag a couple of times, mixing it, then hung it back on the IV pole, opened the line again, and started the pump. He pitched the empty vial and syringe into the red sharps container.

Lynn's mouth moved to one side. "Nectar, huh? I'll call you again if anything happens."

"Trust me, you won't have to." Dr. Sheepstone winked at her and left the room.

CHAPTER ELEVEN

==

At his apartment, Les puttered around making coffee, adjusting the stereo volume, anything he could think of that would postpone the job he knew he had to do.

"Stop avoiding the inevitable. Sit down and talk to us." Jerry patted the couch cushion next to him.

Les plopped down with his body leaning forward, resting his elbows on his legs, rubbing his hands together. "I don't know why I'm so nervous. My hands are sweating."

"Dude, it's all good in the 'hood. You're surrounded by compadres." Jerry slapped Les on the back.

"Okay, but first we need to make a pact. Everything said here tonight stays in this room. Got it?"

"Got it, bro." Jerry picked a piece of rib out of his teeth with a toothpick.

"You have my word." Suzy crossed her heart with her index finger.

Les drew a deep breath. "Remember the other night when I was talking about Star Wars, the Bible, and Jesus? I had a horrible headache that day. It kept getting worse until I screamed out for Jesus to take it away, and he did."

Jerry scratched the back of his head with one of his eyes closed. Suzy's empty gaze left Les feeling insecure. He swallowed back the doubt that crawled across his mind. "I started researching this Jesus guy and his power. The only thing I could compare it to was the Force in Star Wars. I tried to explain it to you, but you kept making fun of me."

Jerry picked another piece of rib out of his teeth and smacked his lips. "Sorry, but it sounded dumb."

"It's okay. I must have sounded like a lunatic. I put

in some mega-research hours that night and came up with a formula that creates what I call the holy force. It's a cross between the Jedi power, 'the Force' and Jesus' power, the Holy Spirit."

The corner of Suzy's mouth turned slightly upward. "I'm lost."

Lester reached over to touch Suzy's knee. "Bear with me a few more minutes. A Jedi master believes that if you have enough faith in something and don't doubt, you can make it happen. When Luke's X-Wing sinks and Yoda raises it from the murky water, Luke says, 'I don't believe it!' Then Yoda says, 'That is why you fail.' Luke tried to use the Force to raise the X-Wing, but he couldn't because he lacked faith in the Force."

"I'm really lost now. I've never seen Star Wars." Suzy folded her arms.

Les wiped his face with his right hand and turned toward Susie. "No way. You've never seen Star Wars?"

"I'm not a sci-fi geek."

Jerry's laugh made the whole thing worse.

"You don't have to be into sci-fi movies to—" Les stopped himself, trying to gain composure as he felt his blood pressure rising. "Okay."

Speak from the heart. "Luke failed because he lacked faith. The book of John talks about Jesus doing all of these incredible things because the people had faith in him. I believe that Jesus did these miracles. It makes sense to me. I don't know why. Maybe because for most of my life, I've wished that Star Wars was real. I have always dreamed of doing something extraordinary. Not that Jesus would turn me into Luke Skywalker or anything, but that I could do something with my life that would matter." Les froze for a few seconds as he realized he had both Jerry's and Suzy's full attention.

"So I figured I would do my own experiment and try to turn water into wine. This was the first miracle Jesus ever did, so I decided it would be a good place for me to start. I asked Jesus to turn that old milk jug full of tap water into wine, and he did. Except it's not just wine. I mean, it tastes like wine, but it has the power of the holy force in it which gives it the power to heal just like Jesus did. That's why when you were sick, I brought you here and made you drink it, and you were completely healed."

"Deep, bro, real deep." Jerry's face bleached, his voice somber.

The cold, sober presence in the room made Les fidget. "Anybody want coffee? I've got French vanilla creamer."

Les grabbed the pot, poured the coffee, and handed a mug to Jerry. "Your turn. Tell us everything you remember."

"It started last night with my neighbor, old man Al. He said that he needed to tell me something. What was it . . . ?" Jerry sipped his coffee. "Oh man, now I remember! You're not going to believe this, but old man Al asked me if I was satisfied with my life. He wanted to give me a Bible and have me answer that question just like Miss Copeland asked you to do. Is that not freaky?"

"Freaky." Les's eyes beamed.

"I'm totally lost about this whole 'are you satisfied with your life' thing." Suzy waved her left hand. "Care to fill a girl in?"

"Long story short, Miss Copeland gave me the week off so I could figure out whether I was satisfied with my life and if I want to continue working at Air Parts. Now Jerry's getting the question."

"I didn't handle the situation too well. I was so freaked out that I ran out of his apartment. The next morning, the ambulance took him to the hospital. I called in to work so I could go to the hospital and see if he was all right." Jerry hesitated. "I smoked some superweed for the first time instead. That's the last thing I remember."

Jerry's mood had shifted, and his shame burned in his eyes. Whatever had happened to him, he no doubt didn't want to talk about it in front of Suzy.

"It's okay, bud. It's all over now." Lester patted Jerry on the back. "I wonder what happened to Mr. Al?"

"I don't know, but it's getting late, and I need to get home soon." Suzy stood and let out an exhausted breath. "This is a little overwhelming, and I wouldn't believe it if I hadn't seen it. I need some time to decompress. The only question I have is what you're going to do with your discovery."

Les shrugged. He needed an answer to that himself.

Thirty minutes later, they dropped Suzy off at her mother's house. As they backed out of the driveway, Jerry snapped off the radio. How had he ever been able to think with that noise going on? Or had he ever spent his driving time in thought? Possibly not. "Dude, what are we going to do about Suzy?"

"Trust her that she isn't going to tell anyone."

"Great. We have to trust a gossip queen not to blab her mouth."

Les rested the side of his face on the steering wheel. "What do you want to do tonight? You want to stay with me or do you want me to take you home?"

106

"Let's swing by my house and pick up some things. I'll spend the night at your house if that's okay."

"It'll be like old times."

They pulled into the Westwood Apartments parking lot. Les waited in the car, and Jerry sprinted to his apartment. As he reached his door, he caught a stench of something foul. He opened his door. "Pee-ew. That reeks!"

He found a large puddle of half-crusted throw-up on his kitchen floor. "Where did that come from?"

Jerry grabbed the bleach bottle under his kitchen sink and sprayed the throw-up to let it soak. He grabbed Suzy's bike from the foyer and leaned it against one of his living room walls. The strong smell of marijuana residue in the living room flared his nostrils.

"Wow, am I glad I'm not sleeping here tonight." Jerry grabbed a bag from his closet, and as he stuffed clothes into his bag, he had an overwhelming urge to get high. He dashed out of the closet, snatched his toothbrush and pillow and headed back to the kitchen.

The stench of marijuana and throw-up made him gag. He ripped a handful of paper towels off the roll, sprayed more bleach on the gross mess on his kitchen floor, and wiped it up. He then nabbed his keys, bag, and pillow and left, slamming the door behind him.

Jerry climbed into the Civic and threw his stuff in the back seat.

"What took you so long?" Les frowned

"I had to clean up a little mess in the kitchen."

Les laughed. "Man, I forgot about that. I puked on your kitchen floor."

Jerry punched Les in the arm. "That's why you didn't want to come in, jerk. Whatever, my apartment reeks right now of a nice mixture of marijuana, throw up, and bleach." Jerry shook his head. "Unbelievable. Let's get out of here."

They drove back to Les's condo, parked, and climbed out of the car. Les punched a button on his key fob and locked the gate. "Do you plan on going to work tomorrow?"

"No, I'm going to call in sick again."

"What will your supervisor say?"

"At this point, I don't care. In the grand scheme of things, my job is becoming less and less important." Jerry tapped his foot while Les unlocked the condo door.

"I know what you mean. I have no desire to go back to work on Monday." Les plopped on the couch.

Jerry sprawled out next to him. "I haven't been completely honest with you." He paused and dropped his gaze, tapping his leg. "I think my superweed opens the doors to another world of weird people I can interact with."

"You mean it lets you see an old gas-station attendant and a big Arian-supremacy-looking dude."

Jerry whirled his head toward Les. "You know?"

"Yeah, I saw them too, at your apartment. Remember, I smoked with you."

"You saw them too? This is crazy!" Jerry sprang to his feet and paced the floor in front of the couch.

"The last thing I remember at my apartment was trying to open my door, then I blacked out."

"What happened after that?" Finally, everything was piecing itself together.

"The door flew open, then you shot backward and were knocked out. They stood there in the doorway, a gas-station attendant with a name tag that read 'Gretchen' and some big, bald-headed dude."

Jerry fell back onto the love seat. "No way! This is

unbelievable."

"They stood there in the doorway asking if they could come in. It seemed strange to me that they kept asking permission to enter."

"You never invited them in?" Jerry stood and paced again.

"No, I was too paralyzed with fear and concerned with you to even speak. Then the big guy pushed the woman out of the way, screaming that he would kill you if I didn't let them in."

"Dude, this sucks. I think I'm having a nervous breakdown." Jerry sat on the love seat again and clasped his hands on top of his head. "I thought I killed both of those people."

"If I hadn't seen those two, I would have thought you belonged in an insane asylum, but I know what I saw and I know what I felt. They were real, all right—too real. Are you sure you killed them?"

Jerry puffed his cheeks out with his eyes fixed on the ceiling. "I'm not sure. This is making me depressed. Let's talk about something else."

The theme from *Rocky* broke the tension. Les surveyed his phone. "I don't recognize the number." He clicked the phone silent and laid it down on the coffee table. He watched it vibrate for a few seconds, then he picked it up and punched the speaker-phone button.

"Jerry, this is Lila." The woman's voice was soft, smooth. "We met at the skater shop the other day when I was with my friend, Darla. This is going to sound weird, but I just had this overwhelming urge to call you."

Les's eyes glazed over, and a bead of sweat broke out on his forehead.

"Give me the phone. That chick is hot." Jerry

109

snagged the phone from Les and turned off the speaker-phone feature. "Hey, Lila. How could I forget you? I was just thinking about you."

Jerry bounced up and strolled to the guest room, giving Les a thumbs-up.

"You were just thinking about me, huh?" Lila said. "What were you thinking about?"

"I was telling my friend what a refreshing, intellectually stimulating conversation I had last night with two intriguing individuals."

"You're such liar. I know you don't talk like that."

"What? I'm insulted." Jerry sat at the end of the double bed that was pushed against the wall. His feet overlapped one another. "Anyway, let's cut to the chase. You want to go out or what?"

"Wow, right to the point."

"Let me put it this way. If I could rearrange the alphabet, I would put U and I together."

"You can stop now. Darla and I will meet you tomorrow at Greenie's off Park Street. Let's say five o'clock."

"Sweet! Five it is." He hung up and pumped his fist. "Yes! Sometimes even I am amazed at my abilities."

Jerry swaggered back to the living room, swinging his body and arms wildly from side to side. He stopped his swagger and stretched out his arms. "Who needs a hug? Who needs it? Come on, give your best friend in the whole wide world a hug."

"I am not giving you a hug." Les rolled his eyes.

What's with him? "Maybe I can change your mind when I tell you we've got two smoking-hot dates tomorrow night." Jerry kicked his legs from side to side as if he was one of the Rockettes and sang like Frank Sinatra. "Bop,

bop, dadada, bop, bop dadada, start spreading the news! We have really hot dates."

Les's laughter encouraged him. "You're crazy. You know that?"

"Come on, dance with me. Bop, bop, dadada, bop, bop, dadada." Jerry yanked Les up by the hand. He slung his arm over Les's shoulder. "All right, one, two, three, four, right leg, bop, bop, dadada, bop, bop, dadada. Start spreading the news, we have really hot dates." They sounded like two dogs howling at the moon.

"Okay, this doesn't feel right. I'm done." Les removed Jerry's arm and chuckled. He moved away from Jerry and back into the living room.

"Party pooper!" Jerry ran and leaped over the couch onto Les.

"Get off me. You have officially reached the annoying zone." Les pushed Jerry onto the floor.

"Hey, I need to tell you something serious." Jerry paused then sang, "We have really hot dates!"

Les crashed his face into a couch pillow. "What do these girls look like?"

Jerry popped his head up from the floor to peer at Les then laid his head back down. "Lila is one of the hottest chicks I've ever met. She reminds me of a real-life Arabic princess, real exotic-looking."

Les's face went limp. "I don't believe it."

"You don't believe what? That we have really hot dates?"

"Nothing." Les pushed his face back into the pillow.

"Her friend is pretty hot too. She's a blonde, and I think she used to be an NFL cheerleader or something. I didn't pay much attention to her. I was so captivated by Lila. We're meeting them tomorrow at five for happy hour at Greenie's off Park Street. Then I figured we could go get something to eat and then maybe hit the bars."

"Fine."

"What is the matter with you?" Jerry mimicked Les. "Fine. You don't even seem excited about this."

"Hey, I danced with you," Les snapped back.

"Easy, big fella. I'm just saying it sounds like something is bothering you."

"It's been a long day. I feel like zoning out into the tube. You wanna beer?"

"Does moss grow on trees?" Jerry grabbed the remote, turned on the TV, and flipped it to a game.

At midnight, the basketball game ended. "I'm beat. Time to hit the sack." Les clicked off the TV.

As they shuffled toward the bedrooms, Jerry grabbed Les by the arm. "Hey, man, I just want to say thank you for what you did for me today."

"I couldn't let my best friend die."

"Man, you're a good friend." Jerry slogged toward the bathroom.

"Hey." Les paused and waited until Jerry turned to look at him. "You need a hug?"

"Shut it."

CHAPTER TWELVE

==

Lynn's watch made a one-tone beep. Twelve o'clock. Her eyes felt heavy as sacks of sand as she squeezed them shut and then open. She entered Mr. Allen's room and noticed more color in his face, but it was probably just the bad lighting. Lynn did a quick scan of his vitals and his IV. Everything looked the same as an hour ago except for his skin.

When she finished her rounds, she made her way toward the break room. There she found Tommie dumping sugar into his cup of coffee. "You look like you could use a cup or two of this weak hospital coffee."

Tommie's perfect smile could have been in a toothpaste ad. His six-foot-eight frame made him always stick out around the hospital.

"I'm considering a straight IV drip of java." Lynn poured herself a cup.

Tommie laughed and sat at a table. "I haven't seen you around the hospital much tonight. Where have you been hiding?

"I'm in Eugene Allan's room a lot."

"Why? His machine needs to be calibrated only every two hours."

"Because Dr. Sheepstone ordered it." Lynn took a sip of her coffee. "He believes Mr. Allen is going to get better."

"Impossible! Maybe if he was thirty years younger. He's eighty-five."

Lynn pulled up a chair and sat across from Tommie. "Why do you think Dr. Sheepstone is so confident that this patient is going to recover?"

"All my encounters with Sheepstone have been good. He always thinks the best in every situation, and I think he is probably just trying to be positive."

"But what about his track record and all the outstanding accomplishments?"

"The man is an amazing doctor, but in this case, I feel he's just trying to be positive."

"Hypothetically, if Mr. Allen got better and walked out of this hospital, then what would you think?"

"I would have to see it to believe it. I don't even know why we're having this conversation about some guy who has one foot in the grave," Tommie said with a smirk.

"You've worked with Dr. Sheepstone before, right? His positive energy seems to have an effect on the patients."

"We are no longer talking about material facts of medicine. We're moving toward hocus-pocus," Tommie snapped.

Lynn stirred the cream into her coffee with a red stir stick. "I'm starting to believe that books don't have all the answers. We have both seen it in our short careers—you do everything right, the diagnosis is spot on, the surgery goes perfect, the timing is impeccable, and the patient dies from some unknown complication. Could there be some other force out there that plays a role in deciding who lives and who dies?"

"Not to be rude, but you're insulting my intelligence, telling me that I went to school for four years to find out that another force is floating around, determining who lives and who dies. For you to diminish what we do every day is insulting." The chair made a screeching noise as Tommie towered.

Lynn's gaze followed him. "That's not what I'm

saying."

Tommie crossed his arms. "Then what exactly are you saying?"

"There could be other factors involved in people getting better, not just medical treatment."

"I have to get back to work." Tommie threw his coffee cup in the trash on his way out the door. He waved and gave her a smile with no teeth as he disappeared into the hall.

That was a look of pity. He feels sorry for me. Lynn finished her coffee and poured herself another cup. *I can't believe he just got up and left like that. What was he so offended about? I was just trying to have a deep conversation.*

Lynn headed back toward Mr. Allen's room. As she advanced toward the nurses' station, Tommie was talking with Anne in the hall. They both looked up and quickly turned away.

How tacky. She opened Mr. Allen's door and peeked in on him. Now Tommie will no doubt tell all the nurses how she thinks modern medicine is a waste of time and everyone should just tap into positive energy to heal themselves.

As she checked the IV pump, she caught movement out of the corner of her eye. She turned her gaze toward Mr. Allen. It looked as though his right hand was moving slightly, but it could just have been the bad lighting or her eyes playing tricks.

She stood beside him, watching his right hand for any kind of movement. There it was. A slight twitch in his hand set her heart to skipping a few beats. She stepped back and took in the sight, then she wanted to touch his hand. She reached over and held it gently.

The skin felt much warmer than before. Lynn pulled a stool over so she could sit next to him, holding his hand with her head down and her eyes closed. Dr. Sheepstone's words echoed in her mind. *Feel his peace.*

It was as if warm honey was being poured on her head and making its way down her body. She felt a slight squeeze from his hand. Lynn jolted, and her pulse shot up as if someone had frightened her.

Sometimes patients spasm right before they die. Was he getting ready to die? His right legged jerked slightly to the right. Lynn checked his vitals: blood pressure 116/64, pulse 68, respirations 14, temperature 97.3, oxygen saturation 98 percent. No change from the last readings.

She stood back and tried to assess the situation like Dr. Sheepstone would. *If Mr. Allen is going to die, he's at least not going to die alone. But if he sits up in this bed, I'm going to scream.*

A soft rap sounded on the door. Lynn grabbed her chest and took a deep breath.

Tommie peered in the door then stepped in. "Sorry if I startled you. I wanted to apologize for the way I ended the conversation earlier. I should have respected your opinion. Can I do anything to help you in here?"

"I'm fine. Thanks for asking."

"All right then. I'll see you around." Tommie flashed his million-dollar smile and closed the door.

A rush of warm air swept through the room, brushing the loose strands of hair from her eyes.

The fingers on Mr. Allen's left hand moved from right to left. Unbelievable. Lynn stood in the half-lit room and crossed her arms. Another gush of warm air, this time from behind her, pushed her gently forward. She spun around to see where the breeze came from.

There was nothing.

There hadn't been any warm breezes or movement from Eugene Allen in an hour. Lynn needed to freshen up after a long shift, so she grabbed her purse and headed toward the staff bathroom. She touched up her foundation, applied red lip gloss, brushed out her hair and made a new ponytail, and spritzed on fruity body spray.

As she cleared out of the bathroom, Tommie bent over the water fountain. Was he stalking her? Part of her hoped so.

"You still hanging in there?" Water dripped from Tommie's mouth. "I've been waiting for you to get off break so I could follow you around."

"Sounds like you're having a busy night."

"It has been kind of dead tonight." Tommie's face reddened. "No pun intended."

Moments later, back in Mr. Allen's room, Lynn pulled back the privacy curtain to examine her patient. The room was brighter than it had been when she'd left. His face looked as if it reflected the lamplight back into the room. Lynn had never seen anything like it.

Her eyelids flickered in rapid succession as she concentrated on the old man. Her cell phone went off, signifying a text message, and almost made her pee her pants. She buried her face in her hands, feeling her blood pressure rise and maybe an ulcer forming.

Get a grip. You're a professional. Lynn closed her eyes, inhaled deeply through her nose, and exhaled through her mouth. When she opened her eyes, the light no longer illuminated Mr. Allen's face. Everything looked like it had all night.

Lynn marched over to Mr. Allen to check his vitals
and take a closer look. To the naked eye, he looked better
and healthier. She scratched her head and checked the dim
overhead light on the wall over Mr. Allen's bed. Then she
prodded his cheek a couple of times. His face radiated
warmth into her fingertip.

She must be losing it. She needed some sleep. Lynn
pulled her phone out of her pocket. She flipped it nervously
in her hand, knowing that if she was caught checking her
messages, she could get written up. She arced her back
toward the door and glanced at the unfamiliar number, then
read the text. *You need to take out the endotracheal tube
now! Eugene wants to talk to you.*

With a weird, creepy feeling of being watched,
Lynn franticly scanned the room. Tommie must be playing
a joke. She popped her head out into the hall but saw no
one.

Lynn dropped her phone. She focused her attention
first on the phone, then on Mr. Allen's motionless body.

She pressed two fingers of each hand onto her eyes.
"I am not going crazy, I am not going crazy, I am not going
crazy." She bent over and picked up the phone, damp from
her sweaty hands. If this was Tommie playing a practical
joke, she'd kill him.

Then another text came from the same number. At
this point, if someone walked in and saw her checking her
phone, she'd deserve the write-up. *If you want to see, you
must believe. Now you have to obey.*

What did she want to see? A miracle. Lynn looked
back at her phone. Believing and seeing was one thing, but
even if he lived, Lynn would be fired and probably go to
jail for removing the tube without a doctor's order. How

could this happen to her? This wasn't even possible, was it?

Does this man need to talk to me? Do I really believe that he'd be able to breathe on his own if I did take him off the ventilator? Her head felt dizzy and suffocated. She rushed for the door. "I need some fresh air!"

Her phone beeped with another text message. She ignored it and informed her supervisor that she was taking a break. Then she made her way outside to the hospital courtyard and sat on a bench overlooking a couple of rose bushes. She took in huge gulps of fresh, cool air. The slight fragrance of roses surrounded her.

A man in his mid-forties hobbled over to Lynne. "You have a light?"

"No, I don't smoke." Lynn examined the man in the stained yellow shirt.

"I don't smoke, either. I found this cigarette on the ground, and I was like, what the heck, maybe it will make me feel better." The man's bright turquoise eyes sparkled like the Caribbean. They were filled with so much life, and they radiated hope. They didn't match his exterior at all. Lynn couldn't help looking past all of that to the hope in his eyes.

He reached out his stubby hand. His gap-toothed smile set her at ease. "I'm Charlie."

"My name is Lynn. Not to be intrusive or anything, but what are you doing out here?"

Charlie paused and admired the roses. A solo tear formed in the corner of his eye. "My wife of twenty years has terminal cancer, and the doctor has given her a month to live. We just got the news today. I couldn't bear to go home without her, so I decided to wait it out in the courtyard for the night. Sounds pretty stupid, huh?"

"No, I think it's sweet that you don't want to go

119

home without your wife. It shows how much you love her. I'm sorry about your bad news today."

Charlie sat beside Lynn admiring the roses again. "It's just life, right? We live for a little while, then we die for a long while. It doesn't seem fair, does it?"

Lynn rubbed the back of her neck. "No it doesn't, unless, of course . . ."

Charlie wiped the beads of sweat back over his badly receding hairline. "Of course what?"

"Nothing. I was just speaking without thinking."

"Sometimes I have my best ideas when I'm not thinking." Charlie stroked the side of his jaw, running his fingernails over his beard stubble.

Lynn hesitated again. "You might think this is silly, but recently I've been thinking that there might be another reason for us living and dying."

Charlie rotated his body to face Lynn. A whiff of his body odor sank into her nostrils like hot garbage. "Like what?"

Lynn cleared her throat and batted her eyes as she tried to scoot a few inches away. She balled her fist and kept it pressed up against her mouth and under her nose as she spoke. "I'm not sure. I'm trying to figure it out. There's this man I've been watching all night. He dedicated his life to serving others, and I feel as if I need to talk to him to find out why he lived that way. I feel as if he could answer my questions if I could only speak to him for a few moments."

"Why don't you just ask him?"

Lynn cleared her throat again as the stench torched her nostrils, making it difficult to focus on Charlie's words. "He's hooked up to a ventilation machine. He can't talk."

A gust of warm air rushed over both of them, taking

the hot-garbage smell with it and leaving a vibrant scent of roses. Lynn closed her eyes and inhaled the inviting aroma.

Charlie swiveled his body back in the direction of the rose bushes. "That is a problem. Let me tell you something. I could be thirty days from losing the thing I love the most and spending the rest of my life alone. If I had an overwhelming feeling that someone could give me an answer to help my wife, I would do anything to talk with him. That's why I asked you for a light."

Charlie reclined back on the bench and rubbed his pot belly. "I had an overwhelming urge to come over and talk to you, so I did. I'm a shy person, but when you're desperate for answers, fear doesn't seem so big anymore."

"I might be able to help your wife. Have you heard of Dr. Sheepstone?"

"Who hasn't in this town? I bet he's expensive, though, and we don't have much money."

"I can't promise anything, but I'll ask him to see your wife as a favor to me. What's her name?"

Tears sprung into Charlie's eyes. "Bonny Blue, like the color blue."

"Huh, like *Gone with the Wind*?"

Charlie wiped his eyes. "No, she's not gone with the wind yet."

"Oh, no. I meant—never mind. I'm glad I met you." Lynn stuck her hand out to shake Charlie's hand, but instead, he gave her a big hug. Charlie squeezed her as her arms stayed tightly crossed in front of her body. Then Lynn stood and nodded toward the entrance. "I have to get back to my patients."

Lynn scurried toward the door. She turned around to wave to Charlie, but he was gone. He must have gone back into one of the corners, poor guy. Lynn couldn't imagine losing someone so close like that.

She reached into her pocket and felt her cell phone, then remembered the text message. She hit "view." *Your eyes have been opened, your heart believes. Now it's time to obey.*

A chill shot down her arms.

CHAPTER THIRTEEN

===

When Lynn reached the nurses' station, Dr. Mancini hovered next to Mr. Allen's room, deep in conversation with another nurse. Lynn slowed her pace to avoid drawing attention to herself.

"How is your patient doing? Never mind, I'll check on him myself." Dr. Mancini pushed the door open. Inside the room, he glanced at the monitor. "Everything looks good. I must have done a pretty amazing job, don't you think?

Lynn rolled her eyes. How pompous.

"Let me ask you a question. Do you find me attractive?" Dr. Mancini's lecherous grin turned her stomach.

Lynn shifted from one foot to the other. How do you answer a question like that?

"Seriously, for my age, you think I'm hot, right?"

Lynn's face heated. "This conversation is not appropriate."

"Yeah, because I'm the doctor. I understand, but if we didn't work together, and you saw me driving my Mercedes SLK convertible with the top down, what would you think?"

I would think you were a greasy old perve. "Get back to the patient, because I don't want to file a sexual harassment suit tonight."

"Lighten up. I'm just trying to have a little fun. It's three o'clock in the morning, for heaven's sake."

A knock came on the door, and Tommie peeked in. "You looking for me?"

"Get in here, Tommie-boy. We need someone who

can lighten up the mood." Dr. Mancini's gold chains clanked together as he moved to greet Tommie. "So, Tommie, have you ever dunked a basketball on an Italian?" Dr.Manicini playfully hit Tommie in the chest.

Tommie's eyes shifted to Lynn, then back to the doctor. "I've dunked on a lot of people, but I never stopped to ask if they were Italian."

Dr. Mancini laughed. "All right, what do you guys think about helping me take out this endotracheal tube and see if this man can breathe on his own?"

"Great idea." Lynn couldn't believe how quickly those words flew out of her mouth.

"Lynn, get over on the other side and give me a hand." The doctor shut off the ventilation machine and had Lynn cut the medical tape that held the endotracheal tube in place. Dr. Mancini carefully pulled the eighteen-inch tube out of Eugene Allen's mouth. Blood and saliva dripped off the tube.

Mr. Allen's mouth stayed open. He drew a breath, then another.

Dr. Mancini spread his arms open with his palms facing up, visibly gauging Lynn and Tommie's facial expressions. "Wow, am I good or what? I guess we've got ourselves a fighter. Keep a close eye on him the next several minutes. He could have some internal bleeding that we don't know about, and if he stops breathing, we'll have to re-intubate as fast as possible."

Lynn could feel each beat of her heart. "I'll take it from here."

"Let's go, Tommie, I need to talk to you about something private." Dr. Mancini eyed Lynn then patted Tommie on the back.

The two men left Lynn alone with Eugene Allen.

She watched his every breath, waiting to see a sign of life. She closed her eyes, and her courtyard conversation with Charlie replayed in her mind. Her pulse raced as his words overwhelmed her. Was she really on the brink of the answers she so desperately sought?

She fixed her gaze on the old man's chest. It moved so slightly, up and down. Small mucus strands came out of the old man's mouth as his right eye faintly opened.

A small cough shook her body as her hands trembled. Lynn bolted around to get a washcloth and wipe his face, but she bumped into the overbed table and sent it sailing into the wall. She glanced at Mr. Allen. Both eyes were open, watching her.

She felt as though someone had punched her in the stomach.

"Be still, my child. I am here for a little longer. Come close so I can touch your face." His voice was sturdy but worn out. Every word danced on her skin, leaving imprints as if she were made of snow.

Lynn let out a long sigh, her pulse slowing again. As she funneled closer to the old man, tears ran down her face. He touched her cheek and sent goose bumps down her left arm.

His hands were tender and soft as he wiped her tears away. "Why do you cry, my child?"

"I was hoping you could tell me."

Mr. Allen removed his hands from her face. "What would you like to ask me?"

"How did you know I wanted to ask you something?"

"Isn't it obvious? Come close, my child, I can't talk very loud." The old man opened then closed his fist as Lynn moved in close. "My physical destiny has not been fulfilled. That is why my father brought me back."

Lynn swallowed the clump in her throat.

How could an eighty-five-year-old man's father bring him back to earth? She must have misunderstood. "Who brought you back?"

"My heavenly father." Mr. Allen put his hand on top of Lynn's. "What is your name, child?"

"Lynn."

The old man smiled. "Ah, yes. You were the beautiful waterfall."

Lynn's eyes grew wide. "That's what my name means. How did you know that?"

Mr. Allen closed his eyes.

"When I was asleep, the Lord took me on a great journey. I saw incredible sunsets on magnificent mountain tops. In the middle of these mountain ranges flowed a beautiful waterfall with all the colors of the rainbow. The Lord spoke to me through it. 'Eugene, my old friend, it is almost time for us to meet, but I need you to go through this waterfall, and soon we will be together.'"

Lynn clutched Mr. Allen's hand.

"So I jumped into a crystal-blue pool of water and swam toward the waterfall. As I got to its edge, the Lord spoke to me again. 'Climb the side of the mountain and walk through the middle of the waterfall.' So I climbed up the side of the rock, jumped onto the ledge, and walked right through the middle of the waterfall. Through the water I could see a dark cave with a single bright light all the way on the other side. So I continued walking through the waterfall and into the cave toward the light when all of a sudden the light extinguished. My world went completely dark. I turned around and there was no more waterfall, just a pitch-dark cave. Then I heard a crashing noise like something ramming into the wall, and that's when I woke up."

Lynn let her mouth slack, then she snapped it shut. "So you're saying that God sent you back to talk to me?"

"Why are you so shocked?"

"Because I'm nobody. I'm a twenty-eight-year-old nurse who's lived to please only herself."

The old man cleared his throat. "It's never too late to fulfill your destiny. God has called you by name, and he brought me back from death to show you life."

Tears cascaded down Lynn's face again. "Can you tell God that I'm sorry for living a selfish life?"

"Tell him yourself."

"What do you mean? I can't talk to God. I don't know him."

"Would you like to know him now?"

Lynn paused as she wiped the tears off her cheeks. She held Eugene Allen's hands tightly. "Yes, I would like that very much." Her voice squeaked.

"You must believe in your heart and confess with your mouth that Jesus is Lord. Jesus is God's son, and he sent him to die for our sins so we can have eternal life. Would you like to receive eternal life?"

Lynn could not speak. She nodded.

"Repeat after me then, and believe in your heart that Jesus is Lord. Dear Jesus, I am sorry for living a selfish life. Please forgive me for all my sins. Please come into my heart and be Lord and Savior of my life. From this day forward, help me live every day for you. In Jesus' name, amen."

Lynn finished repeating the prayer and wept uncontrollably. Then she hugged Mr. Allen. "Thank you."

"Don't thank me, child; thank Jesus. He loves you

more than you will ever know."

Lynn released Mr. Allen's hands and wiped her face. She pulled her hair tie out of her hair and whipped her head down, then up, pulling her hair back in a ponytail with the tie. "Now what do I do?"

Mr. Allen smiled. "You start living. Do you have a piece of paper and pen?"

She pulled a small notepad and pen from her pocket and gave it to Mr. Allen. He wrote several notes. "I don't want you to open this until you get home. You understand?"

Lynn nodded.

"Now go get this old man some pain meds. My head is killing me."

"I need to get an order from Dr. Mancini." As Lynn left the old man, she felt lighter inside. She was starting a new life, and it felt good. When Lynn arrived at the nurses' station, Kate was plugging numbers into a desktop computer.

"Hey, Kate, can you page Dr. Mancini for me? Room 2015 needs a new diagnosis because he's awake, and he's also going to need some pain meds."

Kate scratched her forehead and neck. "Is that Eugene Allen's room?"

A smile broke across Lynn's face. "Yep."

"Are you sure?" Both hands rested on Kate's hips.

"Page Dr. Mancini." Lynn's tone was direct. *Ooh, that Kate burns me. Why does she have to question everything I say? Why can't she just do her job?*

Upon returning to the room, Lynn called out, "I've got your—"

He lay motionless.

"Mr. Allen!" She ran to him and shook him. "Are you okay?"

Lynn pressed her fingers against the artery in his neck. Nothing. She held her cheek to his mouth to feel for respiration. None. Tears poured out of her eyes as she snatched the phone and called a code blue.

She inflated the bed for the second time that night then grabbed a pair of gloves from the box over the sink and pulled them on.

Tommie dashed into the room with the crash cart. The next sound she heard was the solid, monotone beep that signaled death.

The next morning, Les awoke to a commotion in the living room. He sluggishly cracked his eyes and squinted at the clock. Eight fifteen. He was too tired to care where the noise was coming from, so he closed his eyes for just five more minutes.

They opened again at nine thirty-two as he heard what sounded like a coffee grinder in the kitchen. Les must have taken off his clothes in the middle of the night, because he woke up under the covers, dressed in his boxers. He grabbed a pair of sweatpants and a T-shirt out of his closet and progressed to the kitchen.

"Good morning, Leslie!" Jerry's loud greeting this early in the morning sounded like a curse.

Les slapped his forehead. "What did you do to my kitchen?"

"Sit down and relax. Let Papa Jer hook you up."

"You're cleaning up this mess, you know." Les stumbled out of the kitchen. "And stop calling me Leslie!"

A few moments later, Jerry brought Les a cup of coffee followed by two pancakes, two eggs, two pieces of bacon, and a side of toast. "It's just a little appreciation breakfast for saving my life."

"Oh, I thought me buying you dinner was your appreciating."

Jerry did an about-face and marched into the kitchen.

"I have an amazing day planned for us. We have to get you ready for the ball, Cinderella." Jerry fluttered back into the dining area with his plate and the syrup. He wagged his eyebrows up and down while stuffing a piece of bacon into his mouth.

"This doesn't sound good. What did you get us into?"

"Eat up and I'll tell you." Jerry waited for Les to finish his breakfast, then he carried their plates to the sink.

"I have to admit, I'm impressed. I had no idea you could make pancakes. So what's the big plan?"

"You have ten minutes to get ready. I have us booked at Olympia Day Spa for an all-day, full-body treatment." Jerry made two small claps with his hands.

Les flinched his head to the right then narrowed his eyes to try and gauge the expression on Jerry's face. *Either he is acting really well or the weed has finally mutated his brain.*

"Are you serious?" Les's eyebrows rose with his voice.

Jerry's jaw clenched as he stomped his foot. "Do you want to go or not?"

Les rubbed his thumb and forefinger over his left earlobe. "This is something two girls would do."

Jerry stood and raised his right hand, placing his left hand on something invisible, like you would when giving your testimony before a grand jury. "I have a confession to

130

make. A girl I kind of dated off and on for the last two
years works at this spa. She gets me in for half price if I do
the full package: haircut, Swedish scalp massage, paraffin
hand wax, one-hour full-body massage, mud facial,
pedicure, and foot massage. I've secretly been a spa addict
for the past two years."

Les doubled over laughing. "I'm going to pee
myself. I'm going to pee myself! You are such a woman."

Jerry folded his arms and tapped his foot.
"Finished?"

"Yeah, sorry. It's just that . . ." Les burst out into
more laughter. "It's such a girly thing to do."

Jerry snapped his fingers. "Hey. Do you want to go
or not?"

Les finally could breathe again. "I'll try anything
once."

They went their separate ways to get dressed. When
Les came out of his room, Jerry scrambled around the
kitchen, stacking the dirty dishes in the sink and
dishwasher.

"What about the dishes in the sink?" Les scowled at
the still-messy counter.

"Don't worry about them. We're going to be late."

Fifteen minutes later, they pulled in at the Olympia
Day Spa. Jerry pumped his fist. "Dude, you are so going to
love this day. We'll get our Swedish scalp massages first."

"You're a trip, you know that? You think you know
someone, and they end up being a closet spa addict."

Jerry sprinted into the building, acting like a kid at
an amusement park. By the time Les reached the spa doors,
Jerry was already inside, speaking with one of the female
attendants. He gave one of the girls a big hug as he
introduced her to Les. "Elizabeth, this is my best friend,

Les. Elizabeth is a good friend and my spa hook-up."

"The pleasure is all mine." Elizabeth winked at Les. "Why don't you take a shower and put your robes on? Then we can get started."

Could this be Jerry's ex? She's cute. Passing by several other attractive spa attendants, Les ambled with Jerry to the dressing area. They sat next to each other and undressed. Les hung his clothes in a locker. "I see why you love this place. How much did it cost?"

"Don't worry about it. Just promise me you'll listen to my idea for a new business venture."

Les's bottom lip and chin raised slightly. His eyes narrowed. "No harm in listening."

Four and a half hours later, they returned to the dressing room. "My body feels like mush." Les sprawled out on one of the benches. "Unbelievable. I feel like a new man."

"You look like one too." Jerry slid him an I-told-you-so smile. "Give me the car keys. You're in no condition to drive. Make sure you drink plenty of water."

"You're right. Take me to your leader."

As they left, they waved to a couple of cute girls at the checkout counter. "Wait for me in the car." Jerry flipped him back his keys. "I need to pay for the damage."

Les dozed in the passenger seat of his royal blue Civic until Jerry came out. "I'm sorry for laughing at you, bro. That was a good time."

Jerry cranked the ignition and let the Civic warm a few seconds before he shifted into reverse.

Les's head was leaning against the passenger side window, fogging up a small portion of it. "What's the story with that Elizabeth chick?"

"She's my ex," Jerry said casually as he shifted into

fifth.

I knew it!

Les drew his head away from the window. "How come I never met her before?"

"We've dated off and on for the past two years or so, but every time we get serious, she says that I have to stop smoking weed."

"The past two years? What else don't I know about you?"

"Chill, brah. It's been more of a friendship than anything. We talk on the phone mostly. She's a great girl, but she has a real problem with me being a pothead."

"I still can't believe you never told me about this girl." Les crossed his arms in front of him.

"I never told you about her, because I figured it would never come to anything. Do you remember a couple of days ago when you were asking me about the Bible and Jesus? This girl was the one who introduced me to all of that."

Les took a sip from his water bottle. "What happened?"

"It was hard for me to comprehend how something you can't see could give you peace. How could reading a book make you feel good about yourself? How can believing in this Jesus fellow take away my sins? She would always tell me how much God loved me even though I continue to disappoint him by getting high."

Les rhythmically tapped the bottom of the water bottle against the side of his head. He needed the perfect words that would make his friend believe in Jesus, but how could he know what they were? "What about everything that's happened to us the last couple of days, especially you being healed by the wine? You can't deny the power."

133

Jerry jerked the parking brake as the car lurched forward then back in Les's numbered parking spot. Jerry wiped his nose with his hand.

"That reminds me, time for you to listen to my proposal." Jerry playfully reached over and pounded Les on the chest.

A knot squeezed in Les' stomach.

CHAPTER FOURTEEN

==

The next afternoon, Lynn kicked her covers off her bed, still tired from her double shift. She slid her feet into her warm, fuzzy slippers and trudged to the living room. Yoda, Lynn's tan Chihuahua, was waiting for her with mouth open and tongue extended.

"Hey, Yoda bear." Lynn bent over and picked up Yoda. She stroked the top of his head. "Do you need to go potty? Do you?" Lynn opened her sliding glass door that led to her large fenced-in back yard. Yoda leapt from Lynn's arms and streaked off.

Within minutes, she carried her coffee and cream-cheese-topped blueberry bagel to the table in her breakfast nook. She gazed out the bay window and studied the geese swimming in her backyard pond, resisting the romantic daydream that once again unfolded in her mind. Maybe Mom was right. Maybe she set her expectations too high, and the love of her life would never appear. Yoda darted in the yard, chasing a butterfly.

Her phone rang, and she shuffled over and rifled through her purse. She focused on the caller ID, then clicked the phone open. "Hey, Lila."

"You sound groggy. Sorry I woke you. I was just calling to see if you made it through the night."

Memories of last night slammed into Lynn's brain. "I had a rough night taking care of a critical patient."

"What happened?"

Lynn's mind went foggy. "I think he died."

"You think he died? You should know if he's dead or not."

"It's weird, but I can't remember if he died or not."

135

Lynn rubbed her forehead. "I feel like my dreams and reality have collided. Let me call the hospital. I'll call you back."

Lynn hung up and dialed her unit in the hospital.

"ICU. Kate speaking."

Great. Of all the nurses who could have answered the phone, why did it have to be Kate? Lynn rolled her eyes. "This is Lynn. Could you do me a favor and look up Eugene Allen's condition for me?"

A long pause came over the phone. "He was your patient, wasn't he?"

The snarky tone of Kate's voice did nothing to ease Lynn's uneasiness. "You know he was."

"You don't remember what happened?"

"Just give me the report, Kate." *Why, God, must you torture me with this incompetent woman who spurs my impatience?*

"He was pronounced dead at five oh-nine this morning. You were the one who made the last note in his chart." Her sarcasm rankled on Lynn's nerves. "Do you need to up your meds?"

Lynn whipped the phone away from her ear and punched the "end" button. Then she called Lila back. "He's dead. He died at five this morning."

"You don't remember him dying?"

"It was strange. Some parts of the night seemed real, and other moments felt as if I was dreaming."

"You work too much. If you are having problems separating your dreams from real life, there's your sign. You need a break. Come out with us tonight."

"I have to be at work at six. Not all of us have rich daddies who wouldn't mind paying their bills if they lost their job."

"Don't hate! I can't help it that he loves to spoil me."

If only Lynn could have the life Lila has. What a perfect life. Beautiful, rich, successful, and could have any man she wanted. A dad who acts as a safety net—always there with a pile of money to land on if she falls.

Lynn's voice was quiet. "I wish my dad wanted to spoil me."

"Why don't you call in sick and come out with us tonight? Darla and I met a cute guy the other day at the board shop, and we're hanging out with him and his friend tonight."

"Be the fifth wheel? No, thanks."

"It wouldn't be like that. We're just going out to have a good time. Nothing serious like a double date. This guy seems real chill and fun. Not like the business stiffs we've been hanging out with."

Lynn twirled her hair around her finger. "What are the plans?"

"This guy, Jerry, suggested Greenie's off Park Avenue at five for happy hour."

Less than two hours. "I'll let you know." Lynn hung up the phone and set it on the table. She reclined back in her chair and twirled her hair around her finger again. *I've done so much for this hospital. I've never called in sick and always volunteered to pick up extra shifts. Of course, I needed the money, but my social life has been on pause the past year because of the hospital. I deserve this break, even if it costs me my first write-up.*

Lynn grabbed her cup of coffee and purse from the breakfast table and carried them into the living room, where she plopped down onto a beige overstuffed sofa. She needed to make a decision right away so her supervisor

could get someone to cover for her. She had no desire to go
back to the hospital after what just happened to her.

Dr. Sheepstone would be the only one who would
understand what she was going through. She rummaged
through her purse, looking for her notebook on which she
thought she had written his number. She pulled it out and
also found several notes Mr. Allen had written.

Lynn replayed the few moments she had spent with
that man. It felt like the most peaceful illusion, as if her
inner child had been freed from a life of confinement. She
gave her life to God's son, Jesus, this morning. But what
did that mean? She had no clue.

She tried to read the notes Mr. Allen had left, but
the tears in her eyes kept making everything blurry. She
reached for the tissue box, blew her nose, and wiped the
tears out of her eyes. Then she picked up the notebook
again.

> I was brought back from death to show you life.
> Your life is no longer your own, but it belongs to
> God. You are now called a child of the Most High.
> Congratulations on your new life! My dying request
> is that you read the living Word of God, the Bible. It
> will teach you everything you need to know about
> God's son, Jesus. Start with the book of John. Go to
> Westwood Apartments, number 34A. There is a
> spare key under the welcome mat. In the
> bookshelves, you will find several Bibles and
> notebooks. Please take a Bible for yourself and give
> another one to my neighbor, Jerry Humberger, who
> lives across the hall in 34B. Please tell him what
> happened to me and that it was not his fault; it was
> time for me to go home. Take the notebook labeled

May 1986 and read the whole story. You'll need the information in there when the time comes. Go to Celebration Church and tell one of the pastors that I sent you. It's a good church, filled with young people just like yourself. I already hear the angels rejoicing; it's almost time for me to go. I will wait for you at the gates when you're called home. Until we meet again, your brother in Christ, Eugene.

Lynn arranged the notepad on the couch next to her as she remembered watching Mr. Allen scribble his notes. *He knew he was going to die, that's why he sent me out of the room.*

She checked the time on her phone. Three forty-two.

What good are sick days if you're never sick?

"It's worth a shot." She flipped through the notebook for Dr. Sheepstone's cell number and dialed it. After two rings, he answered.

"This is Lynn. I wanted to let you know that I got to talk to Eugene Allen before he died."

"You did? What did he say?" Dr. Sheepstone sounded surprised.

Here goes nothing. "I became a child of God last night. Mr. Allen gave me a list of his dying requests." Her words ran together so quickly, he might agree with Kate that she needed meds.

"That's awesome. I'm happy for you. Not to change the subject, but I just received an e-mail from your supervisor, asking whether I've seen any unusual behavior from you. A random drug test has been issued on suspicion of memory loss induced by drug abuse. I wasn't supposed to tell you this, but I am going to vouch for you on this one."

Lynn covered her hand with her mouth to stop herself from cursing.

Kate.

"I need to speak with your supervisor anyway about a charity golf tournament he needs to play in. Let me explain your circumstance. Then you can follow up. Give me ten minutes."

"Why are you doing this for me?"

"I take last requests very seriously, especially from a brother in Christ."

Lynn's hand dropped to her chest. *He understands?* "You don't think I'm crazy for becoming a child of God?"

"I happen to be one myself. For the last twenty years, God has been changing my life and my practice. If you have any questions, please feel free to ask."

Dr. Sheepstone was a child of God? Amazing.

Lynn waited the ten minutes and called her supervisor. "Hi, this is Lynn."

"Dr. Sheepstone just left my office. You can have the weekend off."

The phone disconnected. That had been easy.

Looking over Eugene Allen's notes, she again noticed Jerry Humberg's name. She grabbed her phone and scrolled down to her last received call.

"Hello, beautiful," Lila said in greeting.

"I've got the whole weekend off. Can you believe it?"

"We're going to love having another gorgeous person to hang out with tonight."

"Did you say we're meeting a guy named Jerry? What's his last name?"

"He didn't say. Do you think you know him?"

140

The way these last couple of hours were going, Lynn wouldn't be surprised. "I'll tell you later. What are you wearing?"

"Casual. Greenies isn't exactly the kind of place you wear a dress to. Jeans, casual top."

"I don't want to show up in jeans and you and Darla are decked out."

Lila laughed. "Girl, I wouldn't do that to you. If you want, come over to my house so we can all ride together. Darla is coming over around five."

"I thought we were meeting them at five."

"I love to make boys squirm."

"You are so bad. I'll be there at five."

Les lounged on his sofa, more relaxed than he'd been since the accident. He could get used to these spa treatments. He raised his lime-green glass of water and sipped from it just as the massage therapist had told him. "So what is this big business proposal you wanted to tell me about?"

Jerry sat forward, hunching over his knees, on the loveseat that was positioned diagonal to the couch. "Do you think you can make any more of that healing wine?"

"I don't know, I haven't tried."

"You know all those network-marketing schemes that sell different juices and health products that they say can heal you of all sorts of ailments? We give the public a product they've never seen before—a product that works instantly with just one shot."

Les sat up and placed his glass on the coffee table, dropping his gaze to the floor. "I already don't like where

141

you're going with this."

"Dude, we could be rich! Think about it. We get a video camera, go into a terminal-cancer ward, start giving people shots of this stuff, slap it on You-Tube, and bam! We are sipping pina coladas in Maui for the rest of our lives." Jerry sat straight up and punctuated his words with sweeping hand gestures. "We can set any price we want. Even if you couldn't produce any more, we could make a million bucks easy with that one jug."

"Sell this stuff per shot to the highest bidder?"

"Or produce more and sell it to Africa for a billion dollars to get rid of their AIDS problem."

Les's mind flooded with turmoil. Images of him and Jerry on a beach in Maui sank into his subconscious. "But what if Jesus doesn't want me to sell it?"

"Jesus has given you the opportunity of a lifetime." Jerry bolted to his feet. He pounded his fist against his hand like a politician beating a podium. "You can give hope to people who are hopeless." Jerry's voice roared as if he was trying to speak over a cheering crowd.

"But just giving the rich hope, right?"Les exhaled through his nose as he leaned back against the couch cushion.

"No, you can give some to AIDS orphans in Africa if you want, but not until after we make a few million." Jerry sat down next to Les.

Les was too relaxed to continue to argue. "I'll think about it."

Jerry paused and waited for Les's attention. "All I ask is that you take a good, hard look at the gold mine sitting in front of your face." There was no smile or goofy grin spreading across Jerry's face now. He jetted off to the bathroom.

Les sat there for a few minutes, not moving, but digesting everything his closest friend in the world was saying to him. Dollar signs flashed in front of his eyes. Images of himself swinging in a hammock, sucking down a mai tai danced in the forefront of his mind. A woman in a grass skirt and a coconut bra asked him if he would like a massage.

"Hey, bro, you going to get ready or sit there and daydream all day?" Jerry peeked out of the bathroom as the toilet flushed.

"Yep, on my way right now." Les dragged himself to his room.

Jerry got done first. Since he had his hair done at the spa, his usual uncontrollable mess was cut down and stylishly combed. His curly hair fell across his forehead and covered the tips of his ears. His face was cleanly shaved, and he was actually wearing cologne.

Les strutted out of his bedroom then stopped at the sight of Jerry. "Whoa, looking pimp."

"Thanks. You look like a heartbreaker tonight, bro." Jerry gave Les a high five.

"Well, you know." Les popped his collar. His light-colored jeans gave the impression that they were old, even though he just bought them two weeks ago. He rolled up the sleeves of his white button-down shirt, showing off his tan and his shiny silver watch with the black face. His hair was the shortest it had been since his college swimming days. "Miss Elizabeth convinced me that the hard, spiky, wet look was out and the more natural short look was in. Shall we roll?"

"We shall."

Les held up his hand, palm out, like a crossing guard. "One more thing. No talking about the business

143

proposal tonight. Promise me."

"Why would I bring that up tonight in front of the girls?"

"Because when you get drunk, you tend to spill the beans."

Jerry chuckled. "You're right. It's sealed in the vault."

"And if for some reason you do start to talk about it, I get to smack you on the back of the head."

"Hmm, no deal."

They both laughed as they coasted out toward the car.

The evening might start out with some awkwardness between Les and Lila, but after a few drinks, it won't matter anyway.

They pulled the shiny blue Civic into the Greenie's parking lot off Park Avenue at four fifty-five. Inside, Jerry got them a table in the bar area at one of the high-top tables. "Sit across from me." Jerry pointed. "That way, the girls will have to decide where to sit. Whoever sits by us is the girl we go after for the night."

Les sat down and shook his head. "I don't like that idea. Sitting across from each other is fine, but we need to let nature take its course with the rest."

"Let nature take its course? You're such a goofball. All right, we will vibe it out. We should know by dinner who is digging who."

"Sounds like a plan." Les winked his left eye and shot his imaginary pistol at Jerry.

Les glanced down at his watch. Thirty-two minutes

late. He tapped his fingers on the table as he munched on the last onion ring in the basket. Was she going to stand him up again?

Jerry waved as Lila crossed the room with the others. "We have a code red. I repeat, code red. There are three of them."

Les whirled around and saw Lila leading the way for the other two women. His stomach dropped. Everything seemed to be in slow motion as Les's eyes were drawn to Lila's beauty. Her dark hair flowed in front of her face, giving her the look of a seductress behind a veil. Her plush lips glossed from across the room, radiating sensuality like kryptonite.

The three of them paraded to the high-top bar table. Jerry and Lila were the first to greet. Jerry held out his arms and gave Lila a big hug. "This is my good friend, Les."

Les reached out his hand as their eyes met for the second time. *Perfect 10.* The room started to melt as his pulse throbbed. His vision distorted from the heat waves rising off Lila's body. *Oh crap. My hands are sweaty.* Wait for it, wait for it. . . .

"Aren't you the guy from the video store?" Lila tilted her head and squinted.

Lester's voice dropped two octaves. "John, Lester John." Oh no. "So we meet again malady." *Malady? What am I saying?*

Lila yanked her hand from Les's grip as her left eyebrow lifted. "This is Darla and Lynn."

Lynn sat next to Les. Lila sat across from her next to Jerry, and Darla pulled up a chair at the end. "I guess I'll sit on the end." Darla shot a you-got-to-be-kidding-me glimpse at the women as she dragged the chair across the floor.

145

Her low-cut, bright orange tank top screamed, *Look at me!*

"When I was an NFL cheerleader and contestant on the pageant circuit, the bartenders always gave us free drinks."

Lynn gave Darla a sideways glance. "Why don't you try and get us some free drinks tonight?"

"Because we have two guys who can pay." Darla raised her eyebrows and simpered in the direction of the boys. Their laugher sounded awkward.

When the waitress came to the table, the guys ordered a pitcher of domestic beer, and the women all ordered girly mixed drinks.

When the waitress left the table, Lynn leaned forward, her elbow on the table and her head resting on the side of her hand. "What do you do, Jerry?"

"I love to take long walks on the beach, cuddle beside a camp fire, and talk endlessly about my feelings."

Les burst out with laughter, almost spitting out his beer. All three of the girls rolled their eyes.

"Seriously, I work in an IT department, but I hope to get my own personal venture off the ground someday." Jerry pouted his lips.

"What does your personal venture consist of?" Lila raised her brows.

Les searched his mind for a change of subject. If he didn't find one soon, he'd have to tell these three pretty girls what he did for a living. He'd give up drinking beer for a month if he could avoid that question.

"If I tell you, I'll have to kill you. It's top secret." Jerry pointed at all the girls.

"Can you give us a hint?" Lila batted her eyes at Jerry.

Jerry seemed to melt inside as Lila gazed at him with her emerald-colored eyes. "Sorry, I can't do it." Jerry waved his arms like an empire calling a runner safe.

"You're no fun!" Darla turned to Les. "What do you do?"

Now Les couldn't dodge the question. "I work for the same company Jerry does, just in a different department. I might also start my own business venture."

"Can you tell us what it is, or is it also top secret?" Lila's sarcasm dripped from her lips.

Just having Lila look at him and talk with him made his hands sweat. "Unfortunately, I cannot divulge that information due to contractual issues."

Jerry smiled and nodded his approval of the game he and Les were playing.

"Enough about us. Let's hear what you do. Lila, why don't you start?" At least this way the attention was off Les.

"I'm a consultant for a pharmaceutical company." Lila flashed her green emeralds at Les.

"Which one?" Les asked.

"That is top secret," Lila answered with a smirk on her face. The other girls laughed as Lila was giving them a taste of their own medicine.

"All right, what about you, Darla?" Jerry kicked Les underneath the table.

"Well, to be honest, right now my top priority is to look pretty." Darla twirled her gum with her finger.

The waitress brought out the drinks and arranged them on the table. Jerry had a confused look on his face but didn't ask Darla another question.

"Okay, Lynn, your turn." Les spoke up quickly in hopes Darla wouldn't talk anymore.

"I'm a nurse at St. Bernard's Hospital."

Jerry didn't make eye contact because he was too busy pouring his beer. "Do you like working there?"

Lynn took a big drink from her glass. "I thought it was everything I ever wanted until yesterday when I met this old man." Lynn's eyes fixed on Jerry as if she was waiting for him to look at her. "He dedicated his life to people. He served his country in World War II and pastored a church for thirty years. Then he moved to Guatemala to be a missionary for another twelve years to set up an orphanage. When his wife died, he came back to the States to work on his son's peach farm."

"Peach farm?" Jerry stared into his beer.

"His son owns a peach farm outside of town, and my patient worked the front desk for him."

"Okay, so an old man wants to be close to his son. Big deal. How does that affect you?" Les sipped his beer.

Lynn swung her head around to make eye contact with Les. Her eyes were big and brown, and her dark hair was cut to frame her cute, petite face. "He sacrificed his life for the cause of helping others."

"Isn't that what you do?" Les gazed back into her soft, auburn eyes.

Lynn drew her attention away for a second, then back to Les. "I do it for the money. He did it out of love."

Lynn spoke with such purpose and depth. There was a frailty and vulnerability to her words. Was she wrestling the same demons Les was?

CHAPTER FIFTEEN

===

Les' mind stirred, catapulting him away from reality for a few seconds as they headed to his Civic to follow the girls to the next rendezvous point. *He did it out of love.*

"Dude, you've met Lila before?" Jerry said as they were getting into the car.

"Yeah, she's the girl I met in the video store. We were supposed to meet up with her at Eazy Eddie's."

"Ouch, and she stood us up." Jerry grimaced.

"But she didn't stand us up tonight, so obviously, she's into you." This was one night Les would rather be at home. His stomach churned like it had during last winter's flu, and his tone sounded as sour as bile.

"Well, who wouldn't be into me? I look pretty dang good tonight." Jerry flipped down the visor and admired himself in the mirror. "I like your style with the whole contractual obligation. That was smooth."

"Just following the leader," Les snapped. Resentment crept in, but Les held his tongue.

"I was trying to give you some props, bro. You okay?" Jerry hesitated. "Are you still mad at her for standing you up?"

Les gripped the steering wheel, keeping as tight a rein on his temper. The tension in the air bothered him more than Lila's betrayal. "I'll be honest. It hurt my pride a little, and—"

"You wanna ditch 'em?"

Les glanced over at Jerry. He was serious. "That's the nicest thing you've ever said to me. But I'm a big boy. I'll deal with it. I'll just have intriguing conversation with Darla all night."

149

Their boisterous laughter lifted his mood. Within minutes, the black Mercedes SUV and the blue Civic pulled into the parking lot of the Japanese steak house.

The men escorted the women inside. The five of them sat with seven strangers around a flat grill, watching the chef slice and dice meat and vegetables. Jerry was seated first, and Darla raced past the other women to sit by him.

Could Les tolerate an hour or more of Darla's self-absorbed chit-chat? No matter that he had joked about spending the evening listening to her prattle. He took the coward's way out and plopped down in the empty chair between Jerry and the stranger to his left. Lynn and Lila sat on Darla's other side.

Lynn and Lila seemed to be having a good time conversing about people only the two of them knew, and Jerry didn't seem to have much to say to Darla, so he mostly directed his attention toward Les. Darla made several unsuccessful attempts to get the chef to give her free saki. Halfway through her meal, the chef caved and rewarded her persistence with a shot of saki. Darla held up her tiny glass, making sure Lynn could see it. She knocked the shot back in one violent jerk of her head.

"Yeah, baby." Darla wiped her mouth then blew a kiss at the chef. The chef caught the imaginary kiss and put in his hat.

"This isn't going very well, is it?" Les whispered to Jerry.

"We should have stuck with my ditch plan."

When the meal was finished, Lila snatched the check from the waiter's hand. "I'll take it on one condition. You guys pick up the alcohol on the way to my townhouse."

"Deal!" Jerry said immediately, smiling ear to ear.

As Lila handed a black credit card to the waitress, Les blew out a hot breath. Everything she did drove him mad. She sat through a whole dinner not saying one word to either of them, yet paid for their dinners and invited them to her house to get drunk?

###

"No way, bro. She lives in a golf-course community." Les down-shifted the Civic as they came to the security station.

"Jackpot." Jerry sang in a baritone voice.

A primitive instinct rose in Les's chest as he followed the SUV. His hands shook as he jerked on the parking brake. Jerry gripped the bottles of liquor and barreled out of the car. Les sat and flexed his hands. He opened and closed them, examining them closely as his fingers pulsated back and forth. He'd had the same reaction when he'd overindulged in energy drinks or one too many cups of coffee. Why did his body act this way whenever he was close to Lila?

Les hustled to the townhome as Lila waited at the door.

"You have a beautiful home." Les stepped through the entrance.

"Thank you. Garage to your left. Screening room to your right. Second floor kitchen and third floor party central." Lila's words trailed off as she bounced up the steps.

Les pushed open the door to his right that led to the screening room. He peeked his head in as he flipped the light. A sixty-two-inch plasma was mounted on the wall,

151

along with black-and-white photos of Marilyn Monroe.

"Hey, what are you doing down there?" Jerry's voice was muffled and seemed far away.

"Coming." Les ran up the steps all the way up to the third floor.

Jerry stood in the middle of the room with a pool stick in his hand. He reached into the pocket for the cue ball. "I like it. Let's play some pool."

"I'll get the Goose and the girls, and you guys rack 'em up." Lila headed down the stairs, leaving Les and Jerry alone.

"This place is amazing." Les snatched one of the sticks off the wall.

Jerry leaned down to take aim. "How much do you think it's worth?"

"This side of town, overlooking the golf course and water, fully upgraded—four, maybe five hundred thousand."

"Five hundred thousand! You think that much?" Jerry's loud voice reverberated off the walls.

"Shhh, don't act like that." What was his problem?

"What's the monthly payment on something like this?" Jerry half-whispered.

"Why are we talking about this? Who cares? Let's play pool." Les scooped a piece of chalk off the ledge of the pool table.

"Hey, I'm just thinking ahead. I might want to pick up one of these babies for myself. You know what I'm saying." Jerry winked and elbowed Les in the side.

"Shut it." Les pointed at Jerry.

Jerry bent over again to take aim. This time he broke up the cluster with a powerful shot.

Darla strolled up the steps with a drink in her hand.

"The goose, the goose, the goose is on fire!"

"You gonna show us some moves?" Jerry smirked as his gaze followed Darla to the stereo.

"You bet."

Darla clicked the sound system and turned on the radio. Hip-hop music blared from the speakers, and Darla took off with a complex series of dance moves. Entrenched in the music, she flung her body with herky-jerky motions.

Jerry's head tilted sideways. "It's so bad, I'm afraid to look away."

How was Lila friends with a person who was a few beers short of a six pack? "Jerry. It's your shot."

Lynn followed up the steps with a tray of glasses and an ice bucket. Lila was right behind her with the bottles of Grey Goose and Red Bull.

"I called Fernando, and he said he'll be here in less than an hour." Darla bobbed her head from side to side.

"As long as he's coming by himself and Mike isn't with him." Lila placed the bottles on the coffee table, catching Lynn's attention. Lila mouthed the words, *I can't stand him.*

"Mike had plans tonight, so Fernando is flying solo."

"You two fight every time you get together, especially if you're drinking. You'd better play nice tonight. I don't want to hear either one of you raise your voice, or he is out of here."

"He's got anger issues. It's not my fault." Darla shook her booty in a Beyonce butt-shake move.

Great. Another dude to muddy up the waters.

"Turn down the music. I want to concentrate on my shots." Lila snatched Jerry's pool stick and slammed the fourteen ball into a side pocket. "Stripes."

"I need a smoke anyway." Darla flipped the knob, and the music volume lowered by half. She slid her purse from the arm of the suede couch with one smooth move, reached in, and pulled out a cigarette case.

As Darla held the case open and ran her manicured nail over the cigarette tips, Les elbowed Jerry then angled his head in her direction. Jerry glanced at her for an instant and rolled his eyes. Les huffed out his breath in a half-laugh. Maybe Darla was counting how many cigarettes she had left and calculating when she would have to con another pack out of one of the men. Or was she trying to figure out which one would make her look better while she smoked it?

As Darla took her cigarette and lighter to the balcony, Lynn poured Grey Goose on the rocks and added a splash of Red Bull. She handed the first one to Jerry, then Les reached for the glass she held out to him.

He sipped his drink. "Good stuff. Thanks."

Les cruised to the corner of the room and set his drink on a glass-topped table. As he gazed at the drink, the Red Bull gave it a red tint. Just like the wine he had poured out of that old milk jug. Les was lost in the liquid. *He did it out of love.* The voices and music in the room grew faint as if he had his ears plugged.

Do I relish the opportunity, or do I push my self-destruct button? What will become of me and my discovery? Deep down, am I Luke Skywalker, embracing the force for good, or am I really like Anakin, detoured by selfish desires, swallowed by disguised evil?

A single bead of sweat trickled the side of his face.

"Hey, are we going to play, or are you going to stare into that glass all night?" Jerry tapped him on the shoulder. "I called your name, like, three times. Are you okay?"

"Am I stripes or solids?"

"Solids."

"Are you guys done warming up?" Lynn's smile only deepened his confusion. How many deaths had she seen? How much unbearable pain? What about her patient, the missionary-turned-peach-farmer—would the wine have helped him?

"You can take my spot. I need to sit down." Les grabbed his glass from the table and wiped the sweat from his forehead.

"You feeling okay?" The concern in Lynn's eyes did him in.

"I just need to chill." Les took a seat on the couch with Lila.

"Do you want to re-rack and play two dollars a ball?" Lynn slid her hands together as if trying to warm them. "Or are you scared?"

"Scared?" Jerry's eyes widened. "Let's do this!"

Les finished off his drink. He dropped a few more ice cubes into his glass and poured in some Grey Goose, then a splash of Red Bull. He took another big swig.

"Easy there, tiger. Haven't you heard of pacing yourself?" Lila brushed her hair out of her face and crossed her legs. Her body was now directly facing Les with both hands securely fastened around her glass.

Les kept his focus on the glass for a moment, then he drank from it again and slammed it onto the coffee table. He turned his body to face her. Her eyes enveloped him in a beam of emerald, reaching down and touching his very soul. His testosterone level erupted as his chest trembled. Everything else faded to black. "Why did you tell me to rent a chick flick when we met in the video store?"

Lila giggled and covered her mouth. "I like that

155

movie. It has a deep, emotional plot about the struggle between a man and a woman and how they cope with losing and gaining love."

"You have got to be kidding me." Les swigged from his drink again. "That storyline is so played out."

"But that's what women want, especially single women, because most of us don't have it in real life. We like our movies to move us, to touch us and make us believe there's a man worth loving out there. Possibility is all some of us need to keep going, to keep trying, and to keep searching." Lila paused for moment. "To keep believing we'll fall in love some day."

Lila gazed into Les's eyes with a seriousness he could feel in his bones. He turned away from it. "I find it hard to believe that you have any trouble finding someone to love you." Les credited the alcohol for his bravery and loss of his natural reserve.

"Why? Because I'm rich, or because I'm beautiful?"

Les paused for a second. This could be a trap, but since the alcohol had already slowed his thinking process, he would have to react on instinct. Les relaxed back with his drink in his hand and studied Lila's face. She was the most beautiful creature he had ever seen. Everything about her was perfect.

"It's because you're beautiful. You're the most beautiful woman I've ever seen. Any man would have to be blind not to see your beauty." The alcohol had destroyed Les's fear and nervousness and his words just flew out his mouth.

Lila dropped her gaze. "And therein lies the problem."

"What problem?"

"Only blind people find true love, because they're the only ones who love without lust, who completely trust someone else without ever being able to see them. That's what I call having faith in love. Living in complete darkness and having no outward expectations, but falling in love with a soul and not a facade. No judgment of the way a person looks."

"Physical attraction fuels passion. Our eyes are the window to our libido." Les slid his left knee up on the couch and pivoted his body to face Lila with his back against the arm rest.

"Yes, but if you are blind, there would be no wondering whether this person loves only what he sees on the outside. I'm beautiful today, but what about fifteen years from now when I start getting wrinkles and when losing weight isn't so easy? Will I have married someone who will trade me in for a newer, shinier model?"

"Hey, Les, can I borrow twenty-six dollars?" Carrying two empty glasses, Jerry sauntered to the coffee table. He set the glasses next to the ice bucket.

"What do you need twenty-six bucks for?" Leave it to Jerry to break up his meaningful conversation with this gorgeous woman.

"Because that's how much Lynn has taken from me so far."

Jerry was making two new drinks when the door bell rang.

"That's for me!" Darla threw open the double doors to the balcony, crossed the room in an instant, and raced down the stairs.

A few minutes later, she returned with Fernando. He had tan olive skin and chestnut-colored eyes and wore a black baseball cap backward. "Hey, everybody, this is

Fernando. Fernando this is Jerry, Les, Lynn, and you know Lila."

"What are we drinking?" Fernando rubbed his hands together. He seemed anxious to get drunk. Darla was his girlfriend, so Les didn't blame him.

"Goose and Red Bull. I need another one myself." Darla placed her glass on the table.

Fernando poured them each a drink, then Darla raised one hand as if making an announcement. "Fernando and I are going downstairs to the screening room."

Fernando handed Darla her drink, then she grabbed his other hand and dragged him down the steps.

"Chica, do I smell cigarette smoke?" Fernando's Spanish accent drifted up the staircase. "You driving me loco. I thought you said you quit."

"Oh, boy, it's starting already." Lila stood and sauntered over to the sound system. She twisted the dial until she found a smooth jazz station. Then she glanced in Les and Jerry's direction. "Is this okay?"

Les perked up. Jazz is what he used to listen to before swim meets to calm his nerves. "I like jazz."

"Since you already owe me a ton of money, would you like to join me out on the balcony?" Lynn asked Jerry. Her eyes sparkled with a flirtatious grin.

"Sure, and I bet you double or nothing I can spit in the lake." Jerry followed Lynn out to the balcony. Jerry gazed over his shoulder as he made eye contact with Les and sent him a quick nod and wink. Their sign. Jerry was giving him the go-ahead to take his shot with Lila.

CHAPTER SIXTEEN

===

A cool breeze blew as Jerry leaned over the balcony railing. Could he hock a lugy that far? Two dim lights burned on the porch, giving it an intimate atmosphere.

"You're not going to make it. It is a physical impossibility for any human to spit that far." Lynn curled up with a blanket on one of the outdoor couches.

"I guess I'll have to find another way to win my money back." Jerry perched on the edge of the couch parallel to the one Lynn snuggled on. He rubbed his hands together. "Okay, now what?"

"Do you always have to be doing something? Can't we just enjoy being alive?"

Huh? She had no idea that he had almost died less than twenty-four hours earlier. She was right. He needed to take time to enjoy being alive. "We should do that more. I take it for granted that I'm going to wake up breathing every day. Just the other day, my eighty-some-year-old neighbor was taken to the hospital, and I was with him the night before. I don't know what happened to him, but it made me think that at any one moment, you could be talking with someone for the last time."

Lynn brushed her bangs behind her left ear. "Being a nurse, I see patients all the time who have only a few months, weeks, or even hours to live. But it took a certain man dying right in front of me to wake me up to the fact that life it isn't always about my needs and my desires. He made me realize how selfish I've been my whole life."

Jerry paused, taking in the awkward silence in the air. "Man, it's getting deep out here. I didn't mean to open up Pandora's box."

159

"Hey, you were the one who said you liked to talk endlessly about your feelings, remember?"

Lynn's musical laughter broke the tension. Lynn sat up straight and leaned forward. "What is your neighbor's name?"

"My neighbor who went to the hospital?"

Lynn nodded as her eyes grew intense. Jerry could feel her focus on every word. She didn't look in his eyes but was studying his mouth.

"I don't know his first name. I always referred to him as old man Al. To be honest, I didn't even know the man." Why was Lynn so interested in his neighbor? "We spoke in passing a few times. He seemed nice, and the other night was the first time I had ever been in his apartment."

"What's your last name?" Lynn wet her lips.

"Geeze. Slow your roll, girl. Do you always ask this many questions?"

"Only when I'm intrigued."

"So, I'm intriguing?" Jerry bobbed his head in agreement. "Would you say that I'm like a mysterious lost piece searching for its puzzle?"

Lynn narrowed her eyes. "Let's play a game. Let's see if I can guess your last name from three clues." Lynn removed the blanket from her lap. "Come sit next to me."

Is she serious? Jerry plopped down on the couch next to her.

"Lie back and relax." Lynn pushed his chest. "Take a few deep breaths and clear your mind of all distractions."

Jerry half-laughed as he exhaled. "This is so rad."

"Is your mind clear?" Lynn rubbed her temples.

"My mind hasn't been clear for fifteen years. You know what I'm saying. Puff, puff, pass."

Lynn placed her hand on Jerry's forehead. "Still your thoughts."

She closed her eyes and began massaging her temples again. "I am going to ask you three questions and you have to answer them honestly."

This was nuts.

"What nationality is your father?"

Jerry drew in a deep breath. "German."

"Does your last name start with a letter ranging from P-Z?

Jerry paused to run the alphabet through his brain. "No."

"Could your last name be associated with some type of food?"

"I guess so."

Lynn popped open her eyes. "Humberger."

Jerry jumped up. "No way. That is totally awesome." He pulled on his curly blond hair with both hands as he paced the balcony then flopped down on the couch with Lynn. "How did you know that?"

Lynn didn't answer right away. Then she took a drink from her glass and cleared her throat. "I don't know how to say this without freaking you out, so I'm going to come out and say it. I can read people's minds."

Was this chick for real? She wasn't laughing. "Did Les put you up to this?"

"No." Lynn smiled. "Would it be weird for you if someone could know your every thought?"

"Are you a witch?" Jerry lifted his glass to finish off his drink.

"No, but I do believe in another realm that exists beyond our view."

Jerry rubbed his chin. "Does this other realm help

you read minds?"

"I believe it does. But in a different way than you think. Do you know what fate is?"

"Yeah, I guess. It's when something happens by chance. Like karma."

Lynn nodded. "Kind of. The last twenty four hours have been crazy. I feel as if I'm on some kind of predetermined course that will change the rest of my life."

"Sounds like a bad trip on acid to me."

Lynn pointed her finger and her eyes brightened as if a light bulb had gone off in her mind. "Think about it as a bad trip. What if you had the power to step outside of yourself and view your life as an impartial bystander? What would you see? Would you see a purpose for the things you do? What if you realized everything you thought was important really wasn't?"

Jerry nodded. "I would say that would be a bummer."

"I had a friend who dedicated his whole life to the well-being of other people."

Jerry shrugged. "Why?"

"Exactly. Why? My friend mentioned a book that can give us these answers."

Oh, gosh. If she says . . .

"It's called the Bible."

Jerry bolted to his feet and stretched his arms, faking a yawn. "All this deep thinking is killing my buzz. I'm going inside."

Les and Lila observed Jerry as he followed Lynn out to the balcony. Lila swiveled her head. "Does he have a girlfriend? Do you think he likes her?"

Here comes the barrage of twenty questions. "I think he is going to propose." The corners of Les's mouth turned up.

"Do you know and don't want to tell me, or do you not know?" Lila shimmied her head with attitude.

What an inquisitive girl. "I have no clue what's going through Jerry's head. Scout's honor." Les raised his three fingers.

"Were you even a Cub Scout?"

"I had friends who were, so . . . I don't know where I was going with that."

Lila's laughter was like a shot of tranquility flowing over his body. Les loved making Lila laugh. With every passing second, he was falling in love with her more and more. He hadn't known it was possible to fall in love by the second, but it was happening to him. Or was it a lust concoction of alcohol and hormones that made him feel this way?

"So what is this secret business you're working on?" Lila inched closer to him.

Les wanted more than anything in the world to impress Lila, but how could he begin to tell her about his discovery? "It's kind of hard to explain."

"What industry will it be in?"

Les stroked his left hand over his sideburn, letting his hand drift all the way down the side of his face. "I haven't thought about that."

Lila's head jerked forward. "You're going to start a business, but you don't know what industry you're going to market to? I'm starting to think you made it up to try to impress us."

"Healthcare." Les blurted out the first thing that

came to him.

"Healthcare? That's my profession. Maybe I can help." Lila placed her glass on the coffee table. As her demeanor changed, she pressed her hands together and sat up straight.

Bad choice. She'd said earlier that she was in pharmaceutical sales. How had he forgotten that? "How do I know I can trust you? I don't even know what company you work for."

Another bad move. He studied her face for a sign that he had offended her, but her eyes radiated the same softness as before.

"Fair enough. I work for EFIL Pharmaceutical. Our primary focus for the past fifteen years has been neurology. We just initiated a phase-two clinical trial for an experimental humanized monoclonal antibody with a targeted indication of immunotherapeutic treatment for cancer patients."

"Whoa. English, please."

"We're trying to find a better way to fight cancer in hopes of finding a cure. Our recent discovery of growth factors opens the possibility of healing or regenerating nerve tissue."

"Interesting. How is phase two coming?"

"I can't discuss details. I can tell you that early studies have shown some promise but not the results we were hoping for."

Her lips were so plump-a-licious. "What made you want to go into that industry?"

She bent forward and finished off her half-empty glass. Her body relaxed against the couch as her eyes gazed at the ceiling. It was as though the question made it hard for her to breathe.

What did he say wrong? "I'm sorry. I didn't mean to bring up a painful topic."

"It was a long time ago." Lila poured herself another drink and mixed it with her finger.

"You don't have to—"

"I want to." Lila's hair had drifted over her left eye, but she made no action to remove it from her face. "When I was young, my mother died from cancer, and it's something that I carry with me every day. It fuels my passion for what I do."

Les swallowed the lump in his throat. "I am really sorry."

Lila held her balled-up fist over her mouth then sniffled and slurped her freshly made drink. "Enough about what I do. What is it that you do again, other than your secret healthcare plan?"

How could he tell the woman he adored that he was nothing more than an assembly-line parts checker making twelve dollars an hour? He avoided her eyes. "I work for Air Parts in the audit division."

"Is that what you went to school for?"

"I have a degree in communications."

"Why aren't you using your degree?"

Lila's bluntness took him back. "If I start talking about it, I'll get depressed, and what's worse than a depressed drunk?"

"Nothing. Excuse me for a minute while I go to the ladies' room."

"I need to hit the can myself." Les checked out Lila until she disappeared behind her bedroom door.

He wobbled himself over to the third-floor bathroom, buzzing pretty good, and steadied himself on the wall next to the door for a moment. In the bathroom, he splashed water on his face while giving himself a pep talk in the mirror. "You can do this. You can make a good impression even if you are a little drunk."

Les wiped his face and hands with the white hand towel and schlepped back into the room. A few minutes later, Lila burst through her bedroom door like a model hitting the runway, looking more dazzling than ever. Her scent reminded him of the wine in his milk jug. "Mmm, you smell good."

"You can stop smelling me now."

Did this girl even like him?

Lila sank down on the couch on the opposite end of the room and crossed her legs. Her plush lips glossed. "Do you want to join Lynn and Jerry out on the balcony?"

"And mess up Jerry's proposal? No way."

Lila picked up her purse that had been resting on the couch and pulled out her iPhone. Immediately she started texting.

You're losing her, Les. Bring out the big guns.

"If your company had a product that could cure cancer with no side effects, what would it be worth?"

Lila finished her text and dumped her iPhone back into her purse. "Billions. My father has been obsessed with finding a cure for cancer for the past twenty years. One of the reasons is for the several billions dollars a cure would be worth."

"Your father?"

Lila exhaled. She reclined in her seat and ran her manicured nails through her hair. She touched her lips with her fingertips for an instant as if she had made a mistake letting out a secret. "My father started EFIL with the life insurance money he received after my mom died of cancer. My father is a neurologist and has been trying to treat cancer through the nervous system for the past twenty years. I sell his drugs and ideas to clinics and hospitals all over the world. He's possessed by the need to find a cure. He works every waking second of his life."

"What if he finds a cure? Then what?"

"He'll probably realize he has a daughter whom he has neglected for the past twenty years. He'd just occupy his mind with another incurable disease."

"What if someone beat him to the cure?"

"Never thought about that." Lila paused and tapped her nail against her front tooth. "It would sink him. He receives a lot of his money from private investors who bank on him finding a cure and reaping huge rewards. If someone beat him to it, I guess the money would dry up, put my father out of business, and leave me without a job."

Every fiber in Les's being ached to tell Lila what he had discovered, but now he couldn't.

CHAPTER SEVENTEEN

==

Lester touched his tongue to the roof of his mouth to wet it, and then swallowed hard. It was if someone had placed cotton balls in his mouth overnight. He wiped the sleep out of his eyes and gazed at a black-and-white photo of Marilyn Monroe hanging over him.

He sat up and rubbed his eyes and face. A sixty-two-inch plasma mounted on the wall jogged his memory to the realization that he was in Lila's screening room. Heavy, dark curtains blacked out the sun. Only the light from underneath the door gave any indication that it was daytime.

When Les's eyes adjusted, he spotted Jerry curled up on the other couch across the room. Les grabbed one of his shoes and threw it, hitting Jerry square in the back.

"What was that?"

"Good morning, sweetheart." Les had a groggy, morning voice.

"I hate you."

"Aren't we cranky this morning?"

"How would you like to be woke up with a shoe to the back?"

Les steadied himself with the couch, gaining his equilibrium. "I have a category three this morning, but I think I just need some water and I'll be fine."

Jerry turned over on his back. "I would say I have a cat four going on. I drank a lot last night."

"Cat four? That bad?" Les see-sawed to the bathroom.

"I can't hear you. Too much pounding!"

"All right, all right. I'm going to freshen up in the

168

bathroom, then we can hit the road." Moments later, Les came out of the bathroom, feeling better that he at least got to wash his face and do his hair. He flipped on the light.

"What are you doing to me? Do you like torturing me?" Jerry snatched a pillow from the floor and planted it over his head. "I hate you!"

Les left the light on as he lumbered up the stairs to the kitchen. At least he didn't have a headache.

In the kitchen, Darla dropped strawberries into a blender. "Want some coffee?"

"I need a gallon of water."

"How about a smoothie?" Darla poured a strawberry smoothie into a plastic cup and handed it to Les.

He leaned against the kitchen counter and slurped the pinkish-red drink. "Where's everyone else?"

"Fernando left early this morning to go to practice, Lynn is still in bed, and Lila's at the gym." Darla tossed more berries into the blender. "Do you like her?"

Les played dumb. "What's not to like?"

Darla pressed the "blend" button then poured herself a smoothie. "She'll hurt you. She is way out of your league. A woman like her needs a man who can offer her something extraordinary. Not just any Joe Schmo is going to get a shot at her. You seem like a nice guy, but nice isn't going to get you a woman like Lila."

Les gulped his smoothie. What a wench.

Lynn stepped into the kitchen and headed straight for the coffee. "I can't believe I have the whole weekend off. It feels so weird. I haven't had a weekend off since I started at St. Bernard's."

"That shows dedication."

"I think it's sad," Darla piped in.

She was so dense. Les swigged his smoothie then

wiped his mouth with his hand. "Do you enjoy your work?"

Lynn opened the fridge. "For the most part. Yesterday a patient died in front of me, which is usually not that difficult to deal with, except this man was someone very special."

"Sorry I can't stay. I have to get my hair done at one thirty." Darla abruptly exited the kitchen.

The front door of the townhouse slammed shut. "If Jerry wasn't up before, he is now." Les shook his head. "What's up with her?"

Lynn rolled her eyes. "Don't even get me started. That girl is a hot mess."

"Hot mess?"

"Let me put it this way, she should change her name from Darla to Drama."

"Yeah, she seems really self-absorbed."

Lynn shut the fridge door and poured creamer into her coffee. "I'm going to drink my coffee out on the balcony. Would you like to join me?"

This could buy me sometime until Lila gets home.

Les shrugged. "Yeah, that would be great."

The two of them shuffled to the second story balcony, where they sat across from each other at a round, glass table. Lester drank his water and smoothie and Lynn savored her coffee. The early afternoon sun felt good on Les's face in the sixty-eight-degree weather. "So tell me about this special man who died the other night."

"Do you want the long version or the short one?"

"The long one." *Just keep talking until Lila gets home.*

"Have you ever looked into the mirror and asked yourself what you're doing with your life?"

Man, had he ever.

"I have a good job, good friends, my own place. I have a decent amount of money. But am I satisfied with my life? What will it take to satisfy me?" Lynn sipped her coffee. "I always thought that getting married and having a couple of kids would satisfy me. But what if I never get married? Then what?"

I knew there was something different about this chick. "This is incredible. I have been asking myself the same question all week."

Lynn's eyes brightened. "Really?"

"Yeah, I'll tell you about. But I want to hear your story first."

Lynn paused and gazed out over the balcony as five baby ducks swam in the lake behind their mother. "My patient made me realize that I will never be satisfied until I give up my life and stop living for myself."

"How do you give up your life?"

"This is the strange part. If you think I'm crazy, that's fine. I understand. But here it is. This old man who had a massive heart attack was clearly going to die. He woke up and told me that his heavenly father sent him to come back and talk to me about my life."

"Heavenly father?" *What?*

"He said God was his heavenly father. God sent him back to talk to me about giving my life over to his son, Jesus."

She moved a loose strand of hair from her face and tucked it behind her ear. Her long eyelashes and high cheek bones accentuated her face's natural beauty.

"I gave my life to Jesus right there in the hospital room. It was a feeling of peace and love that I'd never felt before, and my whole body tingled. I don't know how or why I felt the way I did, but what I felt was real."

A chill swept over Les's body, sending goose bumps all down his arms. He reached his arm over so Lynn could see the bumps. "While you were telling your story, I kept getting a wave of chills all over my body."

"Really? You don't think I'm crazy for giving my life to Jesus?" Lynn's eyes flashed a brilliance of adoration.

Les grinned and rubbed his chin. "I had a similar experience the other day."

"This is amazing. Now I just got the chills! I'll finish my story, then you can tell me yours." Lynn waved her hands in excitement. "My patient wrote in my notebook. This is where it gets wild. His last request was for me to go to his apartment and get two Bibles and a notebook, one for myself and one for his neighbor, Jerry Humberger."

Les's mouth dropped. "That's crazy. Did you tell Jerry?"

Lynn's attention fixed on the ducks on the lake. "No. He kind of freaked out when I mentioned the Bible."

"Sounds like Jerry." Les stretched his neck and finished of his glass of water. "Did you have any idea that our Jerry was the guy the old man was talking about?"

"None."

Les half laughed. "Were you totally tripping out?"

"I didn't know for sure who Jerry was until I got him on the balcony and asked him his last name."

"How did he take it?"

"Well." Lynn paused as her face reddened like a Coke can. She smiled. "He thinks I can read minds."

Les puffed out a laugh.

"I tricked him. I had to find out what his last name was without him knowing how I found out."

"Do you wanna ride over and get these Bibles?"

172

"Wait a minute. I told you my crazy story. It's only fair you tell me yours."

Les popped up from his chair. "I will later. We need to get those Bibles."

"Oh, one more thing." Lynn latched on to Les's shirt as he walked by. "Tell Jerry I'm going to see my friend who lives in his apartment complex and I need to follow you because I forgot where it is."

Les held his gaze down as he towered over Lynn with her big, auburn-colored eyes glimmering in the sun. *She is precious.*

They returned to the kitchen and placed their cups into the sink.

"I'll change and grab my bag, and I'll follow you guys over there."

Les trampled down the stairs and into the screening room. The light was still on, and Jerry lay in the same position Les left him in over an hour ago. He grabbed the pillow off Jerry's head. "Come on, sleepyhead, let's go."

"Dude, why do you keep bothering me?"

"Because it's almost one o'clock, and we need to get going. Get up or you're going to get another shoe in your back."

Jerry methodically flopped his legs to the edge of the couch and lifted his body. His hair looked like a big frizz ball. Les laughed. "Go tame the beast on top of your head so we can go."

"Have I told you lately how much I hate you?" On his way to the bathroom, Jerry playfully slapped Les across the face.

"And can you please squirt some toothpaste in that mouth of yours? You're going to start a fire with that dragon breath."

Minutes later, Jerry came out of the bathroom. "Do I look pretty enough to go now?" Jerry batted his eyes.

"We have to wait for Lynn. She's following us."

Jerry scrunched his forehead and whined. "Why?"

"Relax. She has a friend who has an apartment in Westwood."

Lynn tore down the stairs with her brown leather purse in hand. "I'm ready."

"Can I get your phone number in case I lose you?" Les flipped open his phone.

Lynn recited her number, and Les punched it into his phone. "It's only a couple of miles."

In the Civic, Jerry flashed an I've-figured-out-the-master-plan smile. "Thatta boy. Sneaky way to get the digits, but I'm with you."

Les twisted the key into the ignition. "If you weren't my best friend . . ."

"If I wasn't your best friend, you would think I was Sherlock Holmes."

"Absolutely . . . not."

"So now that you're into Lynn, getting her digits and all, I guess that means Lila is open game."

Les flipped the radio on.

"Silence gives consent." Jerry tilted his head against the passenger-side window. Les kept his focus on the road, going slow enough so Lynn could stay on his bumper. Within ten minutes, they pulled into Westwood Apartments.

Jerry filed out of Les's car and meandered to his apartment. He spun around. "You coming?"

Les stood on the sidewalk that led to Jerry's unit. "I'm going to wait for Lynn."

"Oooo. Whatever." Jerry swung around and ambled in the direction of his apartment.

Lynn unzipped her purse and held out a piece of folded notebook paper. "This way?"

Les nodded and the two of them strolled to apartment 34b. Jerry fidgeted with his key as his attention fixed on the two of them as they drew closer. "Where does your friend live?"

Lynn reached under the mat and pulled out a key. She tried the knob. The door was already unlocked. She pushed open the creaking door.

Les's eyes remained on Jerry's facial expression as Lynn pushed open the door. His face went from relaxed to contorted anger in seconds.

"What are you guys doing? That's old man Al's place." Jerry leaned forward.

"Calm down. Were just getting some Bibles." Les placed his hand on Jerry's chest.

Jerry's eyes began to oscillate. Bit by bit, they glazed over. It was as though Les peered into a dark, empty well. Les swallowed the lump in his throat. "You okay, bro?"

Jerry whirled, jammed his key into his door, and slammed the door shut.

Lynn's face was somber as she removed her hand from her mouth. "What's with him?"

"He's not into the Bible." Les's mouth drew to one side in a half-frown. He eased the door shut, and he locked it behind them. The last thing he needed was getting caught for breaking and entering.

The bookshelves lined the far wall. Lynn ran her finger over the sill then held up a finger full of dust. As they rummaged through the shelves, Les figured out Mr. Allen's filing system. The top two shelves were filled with hard-cover books, and the third was dedicated to notebooks.

Lynn unfolded her paper. "This is the note my patient friend gave me. It says we need to find two Bibles and a notebook labeled May, 1986."

Les pulled one of the old notebooks from the shelf and read the front, January 1988. He contemplated for a moment then opened it up to the first page.

"In everything give thanks: for this is the will of God in Christ Jesus concerning you." I give thanks to my Lord and Savior for blessing me with life and giving me the opportunity to give it back. I give thanks to my Father for giving me such a precious gift and helpmate. I have loved and cherished every moment of life and ministry with her. Madeline has been sick for many months now and refuses to take any more medicine. She says, "Why delay my trip to paradise? I can already hear my father calling my name." My heart rejoices but also grieves for her. Of course, for selfish reasons, I want her to stay here with me. But when the father calls, he calls. I know, my Lord, you have a mansion on a hill awaiting her with many treasures because of her years of faithful service to you. My God, she has also served me well. I did not deserve such a woman, but you gave me everything I needed in a partner and friend. I am writing this letter to you, my Lord, to let you know that my love for you will never fail. It will never waver. I will rejoice in the good times and in the bad, and in all things, I will give thanks. My heart hurts because I know my time with my beloved is short. The last several months have been hard on us and our ministry. She is weak

176

and she yearns more and more to be with you, as
her pain seems never to end. I am going to stop
being selfish and thank you for the gift instead.
Now I give it back to you. With tears I write this
letter, but I know it's time for her pain to stop. Take
her home, my father. Take her home.

Tears stung Les's eyes, and Lynn's reddened, tear-
filled eyes tore down every reserve he had built up over the
years as a man. His macho exterior was drifting down a
stream of serenity that vibrated the walls of the apartment.
This cute Asian girl nudged at a dwelling inside of him that
he had never known.

Her eyebrows raised. "I told you he was a special
man. What does the next page say?" Lynn turned the page.

Les drew in a deep breath.

January 2, 1988: Around six o'clock this morning,
Madeline woke me. The pain was gone and she
wanted to dance. I rolled out of bed, put on a record,
and danced with my beloved. She whispered that
she loved me and that I had been a great husband
and a wonderful dad to our five children. She
thanked me for being the spiritual leader and head
of our family. We held each other tightly, tears
rolling down our cheeks, as we swayed to the
music. Madeline looked deep into my eyes and
spoke these words: "I thanked the Lord every day
for giving me such a man after God's own heart,
loving me unconditionally even though I didn't
deserve it. It's been my life's honor to serve you."
At exactly seven o'clock this morning, my precious
gift was taken from me. I held her in my arms as I

wept. I thank you, my God and my King, for allowing me to say goodbye. You always know what I need.

CHAPTER EIGHTEEN

======================================

Les arranged the notebook back on the shelf and wiped tears from his cheeks. "Sorry for crying like a little girl."

"I like sensitive men." Lynn helped herself to a tissue from the box on Mr. Allen's end table. "It shows that they'll be good daddies."

Les blew his nose and wadded up the tissue then crammed it into his pocket. "I am not a sensitive guy. It's the atmosphere in this apartment. Pulsating through my veins is an overwhelming awareness that I am supposed to do something before I leave this place. It's like the feeling you get when you have to run back into your house to make sure you shut the iron off, because you have this inept fear that if you don't, your house will burn down."

Lynn's soft hand glided over his. Her gentle grip clenched on the side of his hand. "I think I know what's happening."

Les embraced her hand. "Tell me."

The affection in her eyes melted away the callus that years of bitterness had built up around his heart.

Lynn whispered. "Give up your life."

Les let his eyelids close. He was standing at the edge of an ocean. The sand sunk in between his toes, and the sun had just peeked over the still water. As the sun continued to rise, the entire sky was remade into a sheet of red. Wine red. The ocean was magnetizing as it glistened the wine color that radiated from the sun.

A familiar voice spoke, "Come. Come swim in my waters."

That was the voice I heard after I drank the wine.

Where was he? Was he still in the apartment and everything around him had changed? Or did he actually transport to a beach on an ocean?

He sprinted. The water had called his name and he answered. He flung his body recklessly into the air, arching his back and swiftly cutting through the water, diving deep. He dolphin-kicked his way into the depths of the ocean. He held his arms out in front of him, clasped together.

How exhilarating to swim again. There was a release from his soul as if someone had reached his hands in and taken all the anger and bitterness that had been locked inside.

He carved the water with his hands as he glided swiftly. The water was a crystal aqua color, like a swimming pool. He hadn't been swimming in ten years and had forgotten the connection he had with the water.

"Give it up," the familiar voice spoke again.

I don't want to give it up. I just started swimming again.

"Give it up."

Why?

Les's breath ran short as he floated his way up toward the surface. He had dived a lot deeper than he had realized.

"Give it up or you will never get it back," the voice spoke again.

He would never make it. His lungs singed and his body twinged as the red sky bore down on him. He had no breath left. He let his body go limp. His hands broke the surface as he screamed, "I give it up!"

His eyes burst open.

He was in the apartment. Les patted his clothes, waiting for water to splash. *Dry?* He brushed his shirt and pants. *Nothing.*

Lynn had backed away. "Are you okay?"

What the heck is going on? "I could have sworn . . .
Did you dump a bucket of water on my head?"

Lynn pressed her arms against her sides.

Les shook his head and rapidly blinked his eyes. He
cleared his throat as he regained his bearings.

She ran to him and hugged him tight. Les staggered
a few steps back then wrapped his arms around her. She
understood.

"Congratulations. You're a child of God." Lynn
rested her face against his chest for a moment then stepped
away. They had bonded in some kind of unexplainable,
cosmic way. She tugged at her shirt that had scrunched up
from the hug.

"Why don't you get the Bibles, and I'll look for the
1986 notebook."

Lynn nodded. "He must have twenty different
Bibles on the shelf. Which two should I take?"

"I don't know. Wouldn't they all be the same?" *Why
does she look so different?*

Lynn pulled the Bibles from the shelf. She inspected
each one then finally held up two newer leather-bound
editions. "I'll take these."

Les brushed the dust from a bright red notebook
that read May, 1986. "Bingo. You ready?"

"Doesn't it feel peaceful in here? Like you could
just fall asleep."

"If we stay in here long enough, we will."

They reached the linoleum that led to the doorway,
turned, and simultaneously surveyed the room. Part of Les
wanted to leave, but the other part wanted to stay here and
read some more of Mr. Allen's writings and maybe even

experience another crazy vision.

Les placed his hand on the middle of Lynn's back.

"I get the hint." Lynn took one last glance around the apartment and led the way out.

Les locked the door and slipped the key back under the mat. He knocked on Jerry's door across the hall and waited for an answer. Where was this guy? Les knocked again. "Hey, what are you doing in there?"

He tried the door but it was locked. Les shook his head as he banged on the door again. It opened a crack with the chain lock still bolted.

Half of Jerry's face peered through. "I'm getting ready to take a shower."

"Can we come in?" What was up with him?

"Dude, I need to take a shower and a nap. I'm not feeling good. Plus my apartment is a mess."

"I thought you just cleaned it." Something wasn't right here. When Jerry stood there with a blank look on his face, Les shoved the Bible through the crack. "All right, fine. This is for you."

Jerry took the Bible without saying a word and shut the door.

On the way back to Lynn's car, she turned and glanced back at the apartment building. "That was odd."

"I've known that guy my whole life, and I still don't understand him." The years of parental neglect must have caged his mind. "What are you doing now?"

"I need to go home and take a shower and wash my hair. But you can come over later and we can grill out on my patio. I want to hear your story and read this notebook with you."

"You have a grill?"

Lynn scribbled directions on a piece of paper from

her notebook, ripped out the page, and handed it to Les. "How about four thirty?"

"Sounds great. I'll see you then." Les bounded to his car and began the drive back to his condo. His car clock read two eleven. That would give him time to shower, change his clothes, go to the grocery store, and head in the direction of Lynn's house. An indescribable feeling vibrated from his body. *I want to swim again.*

His toes hung over the starting block. He adjusted his goggles one last time to fit snug against his skull. The buzz that trickled over his body warmed his insides that fluttered with butterflies of confidence. His body had been sculpted and engineered for this. On land, his lanky form often made him ungraceful and even clumsy. But in the water, he was an arrow shot from its bow, swiftly cutting through the air until it hit its destination.

He felt at peace with the world. All his problems vaporized for those few moments. It was only him, suspended in his aqua universe. Then his hand touched the wall and jolted him back to reality.

What was he feeling? Was it excitement? Adrenaline? Love? He couldn't pinpoint his emotion or its origin; but it felt similar to when he was in the water, swimming.

At his condo, Les unlocked the door, and as soon as he stepped in, he remembered the mess Jerry had left in his kitchen. His happy feelings soon left him as he tossed a dish towel against the cabinets. That rat Jerry and his "thank you breakfast." Les wasn't thanking him now.

He went to work on the dishes. As he placed the last plate into the dishwasher, he scanned the microwave clock: three ten. He squeezed soap into the dishwasher and closed the door. He did one more wipe-down of the counters and

one last kitchen check. He then hurried into the bathroom
to take a shower and get changed for the night.

Lynn pulled her silver Audi into the garage and
trekked into her cozy, three-bedroom house. Thoughts of
Eugene Allen dominated her mind as she set his Bible and
notebook on the kitchen table. She couldn't name the
powerful emotion swelling through her body.

She pulled out a kitchen chair and sat down. What a
night and what a day. The events of the past two days
seemed surreal, from the double shift with Eugene Allen to
meeting his neighbor Jerry to now spending the day with
his best friend, Les.

How did everything fit together so perfectly? Lynn
traced her finger over the wood grain in her table as her
mind drifted back to the few minutes she'd spent with
Eugene Allen.

God sent him back to give me life. What a sobering
thought, that God would care enough about her to send a
man back from death to help her. And what about Charlie
Blue, the nice fellow she had met in the courtyard? Was he
sent by God too?

Lynn inhaled through her nose and let out an
exhausted breath, letting her lips vibrate together. God was
ordering her steps. She could see for the first time that God
had orchestrated this whole thing. The connection she had
with Les was like no other she had ever had. Deeper than
just a physical interest, it was almost like their spirits were
connecting.

A big grin sprung across Lynn's face. Her eyes
filled with tears. "Thank you, God, for caring enough about

me to send an old man back to life so I could know how much you love me."

At that moment, Lynn realized for the first time what she had been feeling. It was God's love.

CHAPTER NINETEEN

==

"Stupid Les!" Jerry slammed the Bible onto the coffee table. "I hate it when he tries to push this Jesus stuff on me."

Alone again. Of all things, he'd had lost his best friend to some girl who believed in a make-believe storybook. He headed for the shower.

As he got out ten minutes later, the phone rang. He checked the number. Elizabeth. "What up?"

"Hey, Jerry, I just had this overwhelming urge that I needed to call you and see how you were doing."

"I had a pretty heavy drinking night. Just took a hot shower, trying to sweat out the alcohol. But other than this headache, I'm doing great." What was up with her and her questions? He'd been right to leave her behind. If she wanted to know so much about what he had been doing, he'd tell her. "Les and I got drunk off some Grey Goose last night, and we ended up spending the night at some girl's house."

"I'm worried about you."

"Why is everyone so worried about me? I'm fine! And don't start preaching your Jesus mess to me right now. I've heard enough."

"I'm praying for you, Jer." Her voice trembled.

Jerry clenched his fist, flexing his bicep. His teeth gritted together. "Please don't."

"I care for you." Elizabeth started to cry. "Seeing you the other day brought back all the feelings I used to have for you. I never stopped loving you."

"You made that decision, remember? You dumped me because I wouldn't conform to your religious ways and follow your rules. You refused to accept me for who I am."

"Please, Jerry, can't you see you're slowly killing yourself? This way of life leads to one place."

"Maybe I like that place."

"No, you don't. Don't say that." Elizabeth's voice quivered.

The phone went silent for a few seconds with an awkward pause between them. "Is that all you called for?"

"I will never give up on you. Soon you'll realize that God is real and you won't need to get wasted anymore."

He squeezed the bridge of his nose, sucking in a deep shaky breath. "Look, my little Beth-bunny, I care about you too. When you dumped me, you cut me deep. I understand why you don't want to be with me, and it still hurts, because I truly loved you more than any other woman. But I will never believe the things you believe. Being a pothead doesn't make me a bad person. It's just who I am."

"I never said you were a bad person."

"Just not good enough for you."

"Why is this belief in God tearing everyone I love away from me? Why should I have to conform to religion? Why am I the one who has to change?" Jerry snatched one of his shoes from the floor and whipped it against the bedroom wall, marking it with a black scuff.

"'I want you to know that God is real.'" He mocked Elizabeth's voice, pacing his bedroom, his rage burning hotter than it had since he used to lock himself in his room to escape his mother's entourage of strangers. "If God is real, why did he let my mother's low-life boyfriends beat the crap out of me? Where were you then, God? Where were you when my mom was bringing drugs into the house and sleeping with random men? Where were you? How can you be real when I've suffered so much agony?"

Jerry dropped to his knees in the middle of his bedroom and grasped at his hair. "Where were you then? If you are real, God, you have done nothing but cause me pain."

The carpet absorbed his tears. Then they suddenly stopped like a faucet being switched off. Something crawling inside of him needed to be freed. His body became unbalanced for a moment, and he tilted his right hand down to catch himself from falling over. It had to be released.

He lifted himself from the floor, lumbered into his closet, and set up the folding chair. He stood on it and removed the pile of clothes that hid his computer. When he hit the control key, out popped his bud of superweed.

"You have always been there for me when I needed you."

Jerry severed a sticky piece of marijuana off the bud and hit the backspace key to shut the compartment. He climbed down from his chair with a peaceful knowledge that everything was going to be okay once he got high. He just needed to escape for a few hours and not have to think about Les or Elizabeth or even the idea of God. Everything would be fine once he released whatever was writhing inside of him. He could enter his own little world where everything was fun and happy.

A euphoric sensation rushed over his body, leaving his fingertips tingling. He turned his stereo on, and the melody of Bob Marley started soothing his nerves. Jerry sat on his couch, breaking up the weed into smaller pieces to make it easier to roll a joint.

How could Elizabeth ask him to give up rolling joints? It's so relaxing and natural. It made him feel so at one with the earth.

"No woman, no cry," Bob Marley sang.

"Oh, Bob, how right you are." Jerry sang along with Bob. "No woman, no cry."

Jerry finished rolling his joint by licking the paper to keep it together. He set the joint on the coffee table and went into the kitchen to grab a lighter and to wash his hands. His phone rang again, and he ambled into his bedroom, grabbed his phone, and checked the caller ID. Lester.

Jerry punched the ignore button and waited for Les to leave a message so he could shut his phone off. It seemed like an eternity before Jerry heard the solid-tone beep.

"What are you doing, Les?" Jerry scoffed and threw his phone back onto the bed. He stomped into the living room as he eyed the work of art that sat on the coffee table.

"Wow, you are beautiful." It glowed like a glow worm. "Glow worms, glow worms, I love glow worms." Jerry sang his own song. With his joint in hand, he danced into the kitchen.

"Glow worms, glow worms, everyone loves glow worms." He lit the joint with his stove burner again and took a long drag of smoke into his lungs.

He exhaled the smoke and sang along with Bob, "Could you be loved?"

Jerry took another long drag, dancing to the music. He felt so free, like a bird flying high above the world with the whole world underneath him. It was just him, Bob, and his glow worm, a match made in heaven.

Jerry stopped cold. He didn't believe in heaven, did he? If he didn't believe in heaven, how could any matches be made there? Jerry hit the Mary Jane and the smoke filtrated his throat and lungs. His eyelids drooped. There is no heaven, but there are matches. Jerry opened and closed his eyes, barely able to keep them open.

"Matches are used to start fires which in turn are used to light marijuana cigarettes that lead you to experience a state of heaven. Maybe heaven is nothing more than an emotion, similar to the feeling of ecstasy."

Jerry took one last drag from the joint, singeing his fingertips. He dropped it in the ash tray on the coffee table. A fog of smoke rose in his apartment as he continued to dance and sing along with the music. "Three little birds . . ."

A light tapping, like a woodpecker, sounded at the door. Jerry turned down the music and listened to the tapping grow louder and louder. He peeked through the peep hole. Nothing there. He cracked open the door, leaving it on its chain.

The tapping stopped. In the hall, he saw three little birds, chirping away on his doorstep. Jerry slammed the door and laughed. "I'm tripping my brains out, man!"

Jerry unlocked the chain from the door opened it all the way to get a better look at the birds. They were gone.

He stood there in his doorway with his bottom lip protruding. Then he stepped out into the hallway to find them. "Here, little birdies."

A piercing cold hand touched the back of his neck. "Well, hello, Jerry. Don't be afraid. It's your old friend, Gretchen."

Gretchen stabilized herself to face him, leaving her

cold, claw-like hand on the back of his neck. "I brought another friend for you to meet. Her name is Abella."

Abella paraded herself in front of Jerry. Her fiery, curly, red hair flashed against her black leather cat-woman outfit. Her eyes reflected the red in her hair like two tiny torches.

"Can we come in?" Abella spoke with the tone of a seductress as she stepped toward Jerry. She stood two inches from his face. Her breath smelled of the sweetest vanilla.

Jerry nodded, not breaking eye contact with the red-headed beauty.

"Can you say it for me?" Her lips pressed together. Jerry swallowed the lump in his throat.

Jerry snapped out of his trance. "Yes, you can come in."

Abella smiled and kissed Jerry on the cheek as she sauntered inside.

"Okay, let's go," Gretchen yelled.

Seven evil, intimidating-looking people rose from the stairs where they must have been waiting for the word. One by one, they marched into Jerry's apartment.

The first was a six-foot-six Native American with a Mohawk. His eyes were bloodshot, and although he made no eye contact, Jerry could see murder in this man's eyes.

The next two men were identical twins with faces completely tattooed to differentiate themselves. Their pale skin made the perfect canvas, contrasting with their black robes.

Jerry's heart sank into his stomach as these two men hoofed toward him. He opened his mouth to protest, but his throat no longer made sound. He was powerless to stop them from invading his home. Evil oozed from their pores.

As the men drew closer, Jerry got a close-up look at their tattoos. The first man looked like a walking skull with his nose and eyes blackened and his bones tattooed onto his skin. He ogled at Jerry the whole way down the hall. Before he turned to go in, he stopped.

"I will always be watching." The twin then turned his head. Two evil-looking tattooed eyes peered back at Jerry from the back of the man's head.

The second twin was more evil-looking then the first. His neck looked as if fish scales covered it all the way up to his jaw line. His face was ghastly with a black pentagram in the middle of his forehead. From a distance, it looked as if he had hair, but as he drew closer, Jerry saw that the "hair" was a tattoo of a tail of a snake that started on the tip of the man's forehead and ran down the back of his neck. As he advanced past Jerry, he stuck out his tongue. It was split in two like a snake's. Chills ran down Jerry's spine as that tongue wiggled out of the man's mouth.

The fourth was a women dressed in purple, wearing the most beautiful jewelry Jerry had ever seen. She had a shining, gold crown on her head and large pearls and diamonds around her neck and wrists. Judging by the size of the diamonds, she must have been wearing a million dollars' worth of jewelry.

From a distance, she looked like an enchanted princess with beautiful dark hair, dressed in royal purple. She could have been in a fairy tale, riding on a white horse. But as she strutted toward Jerry, she stumbled as if drunk, catching herself on the wall. With every step she took, she aged. As she lugged closer, Jerry saw through her hair a tattoo across her forehead. It looked like some kind of ancient writing, and she had deep wrinkles on her face that gave her a worn look. The women stopped directly in front of Jerry, looking as if she had just aged forty years.

She leaned over and whispered the filthiest, most perverted things he had ever heard. He felt his mouth drop open. The woman laughed as if pleased by his expression.

The fifth man was a wiry, muscular black man dressed in traditional African warrior clothing. His cheeks and neck were painted bright red. He had many piercings, and jewelry hung from his ears and neck. With him he carried a long, sharp spear. His black eyes filled with hate, and as he walked by, Jerry could sense that hatred directed at him.

The sixth was a girl of about sixteen with dark brown hair pulled back in a ponytail. She was dressed like a gypsy, barefoot with several tattoos on her feet. She wore sheer green pants with a golden belt and turquoise jewelry. Her white sculpted top covered her shoulders and chest area, exposing a tattoo of a sun around her belly button. She was a pretty girl, but as she drew closer to Jerry, he sensed darkness all around her. She gazed at him as if she knew his thoughts. She gave him a half-crooked smile as she passed.

The seventh was the white Arien-supremacy guy whom Jerry had met earlier. He had a big grin on his face as he strode toward Gretchen. He rested his hand on her back. "We did it, didn't we?"

"Now let's get to work," Gretchen said. He escorted her into the one-bedroom apartment.

Jerry stood outside for a moment. Should he run? His body was incapacitated. His mind was sending signals to his limbs, but nothing was working.

Abella peered around the corner. "Hey, stud, we're all waiting for you in here." Her voice stunned his system as if someone had taken two electric paddles to his chest.

She reached her hand out. Jerry took it, and she pulled him inside.

Les latched onto his shopping basket, hustling through the supermarket with his cell phone to his ear. "Hey, Jerry, I didn't mean to put you in an uncomfortable situation. I'm in the grocery store." Les examined a package of frozen chicken. "Do you want me to pick up anything for you? I'm going over to Lynn's tonight to cook dinner. It's not a date or anything, just hanging out."

He dropped the package into his basket. "Don't start with me. I already know what you're going to say. We're just friends with a common interest, that's all." Les laughed. "I don't know how late I'll be at Lynn's, so if you want to do something tonight, let me know."

Les ended his phone call, finished grabbing the groceries for the night, and checked out. Fifteen minutes later, his shiny blue Civic pulled into the drive at 4423 Ash Way.

It was a cute little house with its green shutters and yellow flowers in little boxes below the windows. As he filed up the stone sidewalk, a couple of butterflies floated in and out of his stomach. He rang the doorbell, and seconds later, Lynn answered the door in a grey t-shirt, light-colored jeans with different holes in them and pink, fluffy slippers.

"I brought chicken." Les held up one of the bags.

"Make yourself at home." Lynn's beautiful smile lit up her whole face. "Set the bags on the counter."

Les deposited his bags and took out the package of

chicken. "I wasn't sure what you had, so I brought a bunch of stuff just in case. Chicken and marinade, potatoes and corn, lettuce and salad stuff."

"You went all out. You did a great job."

"Now the question is, do you like any of it?"

Lynn laughed. "Let's get to work. Do you know how to make potatoes?"

"Other than throwing them in the microwave, no."

"Neither do I. I'm Japanese, and we don't eat a lot of potatoes. I'll Google them and find out how to make them."

"I should have called first. I was in a hurry and leaving Jerry a message." Les slapped his forehead covering his eyes. "I can do some Uncle Ben's rice."

"I'm Japanese, remember? We don't do instant rice."

"Non-instant rice it is."

"Why don't you do the meat thing, and I'll handle the rice and salad." Lynn reached into the cabinet above the stove and pulled out a glass bowl. "You can marinate in this."

"Sounds like a plan." Les made the marinade and then plopped the chicken into the bowl. He stepped onto the back porch and fired up the gas grill. While it heated, he watched Lynn through the sliding doors. She had pulled her hair back, and she seemed to have focused all her attention on her rice preparations.

Watching her at the kitchen counter, Les had a déjà-vu moment.

What was going on with him? He pulled his gaze from her. He had just met this girl. A few hours earlier, he was falling for her friend. But he still couldn't shake the sense of how familiar everything felt.

Lynn peeked her head out onto the back porch. "It's going to take about thirty-five minutes to cook the rice. How long for the chicken?"

"I wanted to let it marinate for at least twenty minutes. Let's go ahead and eat the salad while we wait."

An hour later, they relaxed in the candlelight and watched the sun set over the lake. "That was great. I think we make a good team." Les wadded up his napkin and pitched it beside his empty plate.

"How'd you like the rice?"

"Best I've ever had. I grew up on instant everything. Push a few buttons on the microwave, and presto—dinner."

"We're leaving the dishes. I'll do them later. What would you like to do first—tell me your story or read the notebook?" Lynn grabbed his hand and pulled him to the living room.

"I think we should read the notebook."

They brought their water glasses into the living room along with the bright red notebook labeled "1986." Les sat close to Lynn on the couch, and she handed him the notebook.

Les grasped the red binder. "You want me to read it?"

"I enjoyed listening to you in the apartment this afternoon." Lynn swiveled in her seat so she was directly facing Les, with her legs crossed Indian-style, looking ready to listen.

Les opened the notebook then paused and observed her for a moment. She looked cute and sweet with her legs crossed, gazing back at him.

Lynn's phone rang then, and she glanced at Les for a second as if trying to decide whether to answer. "Let me see who it is."

She got up, grabbed the phone, and scanned the ID. She hit a button and raised the phone to her mouth. "Hey, girl, I just finished eating dinner with Les."

After a short silence, Lynn's brows furrowed. "Sure. Just a second."

Lynn held the phone out. "Lila wants to talk to you."

Les took the phone from her and answered.

"Hey, cutie, hanging out with my girl tonight, are you?" Lila's voice sounded as smooth as it had last night. It was if she was his ice cream on a hot day.

"Yeah, we're chilling at her house." Les stood from the couch and paced toward the porch. It was too awkward, talking to Lila with Lynn staring at him, nervously biting the side of her cheek. Her doe eyes whispered, *don't do this to me again, Lila.*

"I had a good time last night, and I felt a connection between us. Your new business venture also perked my interest. I think I can help. What are you doing for lunch tomorrow?"

Les wiped his sweaty palms on his jeans. "Nothing. What time?"

"How about around noon? I'll call you. Lynn doesn't need to know. Let's just keep this between me and you."

What was that about? For some reason, he felt like a coward, agreeing to that.

"Now let me talk to Lynn again."

Les scuffed back into the house and handed the phone to Lynn.

She took the phone from him. "Hey, what was that all about?" After a pause, she frowned again. "What do you mean? I can handle myself."

Lynn set her phone back on the counter and moved back to the couch next to Les. "I shouldn't have answered that. She didn't say anything weird, did she?"

"No, nothing weird." Les couldn't hold her gaze. He held up the bright red notebook. "Let's get to the notebook."

He felt like a rope that was being yanked between two women, digging in their heels to take their ground in a tug of war. He was not going to deny his feelings for either woman; he liked them both. Not to mention it was a major stroke to his ego. He enjoyed Lynn's company very much. He could be himself. There was no facade or act. But with Lila—she was his dream women. He was smitten by the very sight of her.

I wonder who is going to win?

CHAPTER TWENTY

June 6, 1986: Madeline and I are in Villa Nueva, south of Guatemala City. This is our fourth time to conduct an open-air tent meeting and hand out food, clothing, and Bibles. Then we invite them into the tent to hear the word of God. The last three meetings were very successful as we handed out two thousand Bibles and had 386 decisions for Christ. Madeline and I believe this will be the biggest turnout yet. Pastor Rios from the local church warned us about a witch doctor coming to his church services. He stands outside the church, writing things in the dirt, and a circling black bird seems to travel with him. He came to our last two meetings and stood outside the tent, watching. Madeline saw him this morning, drawing things in the dirt just outside the tents. She also saw a black bird circling the area around noon. One of the locals told us that he came today because in our first meeting, we broke the spell he had cast on his top fortune teller. We have cost him a lot of money, and he is here to make sure that doesn't happen again. This twelve-year-old girl came to our first meeting and was possessed by a demon that gave her power to see into the future. When Pastor Rios and I gave the altar call for people to accept Christ, she came forward. She stood in front of me with her black eyes and her face contorted. The Lord whispered to me, "Don't be intimidated. Have no fear, for I am with you." I placed my hand on her head, and she shoved it away. She hissed at me, but she did not try

199

to escape. I then set my legs apart, placed my left hand on her shoulder and my right on her head. She tried to slap it away several times, but my hand was firmly planted on her forehead. The Lord told me to cast out the evil spirit of fortune telling. I said, "In Jesus' name, demon of the dead and divination, come out! In the mighty name of Jesus!" The demon picked her up and threw her to the ground. She writhed on the ground like a snake. Pastor Rios saw then what was happening. He came over, held her down, and agreed with me in casting out the spirit. We rebuked the spirit three more times before it gave up and left her. She then stood, hugged us, and asked to stay with us. Then a woman from the crowd came running toward us, weeping, saying this was her daughter who had disappeared two years ago. We watched as mother and daughter held each other in a long embrace.

"This is a crazy story." Les focused on Lynn. "Why do you think Mr. Allen wanted us to read this?"

"Maybe he wanted us to be aware of evil."

"That makes sense because Jesus cast out a bunch of demons in John. Maybe Eugene Allen was telling us through this story that it can still be done."

"Do you think he could be warning us of what's to come?" Lynn spun her body around.

"I just got creeped out." Les shuddered.

"Can you imagine seeing a person fall to the ground, writhing like a snake?"

Les shook his head. Then he thought of Jerry and everything that happened after he smoked his superweed. "Oh my gosh. I don't know if that's what I saw, but I was scared to death."

Les turned to look into Lynn's eyes. Such compassionate eyes, and pretty. "If I tell you this, you have to promise me to keep it between us."

"Is this part of your story that you were going to tell me?"

"Actually, it's the whole story." Les bounced up off the couch.

"I promise to keep it to myself." Lynn made a cross over her heart.

Les paused for a moment, collecting his thoughts. "Jerry had been acting weird and selfish with his time lately. I got mad at him about that, then I felt bad about some of the things I said, so I wanted to make it up to him. When I called, I got a deep breathing sound on his phone."

"That's odd." Lynn tucked her legs under herself again and rocked back and forth.

"Before I called, I had a crazy feeling that something bad was happing to him. So I get over there and I get out of my car, and he's sitting in his van, staring blankly out the window like a zombie. It was like he didn't even see me as I walked over to the van."

Lynn's eyes grew wide as she intently watched Les's every move.

"Eventually, he opened the door to his van and acted as if he'd snapped out of a trance. He was all sweaty and dirty, like he'd been crawling in the dirt. I helped him inside, and he was so thirsty, he drank right out of the faucet."

"That's kind of unusual."

"Anyway, we get into his apartment and he starts acting really strange, begging me to get high with him. I don't know how he did it, but somehow he ended up guilt-tripping me into getting high with him." The concern in Lynn's eyes cut through him. "Yeah, big mistake. I hadn't done that in years, but somehow he talked me into it. He said he couldn't tell me what happened to him that day until I got high with him."

"That's real manipulative."

"He can be that way. So we get wasted on his superweed, as he calls it. It's a hybrid, glow-in-the dark concoction he created. Jerry is actually a highly intelligent guy. He's a self-taught computer programmer."

Eyebrows raised, Lynn nodded. A slight smile broke across her face. He could tell she was entertained by his story.

"Before he could tell me what happened to him that day, someone starts banging on the door. He opens the door and goes flying backward, unconscious. An old lady and a large, bald, mean-looking white man are standing in the doorway."

Les paced the room. "At this point, I just about poop my pants. I can barely move. The two of them are standing in the doorway, asking to come in and help."

Lynn's bottom lip raised. "Why didn't they just come in?"

"I don't know. Then something over came me. In the book of John, Jesus worked through the power of the holy force. It works like the Force in Star Wars. When you believe in something through the force, it happens."

"You're confusing me." Lynn bent her neck to the side.

"I didn't even think about it. I just reacted. I jumped up and slammed the door in their faces."

"Did they get mad?"

"Yeah, they started banging on the door. Something

inside of me told me to tell them to go away in the name of Jesus. So I did, and guess what? They left."

Lynn unfolded her legs and set her feet on the ground as her gaze dropped to the floor. "There must be some kind of connection with that name Jesus." She then covered her mouth with both hands as they pressed together in front of her lips. "What do you think they were doing there?"

"I don't know, but they acted as if they knew Jerry."

"I wonder if they were drug-dealing friends of his."

"Could be. He sold a lot of weed in college."

"So what happened to Jerry?"

Les plopped back down on the couch next to Lynn. "I took him back to my place and got him cleaned up and he was fine."

"Just like that?" Lynn jerked her head back. Loose strands of hair fell across her face.

I can't involve her. He had to lie. "I got him into the shower and gave him a good meal, and he was good as new."

"Do you think those drug dealers were scared of the name of Jesus and that's what made them run?"

"I don't know. It's overwhelming and crazy." Les swiveled his body to face her as he reached out to move a few of the loose strands of her hair.

"There's a connection between Eugene Allen's stories and the Bible. Do you have any plans tonight? If not, we could read through the book of John together."

A slight smile shone on Lynn's face. "Sure, do you like coffee?"

"Does moss grow on trees?"

"Are you trying to impress me with your corny jokes?"

"No, but I would like some coffee, please."

"That's a better answer."

Les's gaze followed Lynn to the kitchen. The red handkerchief that was tied to the rope was being pulled in her direction.

Abella looked deep into Jerry's eyes as she led him into the living room. There on his coffee table were three candles that somebody had lit. They produced the only light in the room. The door slammed shut. Jerry jerked his head to see who had done it, but no one was standing by the door. What did these people want with him? Where they going to torture him? Where they going to kill him and sacrifice him to their god?

Abella squeezed his hand tighter as she pulled his body close to hers. She wrapped both arms around his waist and moved his left arm to drape across her back. Her head rested between his chest and chin, and his right arm dangled by his side. With Abella snuggled close, he felt a little better, but not much.

Eight other sets of evil eyes stared at Jerry in the small, dark apartment. The Native American man sat on the couch with the lady dressed in purple and the twin with the pentagram tattooed on his forehead.

The temperature in the room dropped, and Jerry felt colder and colder by the second. Abella rubbed his chest in the silence. Jerry took a deep breath and exhaled. He could see his breath.

"Some of you are probably wondering why I have summoned you all here today. I want to introduce our newest weapon in the kingdom: Prince Humberger of the

ancient line of Eldridge Humberger, who was a great
wizard in the early nineteen hundreds. Eldridge was one of
the few wizards who had the power to summon many
entities together at one time." Gretchen stepped forward,
and the others formed a half-circle around Jerry and Abella.
"Here, in the line of the great wizard himself, stands before
us his offspring, Jerry Humberger, the new prince of
Gerberville. It has come to our attention that he also has the
power to do the same as his ancient mystical grandfather."

Gretchen took the crown from the head of the
women adorned in purple and placed it on Jerry's head.
"We now crown you prince of Gerberville!"

Everyone in the room clapped as Abella hung close
to his side. Jerry tried to speak, but his teeth chattered from
the cold and his whole body shivered. *A wizard that
summons entities?* "Who are you people?"

The woman dressed in purple stepped forward and
bowed her head. "We are here to help you with anything
you need, my lord."

The African warrior spoke next. "We are here to
help you win the battle."

"What battle?" What were these people talking
about?

The African warrior hurled his spear into the floor.
"We fight many battles all around you every day. Until
now, you haven't been permitted to see them. We will now
go before you, paving the way for your victory."

Jerry held Abella close to him, his heart beating
violently to keep his body warm. "What are you talking
about?"

The warrior glared at Gretchen with blood-red hate
in his eyes. "This is who you pinned our hopes on! This
Jerry is merely a boy who knows nothing. He is no prince!"

Gretchen stood her ground, pointing her claw-like hand at the warrior. "You have no vision! You see only what is in front of you. You see a boy with a mystical talent. I see a god with a vast kingdom."

The warrior stepped back as he examined Jerry up and down with those hate-filled eyes. He yanked his spear from the floor. "Actions speak louder than words! We must see him act!"

The twins spoke up in an evil and chilling unison. "For us to follow, for us to serve, for us to call you our master, you must prove to us you are worthy."

Jerry, frozen with fear and the numbing chill in the air, tried to comprehend what was happening.

Abella touched his cheek with her left hand and kissed him on the lips. She then turned to the eight others, held out her hands, and spoke with the elegance of a trained public speaker. "This is the chosen one, picked from the beginning. We can not change that, but what we can do is embrace it with all our might and strength. Jerry knows about a healing potion that can heal any man or woman of any ailment. Do any of you understand the power and the wealth that would come with that?"

She paused to study the room to make sure she had everyone's attention. "He would be a walking god on earth, deciding who lives and who dies. Through this, we could build a kingdom that would never crumble, a kingdom that would lack nothing. We will all receive prestigious responsibility within this kingdom, and it starts today when we give complete allegiance to our new prince. Prince Humberger, we bow before you."

Abella bowed to one knee in front of Jerry, and the rest of the group followed. Jerry cast his eyes around the room at the nine of them bowing before him, and an electric power surged through his body. He was their prince, Abella was his princess, and they were his loyal subjects.

"You may rise." Jerry spoke with the commanding, deep voice of a general. It surprised even him. He was their leader now, and he would not let them down. The earlier chill had left, and his mind was sharp, as though he could process a thousand thoughts at once.

"Pay attention to my plan," Prince Humberger commanded.

Les and Lynn took turns reading chapters of the book of John to each other. When they didn't understand a section, they stopped and discussed their opinions and how each chapter made them feel. It was a time like Lynn had never experienced.

Lester finished reading the last verse in chapter twenty-one: "'Jesus did many other things as well. If every one of them were written down, I suppose that even the whole world would not have room for the books that would be written.'"

Les glanced up from the Bible, shaking his head. "Wow, the whole world wouldn't have room for these books to be written. The whole world."

"What else do you think he did?"

"I'm sure he did other similar miracles, but I can't see him topping the last one—coming back to life. Let's see David Blaine try that one."

Lynn laughed. "What do you think Jesus would be doing right now if he was on earth?"

Les massaged his forehead. "I think he would go

from city to city, visiting all the hospitals around the world, the children's hospitals first, then the terminal wards. He would heal everyone who received him. I believe that's what John is taking about in the end of his book. I bet Jesus healed thousands upon thousands of people. Think about it. Medicine was primitive, and lots of people died young back then."

"Did you know that more than five hundred thousand women die in pregnancy or childbirth in developing countries every year due to lack of proper care? That's today's stats. Think about Jesus visiting all of these third-world hospitals and bringing these women back to life."

"You're passionate about women, aren't you?" Les's grin warmed Lynn's heart. *He gets me.*

"Can you imagine a child being raised without his mother, knowing that when he was given life, his mother's was taken?" Lynn studied every line in Les's face. His strong jaw line made him look so powerful and in control.

"You're right, I think he would hit the children's hospitals for sure. So many children suffer with pain their whole lives and die at a young age. I think Jesus would want to heal them first and give them a better life."

"Sometimes I work in the pediatric center at St. Bernard's. I struggle to make it through the day without crying." Lynn's bottom lip quivered. "The children there go through so much at such an early age."

Les placed his hand over hers.

"I'm sorry. I get choked up sometimes, thinking about the children."

"It's okay." Les squeezed her hand then gazed down at his watch. "It's eleven thirty. I enjoyed tonight, but it's getting late. The time flew by."

Les stood and opened his arms. Lynn gravitated toward him and allowed him to engulf her in his arms. She felt safe and comfortable with his big arms wrapped around her. She never wanted this moment to end. But she had to let go. She didn't want to come off as clingy. Lynn stepped back, staring up into Les's eyes.

"Come here, you." Les held up his right arm like a mother hen to one of her chicks. Lynn snuggled underneath his arm as they meandered to the door.

"Today was amazing and I had a great night."

"I had a great night too." He smelled good.

When they reached Lynn's front door, Les turned Lynn's body to face his.

Please kiss me. Please kiss me. Please kiss me.

"Something is telling me to go on home." Les twisted the door knob.

She needed to let him go.

"I'll call you tomorrow." Les opened the door and stepped through the entryway.

"What are you doing tomorrow?"

Les was already halfway down the sidewalk. He spun around. "I have plans with a friend."

"Okay. I wondered if you wanted to go to church with me."

"Maybe next week." Les waved.

Lynn closed her front door, locked the deadbolt, and rested her back against the door. God, Jesus, the Bible—it was all so invigorating. How great it was to share these moments with Les. It also didn't hurt that he was attractive and they had a great connection.

Had God put them together? Was Les the man God had sent to be her husband? Is this why she'd never found a man worth marrying? The feelings she had for him were like no other, and she'd known him only twenty-four hours. They connected on a deeper level, a level that she had never experienced, and it was wonderful.

What would tomorrow bring?

CHAPTER TWENTY-ONE

===

"Everyone be seated." Prince Humberger's deep, commanding voice belted out in the silent room. He stood with his arms crossed, peering deep into his subjects' eyes, gaining strength and confidence from every evil stare.

He felt himself evolving. A dynamic power pulsed through his veins as if he had just finished a hard upper-body workout. But he could sense an uneasiness about the room. Some of them still did not fully believe in him and were not quite ready to pledge their allegiance.

"Doubt plagues this room!" The prince slammed his fist into his hand. "You are either for me or against me. You need to decide before I get into the depth of my plans."

The pentagram twin rose from the couch.

"Did I give you permission to stand?" The prince picked up the coffee table and threw it against the wall, shattering the table into tiny pieces as if it were made of Legos. In an instant, he was in front of the pentagram twin, who still stood in front of the couch. The prince grabbed the twin by the throat and, with one continuous motion, slammed him against the wall as if he were some kind of rag doll.

Then the prince stood on the couch and held the twin up with one arm, pinning his head against the ceiling. "I didn't give you permission to stand."

The prince calmly squeezed his hand around the twin's throat, cutting off all air to his lungs. No one said a word or made a move as the twin's face turned from red to purple to a light shade of gray. The twin smiled back at him. Then the prince released him.

The twin collapsed. He crashed down on the arm of

211

the couch, flipped over it, and rolled with a limp thud onto the floor. He lay there motionless.

"Anyone else want to move without permission?" The prince strutted back to his spot in the middle of the room. He looked around and sensed that he was gaining control. The large Native American man sat on the couch with pieces of wood scattered all over him, his head raised toward Prince Humberger. The prince knew he had gained his respect.

The African warrior sat on the floor with his legs crossed, not at all fazed by the ordeal. The prince took deep breaths now, and his heart felt as if it wanted to jump out of his chest.

Abella sat at his feet. She was a vision of beautiful submission, ready to serve his every need, and that calmed his nerves.

"We'll have two plans. In Plan A, I will regain my old friend Les's trust and get him to leave me alone in his condo. There I'll switch the healing potion with a jug of regular wine from the grocery store. The healing potion sits out in the open, in an old milk jug. When Les tries to use the healing potion, he'll think its gone bad and has no more healing power. But I'll have the real potion, and this will be the start of our legacy."

"Plan B is for me to walk into Les's condo and take the healing potion by force. If I have to hurt him, I will. But I will get what is rightfully mine." He gazed around the room. From the looks on the others' faces, his plans were pleasing to them.

"May we rise, your majesty, and give you our allegiance?" Abella beamed up at her prince.

"You may."

The woman adorned in purple was the first. She slid

a gold ring off her finger and placed it on his. One by one, each bowed on one knee and kissed Prince Humberger's right hand to signify their allegiance to him. With every bow and with every kiss, their atrocities infiltrated his soul. An untamed endowment of hate spread over his skin, leaching onto his mind as would a parasite to a host. Abella was the last to give him reverence, kissing his hand then his lips. He pushed her aside and raised his arms.

"I will conquer!"

Les's drive home was one of mixed emotions. He had connected with Lynn on a new, lofty level as never before. She was deep and refreshing and made him feel alive.

So why did his thoughts drift back to Lila? Why did his stomach twist in knots every time he thought of her? Last night, everything inside him wanted to please her.

Les exhaled a big breath that vibrated his lips together. Was it truly a spiritual connection that made him feel this way? Or was it that they'd spent all day together, striving toward a common interest?

I'm giving myself a headache. He turned on his stereo so he wouldn't have to think about it anymore. He numbed his mind as he drove, singing along with the music on the radio. Soon Les scuffed into his condo and set his keys and phone on the dining room table. His throat was parched from the long drive, so he raced for the fridge to get a bottled water. As he chugged the water, he made a quick scan of his kitchen to admire his cleaning skills.

The jug of healing wine caught his eye, sitting in the back corner of the kitchen. Should he have refrigerated it?

What if it went bad? What if it doesn't work anymore? Les dashed over to the jug and pulled off the top. The sweetest aroma he had ever smelled hit him.

"Wow, this stuff is amazing." Les felt a little dazed from the scent. "I should put this stuff in a better container."

That wine could be the key to Les making something of his life, and he was keeping it in an old plastic milk jug. Les rummaged through his Tupperware but found nothing fit to contain this wine. "I need to go to Super Mart."

He grabbed his keys from the kitchen table. In a matter of seconds, he was behind the wheel of his car, feeling torn between two women and two worlds. Could he ever bring himself to tell either one of them about the healing wine? If he were to tell Lynn, she would understand the magnitude of the power and would want to use it to help the world.

He thought of their conversation about Jesus and what he would be doing if he were walking about the earth today. He would visit hospitals and heal the sick, starting with the children.

Then again, Les could do that. He could be a modern-day Jesus, healing the sick, going from city to city with Lynn by his side. But why did such a big part of him want Lila to love him? Maybe Jerry was right; this could be the chance of a lifetime to make a lot of money. Les would never have to worry about his finances again.

What if Les, Jerry, Lila, and her dad worked together to commercialize and market the healing wine? They could all make millions. No, billions, and Lila would be his. He could have everything he had ever wanted within days or even hours.

His lunch with Lila was going to be pivotal. He would tell her and even show her if he had to. Then she would need and want him, then hopefully make out with him. Les smirked. Imagine him, locking lips with his Arabian princess.

The blue Civic pulled into the large but almost-empty Super Mart parking lot. At least he wouldn't have to wait in line.

Les paused as the automatic doors opened, then he wandered into the deserted-looking store. He didn't see anyone around, not even the greeter.

He turned to the right and headed toward the kitchen section in the back of the store. When he arrived at the storage-container aisle, he found so many different shapes and sizes, he wasn't sure what to get.

Les took a deep breath and started searching. He opened the lids and flipped the containers upside down, checking to see how many ounces each one held. He found a six-piece set of twelve-ounce containers with screw-on lids. "These will be perfect."

"Yeah, those are good." The man's deep voice startled Les, and he dropped the box of containers.

"I'm sorry. I didn't mean to startle you." The man rubbed his belly that peeked out underneath his shirt then swished his mop around the floor a few times. "I'm just mopping up the floors. Night time is the best time to do the mopping. Name's Charlie."

Charlie wiped whatever was on his hand onto his shirt and reached out to shake Les's hand. The guy smelled like he'd just bathed in Pine-Sol. Les shook Charlie's hand as Charlie gave him a big grin. He noticed he was missing more than a few teeth. Les gazed up into his bright, turquoise-colored eyes, unable to look away. It was almost hypnotizing, looking into them.

Charlie stroked his comb-over. "Did you need help with anything?"

Les bent down to pick up the box of plastic containers to examine it. "Do you know how many ounces are in a gallon?"

"One hundred and twenty-eight," Charlie replied without hesitation.

Les glanced back at the man. "Are you sure? You answered that kind of quick."

Charlie brushed his beard stubble. "One hundred percent sure."

This guy is a slob. "How many of these twelve-ounce containers do I need to buy?"

"Two sets of six. That's the only way they sell them." Charlie swung the mop closer to Les's feet. "What do you plan on putting in those containers?"

"I don't know, food."

Charlie rested his hands on top of the mop. "Why did you need to know how many ounces make up a gallon if you're just going to put food in them?"

Who is this guy? Why is he being so nosy? Les crammed a box under each arm as a lie formed in his mind. "Food in liquid form."

Charlie stood there squinting at Les as if he understood more about the situation than Les did. "I need to tell you something. I was praying to God this morning, and he told me that he was going to send someone who could help my wife."

The desperation in Charlie's tone tore through Les. "Why do you think God would want you to talk to me?"

"My wife was diagnosed with terminal cancer

216

yesterday. She's been given thirty days to live. She has exactly one hundred and twenty-eight cancerous tumors throughout her body. She could die at any moment, but the doctor gave her a month at the most." Tears ran down Charlie's face. "I wrote in my journal this morning that the man who can help us will answer me with a question, and the confirmation will be in the number. I spoke to eleven people today. You were the only one who has asked me a question that had anything to do with a number."

Les's hands had no more strength in them. He dropped the box. This was beyond his imagination. Was this merely a man crying out for attention or was it the hand of God determining his fate?

"I don't know what I'll do if I lose my Bonnie. She's all I got. I don't know if I could live anymore." Charlie wiped his eyes, his voice now a squeak. "I know this probably sounds stupid to you, but can you do anything?"

Les swallowed the lump that had collected in his throat. "Where is she?"

"You mean you can help?" A ray of hope filled Charlie's eyes. "I brought her home today."

"What time does your shift end?"

"I got done five hours ago. I asked if I could work the rest of the night for free."

This guy is insane. "I need to go home first, but I'll meet you outside in twenty minutes."

Charlie dropped his mop. "I'll be there."

Les took his containers to the only open line. The checkout lady's name tag read, "Sandy."

"Staying out of trouble tonight?" Sandy scanned the containers, scratching her brown greasy hair.

Les opened his wallet. "It's kind of slow, isn't it?"

217

Sandy gazed up at Les through huge, coke-bottle glasses that magnified her eyes. "We get a big rush at three o'clock when all the bars close."

Les swiped his credit card though the machine and signed his name. "A lot of drunk people come in?"

"Huh." Sandy smirked. "You could say that." She handed him the receipt. "Not everyone is what they seem to be."

Les stuffed the receipt into his pocket. "What do you mean?"

"Be careful. Not everyone is what they seem to be."

"Right." What was she talking about? Were all Super Mart employees nuts?

Tired of carrying the two boxes, Les dumped them into an empty cart. He wheeled the containers to the back of his car and pitched them into his trunk.

He checked his watch. He had fifteen minutes to get home, fill a container with the wine, and get back. No way would he make it in time. It would take more like thirty minutes.

He's waited the past five hours. He can wait another ten minutes.

Les pulled out of the parking lot and turned toward home. He glanced at the sky. The cloud cover obscured the stars from his view the same way something untouchable, unfathomable had blocked his understanding of God.

How had God spoken to Charlie? What did God's voice sound like? Les should have asked Charlie.

Maybe I should try to talk to God and see if I can hear him. Les gripped his steering wheel with both hands until his fingers ached. He swallowed then cleared his throat. "Hello, God, I know you're up there somewhere and you can hear me. I was wondering if you wanted to talk to me."

Les waited to hear a booming voice. After several minutes of silence, he pulled into his parking spot and grabbed the two boxes from his trunk. He must have done something wrong.

Inside, he dropped the boxes onto the kitchen counter. He opened one, took out a container, and rinsed it in the sink. Carefully pouring the wine from the old milk jug, he filled the new container to the eleven-ounce line. Then he screwed the blue cover on tight.

"What should I use to administer it?" He opened his cup and glass cabinet. An old shot glass stamped with the words "Spring Break 1999, Daytona Beach" caught his eye.

Les grabbed the shot glass and the wine and headed back to his car. As he unlocked the door, the immensity of the moment hit him: God was unlocking him.

Was this God's way of telling him this was what he wanted him to do with the wine? But what about Lila?

He needed to do this for Charlie and his wife then reassess. Maybe he could do both: help people in the hospitals with Lynn and make money with Lila.

As he parked his car in front of the Super Mart, his car clock read one forty-one. He'd been gone thirty-four minutes. Les inspected the parking lot for Charlie. There was no sign of him anywhere.

After five more minutes, Les parked his car and sprinted inside. A young man with long hair sat at the door, greeting customers.

"Have you seen Charlie?" Les said trying to catch his breath.

"Who's Charlie?"

"He works here, mopping the floors."

"I don't know any Charlie." The young man

yawned through his words.

"Thanks a lot. Big help." Les charged through the store, but Charlie wasn't there. None of the employees even knew him.

Back at the front of the store, Les passed the check-out line. If Sandy was still there, she might be able to tell him something about Charlie. When Les got to her register, a man was working at it instead.

That's weird.

"Thank you for shopping at Super Mart," the young man said as Les jogged through the automatic exit doors. Surely he didn't miss him. Maybe Charlie got confused and thought Les was going to meet him in the back.

Les climbed into his car and drove around the back. Three security lights cast a soft glow over the rear of the store. Les inched past the warehouse docks where the trucks unloaded. He saw no one. He banged the palm of his hand on his steering wheel and let out a mild curse.

Les headed back toward the front of the store. Near the entrance, a woman puffing on a cigarette caught his eye. As he budged closer, he saw it was Sandy.

Les rolled down his window. "Hey, Sandy, have you seen Charlie? The bald, short guy who works here?"

Sandy took another drag of her cigarette before advancing toward the car. "No, but do you remember what I told you?"

"That people aren't always what they seem?"

"Be careful." Sandy pointed at Les then turned and strolled back into the store.

"What is with this place?" He shifted into first gear and coasted toward the exit. When he got to the intersection, he looked both ways and pulled across the three lanes onto the other side of the street. As he drove

220

down the road, he glanced in his rear-view mirror. Charlie sat on the bus-stop bench.

Les swerved to the side of the road. He slammed into neutral and pulled the brake, checking the man in his mirror. The guy sat with his head down, not moving at all.

That totally is Charlie. Should I go pick him up? I told him I would help him. Is it my right to choose whether his wife gets to live or die? Shouldn't that be God's choice? But what if God wants to use my wine that the holy force created?

Then Sandy's words rang in his ear. *People aren't always what they seem to be.*

What did she mean by that? Les glanced in the mirror again. Charlie was gone.

Somebody rapped on the driver's side window. Les let out a yell.

"Do you need help?" There was Charlie, standing at the door.

He couldn't see that it was Les because of his tinted windows. Les could just take off. He hesitated for a moment then lowered his window. "I'm looking for a guy who wants me to help his wife."

"Hey, it's me, Charlie." He waved his stubby little hand.

"Where did you go? I've been looking all over for you."

"I thought you weren't coming, so I went to the bus stop to wait for the next bus."

"Get in. Where are we headed?"

Charlie climbed in the passenger side. "Make a U-turn and go right at the third light."

As they drove toward Charlie's house in silence, Les stole a glimpse of him. What was Les doing? What if

221

Charlie was a serial killer and was luring Les back to his place so he could chop him up? Maybe that's why no one at Super Mart knew who he was.

A trickle of sweat ran down Les's neck, and he swiped it away with the palm of his hand. He had just picked up a strange man and was going to his house in the middle of the night. What an idiot he was! Now what was he going to do?

Could God have sent Sandy to warn him? Did he ignore God? Les's face broke out in a sweat, and he rolled down his window.

"You okay?" Charlie asked.

"Yeah, it's late and I'm tired."

"Sorry, I didn't mean for you to ruin your whole night trying to help me. You can pull over and I can walk home from here."

Les looked into Charlie's bright, turquoise-colored eyes. "I'm not going to do that. It's already past two o'clock."

"I appreciate you doing this. I don't think I ever got your name."

Les paused. "I don't want to be rude or anything, but I'd rather not give you my name."

Charlie laughed. "You're an angel, aren't you?"

Les glanced at the sloppy-looking man, then back at the road.

Charlie laughed again. His laugh was a cross between Santa Claus and the Joker. Les couldn't gauge the emotion behind it. "I knew God would send me an angel. I knew it! Just wait until I tell Bonnie. She's not going to believe it. So what's heaven like?"

Was this guy playing head games with him? Was he that diabolical or just plain ignorant? Whatever he was, Les was going to play along. "God says for you to stop asking me so many questions."

"I didn't mean to upset you. It's just so exciting to be in the presence of a holy messenger."

"Why do you think I'm an angel?"

"Well, you're big. Angels are usually big, so I've heard. You're good-looking, and I've also heard that angles are very attractive. You want to take your next right at Kite then a left on Gorton road. You also have the ability to heal, just like the healing angels in the Bible."

Healing angel? There wasn't a healing angel in the book of John. "Tell me about this healing angel you believe I am."

"You're going to want to turn into Treewood Trailer Park. We're the third trailer on your right."

Les turned the Civic onto the gravel driveway and pulled into a parking spot.

"The angel of the Lord would stir up the pool once a year, and whoever jumped in first would be healed. Are you the angel that stirred the pool?" Charlie's eyes grew wide.

"Let's go help your wife." Les smiled.

"I knew it!" Charlie said with a loud shout of joy. He jumped out of the car, ran to his trailer, and flung open the door.

Les grabbed his plastic container and shot glass. *I am a healing angel who walks around with Tupperware and a shot glass.*

When Les stepped inside the trailer, Bonnie lay on the couch with a blanket over her skinny body. A small television flickered on a wooden crate, providing the room's only light. The place stunk of mildew.

"Bonnie, dear, this is an angel of the Lord coming

to heal you. He found me in Super Mart, and I brought him to heal you." Charlie lightly shook his wife.

Bonnie eased her eyes open. "Charlie?" Then she turned her bright, turquoise-colored eyes to Les.

Les stepped back in shock. He looked from Charlie's eyes back to hers. *The same eyes.*

"It's okay, I'm not contagious."

Les drew a deep breath and knelt down close to Bonnie. Other than those piercing eyes, her face looked hollowed out and tired. She couldn't be over forty-five, but the cancer had aged her twenty years. But something about her eyes projected an overwhelming feeling of hope.

Les unscrewed the top to the wine container and trickled it into the shot glass until it was filled to the top. He twisted the top back on the container. "Can you sit up for me?"

She didn't move, so Charlie pulled her up by the armpits.

Les lifted the shot glass to her lips. "You have to drink this."

Bonnie positioned her hand on his and drank until the wine was gone. She lay back with her eyes closed.

"Did it work? Is she healed?" Charlie was fixated on the container.

Bonnie lay on the couch motionless for ten seconds.

"Is it working?" Charlie's voice held a tremor.

Bonnie giggled once, then laughed. Within moments, her laughter flowed uncontrollably. When she doubled over, laughing hysterically, Charlie pulled Les into a hug.

Bonnie restrained her laughter long enough to look up and Les. "Thank you." Then the laughter took over again.

On his way home, Les felt good inside. He had helped someone. No, changed someone's life. No, he gave life. He just gave someone her life back. What an amazing feeling. God had made him an angel of healing here on earth. He was walking in the power of the holy force. A Jedi master disciple he would soon be. He could perform heroic, anonymous deeds and leave a business card that read, "The healing angel was here." Maybe he could even wear a Jedi knight robe. That would be awesome.

When Les pulled into his condo development and his numbered parking spot, his car clock read three fourteen. He ran his hand through his hair and let out a deep exhale. What a night.

Inside, he threw his keys onto the table next to the unopened box of plastic containers. He placed the sealed container of healing wine on the counter then stepped into the kitchen and picked up the old milk jug. After the events of the night, he needed to Tupperware the rest of the wine immediately. He filled all eleven of the plastic containers.

But what if something happened to the wine? He needed to hide it. He hid four of the containers in different cabinets in the kitchen. He froze one behind some burgers and crammed four more into the fridge, all the way to the back, behind the ketchup and barbeque sauce. Then Les stashed one under his bed and another under a pile of clothes on the closet's top shelf. That left the one he had used on Bonnie. He'd store that one in his car for emergencies, so he left it on the counter. Satisfied with his choices, he crawled into bed.

CHAPTER TWENTY-TWO

==

The *Rocky* song sounded faint and far-off, as if it played in another world. Les opened and closed his eyes a couple of times as the song ended. The double beep signified a message.

"Lila!" Les jolted up, grabbing the alarm clock. It's Sunday. Twelve forty-two. He must have forgotten to set his alarm.

Les ran into the living room and snatched his cell phone from the dining room table. He hit the voicemail button.

"Hey, Les, this is Lila. Do you still want to do lunch today? I was thinking we could go to the Max Bistro off Clement Street. Call me when you get this, bye."

Les's heart pounded in his ears as he tuned in to every syllable. He dialed the last missed call. "Come on, come on, answer the phone."

"Hello, you have reached Lila with EFIL Pharmaceutical."

Les listened to the rest of her greeting. His mouth went dry. "Lila, its Les. I didn't forget about our lunch date, I mean meeting, today. If you can call me back with directions to the bistro, that would be great."

Les balled up his fist and shook it with frustration. "Stupid, stupid, stupid!"

He raced to the bathroom, tossed his phone on the sink, and jumped into the shower. Three minutes later, when he had a full lather of shampoo on his head, the phone rang. In his panic, Les could comprehend only one thing: answer that phone. He flailed his arms, searching for the corner of the shower curtain. Shampoo poured down the side of his face and stung his eyes.

He finally found the shower curtain's edge and jumped out of the tub. He didn't step high enough, and his foot got tangled in the curtain. Les slammed to the floor, pulling the curtain rod out of the wall. Water sprayed the bathroom floor and walls as Les grabbed his phone.

"Hi, Les, this is Lila."

"How's it going?" Les lay there on his bathroom floor, tangled up in the shower curtain with water spilling all over the floor and shampoo covering his face and hair.

"Are you okay? You sound like you're in pain or something."

"I'm fine."

"Me too. I had a great run this morning, and it was so invigorating. Are you sure you're okay? It sounds like there's water running."

"I'm fine. Where is this place you want to meet for lunch?" Les said, grabbing his towel off the toilet seat and wiping the soap out of his eyes.

"Do you know where Leaping Loe's Subs is? You pass that, go three blocks down and turn right in the Universal Shopping Plaza off Clement."

"Got it. What time?" Les's knee throbbed. He needed to get off this phone.

"It's twelve fifty now, so let's shoot for quarter after one."

"See you in a little bit." Les clicked his phone shut and threw it into his closet. Then he grunted and clutched his knees. He crawled over to the spigot, turned off the water, and flung the shower curtain inside the tub.

He wanted to cry. He had thirty minutes to fix his bathroom, clean the water and blood from the floor, stop the bleeding, and make himself look respectable.

He climbed back into the tub and turned on the water. He stuck his head down by the faucet and washed his hair. When he had dried off, he pressed a washcloth against his bleeding knee and elbow until the flow stopped. His other knee looked like it would be badly bruised and swollen too. "Why am I such an idiot?"

He bandaged his wounds the best he could and dressed in jeans, a long-sleeved t-shirt and a light jacket. He picked out a hat from his rack and slapped it on his head since he didn't have time to do anything to his hair.

Walking to the living room, he realized how much pain he was in with every step. However, he had to press on. He couldn't let Lila down.

Les grabbed his keys then limped back into the bathroom for his phone. As he shuffled out the door, his watch read one ten.

Since the restaurant was a good fifteen minutes away, he needed to give Lila a courtesy call to let her know he would be late. She didn't answer, so he left a message. As soon as he hung up, his phone rang.

Jerry. Les tossed the phone onto the seat. He didn't feel like talking to him after Jerry blew off Les's call yesterday. Minutes later, Les pulled his blue Civic into the bistro parking lot and gimped his way inside. There was no sign of Lila. He checked his watch: one thirty. He was fifteen minutes late.

The hostess smiled at him from behind the reservation stand. "Table for one?"

"No, I'm waiting for someone." Les took a seat near the door and noticed a blood stain on the knee of his jeans. The door swished open, and he glanced up.

"Hey, good looking." Lila, in all her beauty, hid her eyes behind a pair of dark, oversized glasses. She looked gorgeous as always, in a navy blazer over a white v-neck t-shirt, skinny jeans, and suede-colored heels.

Les raised his hand as a big smile spread across his face. "You look stunning."

Lila walked past him to the hostess. "We're ready to be seated now."

"What's the name?"

"Lila." Her disgust showed in both her tone and the drawing of her mouth.

The hostess scanned her computer screen. "I'm sorry, but I don't have you down for a reservation. You'll have to wait, but it will be only ten minutes—"

Lila stalked past her into the dining area. The hostess's eyes widened, then she took off after Lila. "Ma'am, just a moment—"

"I'm sorry. I'm sure it won't be a problem for us to wait." Les limped his way behind them, but Lila had already found the manager. When Les reached them, the manager was all but bowing to Lila.

"I apologize for the hostess's mistake. She just started this week and doesn't know you yet."

"You need to let her know who your best customers are." Lila's tone was half-serious, half-flirtatious.

"Come and sit in our VIP area with your friend so you can have some privacy."

"Great idea." Lila flashed him an I-knew-you'd-do-it-my-way smile.

The manager led them to a back room "We use this room for corporate CEOs when they hold business meetings. It'll be like your own private restaurant."

The room held two long, comfy booths that looked like large couches with glass tables between them. They chose the booth opposite a built-in saltwater fish tank that must have held a thousand gallons. A shark swam to the front of the tank and seemed to bare its teeth at Les.

"I come here two or three times a week. The food's great." Lila tilted her head and tapped her manicured finger on the table. "I wanted to talk to you about Lynn. Are you into her?"

Les pulled his gaze from the fish and gave Lila his attention. "It's too soon to tell."

Lila's frown struck a cord inside of Les. Was she jealous of Lynn?

"Either you like someone or you don't. There's no gray area."

"I like spending time with her. I like talking with her." Les could sense the tension behind her questions. She was fishing for info.

The waitress entered the room with two menus. Lila held up her hand. "We don't need them. I want the seared tuna. He'll have the crusted mahi mahi."

Les eyed Lila, not liking this controlling streak she showed.

"It's good. Trust me."

"Okay, I'll have a steak." Les smiled at the waitress.

The waitress smirked but kept her eyes on her notepad. "How would you like that cooked?"

"Medium rare."

"Mashed potatoes or baked?"

"Mashed."

The waitress flipped her notepad. "What would you like to drink?"

Les locked eyes with Lila as if they were two gun-slingers waiting for the other to make the first move. "A bottle of Araldica Gavi 2000 and water." Lila dismissed the waitress with a nod and turned back to Les with the air of giving a lesson to a child. "It's a modern-style Piedmont white, delicious with fish."

Les wouldn't have admitted he'd never heard of Araldica Gavi, nor what year to order, but it didn't sit well with him that she assumed he didn't know. His jaw clenched a little with his annoyance. She was pretty, but brutally dictatorial. "You drink a lot of wine?"

"It depends on what I'm eating." She leaned against the back of the booth as if settling in for a long talk. "Are you interested in taking your relationship with Lynn further?"

To Les's relief, the waitress brought their waters and bottle of wine, popped the cork, and poured. "Thank you." *For the wine and for the extra minute to think through my answer.*

"Well, I kind of like someone else too."

Lila sipped her wine, swished it around in her mouth, and swallowed. "That's so good."

The waiter served a basket of bread and two garden salads. Les reached for a slice of sourdough. Had she heard what he'd said about liking someone else?

Lila set down her glass and pierced him with her eyes. "Let's talk business. Do you have something I want?"

Les smiled and speared a chunk of lettuce. "So it's like that? I lay all my cards on the table and let you decide if I have something you want?"

Sipping from her wine glass again, Lila leaned forward as if trying to close any emotional distance between them. She was calm and collected, and her beauty drew Les in. He had no choice but to stare at her gorgeous features, captivated by her beauty. He was putty in her hands, and she knew it.

"I'm confident that I have something you want."

Lila spoke with the tone of a seductress.

Les swallowed his lettuce. His heart beat faster.

Lila leaned her body up against the glass table, her face close to his. "You want me, don't you, Les?" she whispered.

Les reached for his wine glass but missed and knocked it over, spilling wine all over the table.

Lila shifted to avoid the dripping wine, but she kept her gazed fixed on Les. She had him.

"Sorry. I just—I'll get the waitress."

Seconds later, Les came back with a couple of towels and the waitress, and they cleaned up the mess. His pulse slowed as he settled back into his seat. What else could go wrong to make him look moronic? "I've been so clumsy today."

The waitress left to get Les a clean glass, and when she brought it, Les filled it to the top and took a swig.

Lila leaned back in the corner of her booth, her wine in her hand and a tiny smile on her face. Her dark hair now covered half her face, giving her a mysterious, sultry look.

"You're right; it's pretty good." Les fiddled with his salad fork but didn't feel like eating.

"You don't have to be nervous with me. I know how you feel about me."

"What do you mean?" Les tried to blow off Lila's last statement.

"You think I'm the most beautiful woman you've ever seen." Her tone held all the confidence a woman like her should have. "I know by the way you look at me. And you told me last night while we were drinking."

She was a bulldozer, bullying him into a corner. There was a very high probability that he'd said those exact words to her last night. But why would he admit it now and give her the upper hand?

They ate a little of their meals, then they took what was left of the bottle of wine and moved to the leather couch in front of the fish tank. Lila had three glasses already. Les poured himself another then tipped the bottle upside down. "That's it."

"Let's get another bottle. We can drink it tonight, unless you have other plans." Lila tilted her head back, opening her mouth slightly.

"No plans. But I wonder about yours." Les raised his eyebrows.

"I'm trying to help you get over your nervousness so we can talk."

She was right. He was nervous. "Fair enough. Another bottle of this stuff?"

"One check or two?" The waitress gathered dishes from the table behind them.

"One, and can we get another bottle of Araldica Gavi 2000?" Lila answered before Les could get anything out of his mouth. She turned to him. "Don't worry about the bill. EFIL will pay for this one."

Is she setting me up? Using her sexuality to swoon me into spilling my secret?

Lila hit a button on her cell. "Hey, Daddy. I'm at the Max Bistro having lunch with a potential client."

Les sat back and watched. She was an authoritarian, but angelic. Ravishing, but rude. Did the exquisiteness outweigh the ugliness?

"Yes, I understand. I also need the company limo because we've been drinking. The Max Bistro off Clement. Twenty minutes, that sounds good. I'll let you know." She hung up and slid her phone into her bag.

233

"We're taking the company limo?"
"My father does it right for potential investors."
"So you think I'm a potential investor?"
"No, I think you're a potential partner."

CHAPTER TWENTY THREE

Jerry's vision was badly blurred as he tried hard to focus on the object standing at his bedroom doorway. It looked like a woman dressed in black with flowing red hair, but he couldn't focus long enough to find out.

He laid his head back down, squeezing his eyes shut, then opened them again. The image was gone. Jerry slowly rolled himself out of bed and sat with his feet against the floor. He felt as groggy as the time he had a dose of laughing gas at the dentist's office. He tried to stand up and proceed toward the bathroom, but his head spun, and he saw little black spots all over the room. He dropped to the floor.

Closing his eyes, he rubbed his temples for a few seconds then eased to his feet. He shuffled his way to the bathroom and splashed cold water across his face for several seconds. He dried his face with a hand towel, and as he pulled it away from his face, he thought he saw a faint, black, shadowy image behind him in the mirror, similar to the image he always saw after someone took his picture.

He looked behind him and then peeked into his room. Nothing. He hung the towel back on the rack and slogged toward his living room. A great sense of depression fell on him as he walked into that room. His coffee table lay smashed to pieces on the floor, surrounded by bits of candle and wax. A nice-sized hole was in the drywall over his couch.

"What the heck happened?" Jerry grabbed a chunk of his hair. He ambled into the kitchen for his cell phone and scrolled down to Les's name. He got his voicemail.

"Hey, dude, I was just wondering if we had a party

at my place that got a little out of hand last night. For some reason, my memory is a little foggy. Give me a call when you get this."

He grabbed a soda from his fridge and plodded back into his living room to examine the damage. He stood on the couch to take a look at the large hole in the wall. "Unbelievable."

The phone rang, and he scanned the ID. Elizabeth. "Hey, girl what's up?"

"Can you meet me at Brendan's? I need to talk to you."

"I'll meet you there in thirty."

As Jerry dipped into his closet searching for jeans and a shirt, his gaze landed on his computer. His body shuddered as he had a sudden urge to get high. His hands became ice cold, so he started clamping them together.

He couldn't get high now. But it would make his food taste better. He shivered and his teeth chattered. He rubbed his arms to get over his cold nervousness.

You need to get high to make this feeling go away. Just get high and you'll feel better. Over and over the voice in his head repeated those words.

Jerry ignored the voice as much as he could, but when he turned around, he swore he saw a dark figure lying on his bed. He stopped, frozen, as another chill shook his body.

As soon as he took a step out of the room, the dark figure was gone.

Maybe he was getting sick. He'd been seeing dark spots the last couple of days. He grabbed a towel and washcloth and stepped into the shower. The hot water felt good as it splashed on his head. He felt better already. A good, long, hot shower was all he needed.

When he turned off the water, the bathroom was completely steamed up. Jerry reached for his towel. It was gone.

"I could have sworn I left my towel on the rod right outside the shower."

His clothes were gone too. "I'm going crazy. I can't remember anything anymore."

Jerry swiped off the water as best he could, trying not to make too big of a mess on his bath mat. He opened the door to his bathroom. Distorted, muffled voices drifted in from the living room.

He swung the door shut and grabbed the hand towel. Covering himself, he maneuvered out of the bathroom and into his closet. He grabbed a dirty towel from the laundry basket and dried off as fast as he could then got dressed.

Grabbing a golf club from the closet, he backed up against the wall. He crept closer to the doorway and listened.

Two women spoke fast, and it didn't sound like English.

He stood there in complete silence, taking deliberate, slow breaths, golf club in hand. This was some kind of foreign language that he had never heard before.

What should he do? What were these women doing in his house? Maybe he had forgotten to lock his door, and they were cleaning ladies.

That didn't make sense.

Inching his head around the corner, he saw two shadowy figures underneath the bar area that looked into the living room. Jerry decided he just need to bum rush them and catch them by surprise. He took a deep breath, ready to slam into the living room, when the voices stopped.

He turned his head, and five feet from him stood a red-headed woman.

"Who the heck are you?" Jerry pointed his golf club at her like a sword.

"Take it easy there, tiger. We met at a bar last night."

What was she talking about? He'd never seen her before.

"I brought my friends over, remember? The party got a little out of hand, and you threw your coffee table against the wall." The redhead folded her arms. "You don't remember?"

Jerry rested the golf club on his shoulder. "Did we . . . ?" He looked the redhead up and down.

She clinched her jaw while tapping her foot. "Did we what?"

"Never mind. How did you get in here?"

"I never left, except to take a walk this morning to get some fresh air."

Jerry scratched his head with the club. "So you're saying that you spent the night here?"

"If you want me to leave, you can just say so! You don't have to act like a jerk and keep pretending you don't know me." The redhead swung toward the door.

Jerry followed her. "Wait, I'm sorry. I must have gotten really wasted last night. I have to meet someone for lunch in twenty minutes, but maybe we can hook up later tonight for dinner."

"You don't have to be nice to me because you feel bad."

"No, I want to see you. I had a great time last night."

238

"You're not just saying that?"

"Of course not. How could I lie to such a gorgeous knockout like yourself? Give me your number, and I'll call you in a couple of hours."

She grabbed a pen from her purse and scribbled her number on the back of one of Jerry's bills lying on the counter. She opened the door then looked back with a devilish grin. "I'll see you soon."

Jerry tried to concentrate on something other than the fact that he couldn't recall anything from the night before. Also that Les hadn't called him back yet. It was almost one thirty when Jerry arrived at Brendan's Family Restaurant . He looked at himself in his rear view mirror and then did a quick boogie check. He was clean.

As he drifted toward the restaurant, footsteps sounded behind him, then somebody's arm swooped around his waist.

"Hey, friend." Elizabeth gave Jerry a side hug, then she opened the door for him. "I thought it would be a good idea for us to hang for a little bit. And I'm paying, because I invited you."

"No argument here, cutie."

Within minutes, they were seated in a booth. Elizabeth plunked down in her seat and banged on the table to get Jerry's attention. "I wanted to clear the air. I'm sorry for getting all emotional on you last night. I was having a girl moment."

"Some days I wish I could be everything you want me to be."

Elizabeth paused then shook her head as if she had

239

been ensnared in a trap. "Why do I let you do this to me?"

"What do you mean?"

"That statement you just made, that you wish you could be everything I want you to be. You don't understand how that makes me feel."

The server came to the table, and Elizabeth dabbed at the corner of her eye with her small finger. "Water with lemon, please."

"I'll have whatever is on tap, and can we order? I would like a bacon cheeseburger with fries."

Elizabeth flipped through the menu. "I'll have the salmon with rice."

When the server left, Elizabeth fanned her face with her hands. "I don't want to feel this way toward you any more. I just want to be friends with no emotional garbage."

"We've always been friends."

"When I look at you, I see everything that you could be. Your potential is buried deep down and needs to be dug up. You're the sweetest guy I've ever met."

Jerry nodded. "We always have a good time when we're together." *Why can't I be stronger for her? Every word out of her mouth makes me want to be with her.*

Elizabeth spun a spoon that was on the table. "Maybe I could live with your marijuana habit."

"It might become legal in a few years anyway." Jerry wiggled his eyebrows. He examined every detail of her face. She stopped playing with her silverware to glance up at him. Her hazel-colored eyes penetrated his walls, leaving them as rubble. He wanted to protect her, provide for her, and most of all, he wanted to love her.

The server brought their food, breaking up the moment. Elizabeth took a bite of her salmon. "I'm not a faucet. I can't shut off my emotions for you. I've prayed countless nights for God to take these feelings away from me. I've spent hours on my knees, praying for you to change your life, but the more I prayed, the worse you got."

Maybe their love for each other was strong enough to overcome anything.

When they'd both finished their meals, Elizabeth got a dreamy look in her eyes. "What are you doing the rest of the day?"

Oh no. Here comes the part where she suffocates me. "I don't know. I need to clean my apartment."

"Do you want me to come over and help you?"

I am too ashamed for you to see my apartment. "Aren't you a sweetie? Thanks for the offer, but I need to see what Les is doing today. Can I take a raincheck?"

"No raincheck." Elizabeth face went somber as she stared at the table top.

The server brought Elizabeth's credit card back and she signed the bill and stood up.

"You okay?"

"Fine," she said in a fake voice.

"No, you're not. I know you better than that."

She filed past Jerry and out of the restaurant with him following close behind her. They didn't say a word until they got to her car. She leaned her back against her car door, and he stood about two feet in front of her. She looked up at him with these big, teared-filled, brown eyes.

"Don't give me that pathetic, feeling-sorry-for-yourself look."

"Oh, now I'm pathetic." She stomped her foot.

"No, I didn't mean it like that. Give me a hug." Jerry wrapped his arms around her. Elizabeth moved toward him but didn't embrace him, and the awkwardness of the situation made him back away. "Thanks for dinner."

241

She got into her car. Jerry watched the car back out then drive off. His sense of emptiness was so strong, he wanted to run after the car and stop her, tell her he would do anything to be with her.

He hated himself for not being able to open his heart and let go of the bitterness he harbored toward her for hurting him. But he couldn't move. It was as if his feet were stuck in cement. He pulled out his phone and sent Les a text message. *Hey, Jerk, why can't you return a phone call? Oh, right, that's me. Sorry, call me when you get a chance. Maybe we can hang tonight.*

CHAPTER TWENTY-FOUR

==

Les and Lila waited for the limo outside the Max Bistro when Les's phone beeped. He opened his phone and found a text from Jerry. He read it then texted back. *Sorry, I'm busy. Maybe we can get together tomorrow.*

He sent the text and slid his phone back into his pocket. The sun was shining, he was buzzed, and he was standing next to the most beautiful woman he'd ever seen. Could life get any better then this?

"You're bleeding. You've been limping too." Lila pointed to the blood stain on Les's knee.

"I forgot about that. It's nothing."

Lila touched Les's back. "Do you want to go home and change the bandage? Maybe get a clean pair of pants?"

Les bit his thumbnail. He could take her to his condo and show her his healing potion first-hand. He could drink it and she could watch his wounds heal right in front of her. Talk about a selling point. But could he trust her? "We can do that."

The silver H2 Hummer limo arrived. Les laughed. "When you guys do it, you do it big, don't you?"

"My father does it right."

The chauffeur opened the door, and they climbed in. Les relaxed on the black and gray leather seats.

"Wow, this thing is huge." Les pointed to the fully stocked bar. "Are you kidding me?"

"Pretty sweet, isn't it?" Lila sat close to him, all the way in the back. "Pick up the phone and press zero, then you can give the driver your address."

Les grasped the phone and followed Lila's instructions.

243

"What is your desired destination?" the limo driver asked in a thick Australian accent.

"Good day, mate. Let's throw another shrimp on the barbie." Les said in his best Australian imitation.

"No worries, mate. What is your destination?"

Les gave the driver his address then hung up the phone.

"How long until we get to your house?" Lila caressed her lips with a cherry lip balm.

"Twenty or thirty minutes if we go the speed limit."

"Good. Tell me what you really do. Are you a scientist of some sort?"

Les jerked his head back and swallowed the lump in his throat. "What do you mean?"

"The last time we hung out, you said you were in the health-care industry, working on starting your own company or something."

"That's true."

"You asked me a lot of questions about what my father does, so I thought you might be a scientist." Lila positioned her hand on Les's thigh.

At her touch, Les stiffened his body for a second then relaxed as if she had injected him with a truth serum. "Okay, I'm not going to lie to you. It's big. Real big. But I need to know I can trust you." Les turned to look into Lila's eyes. He saw two emerald orbs vibrating assurance.

Before Les knew what was happening, she leaned over and kissed him on the lips. He closed his eyes, then they kissed again, this time passionately. Her lips were soft. He cupped her face as they kissed for the third time. He felt the world disappear around him. Nothing else mattered. Finally Les leaned back to let it all sink in. She had kissed him.

244

Lila held his hand against her cheek. "Do you trust me now?"

Her lips allured him like a fish to the bait. "I'm not convinced yet." He gathered her close and closed his eyes. Her lips were delicate, agreeable, and yet the kiss in some way felt desperate.

His eyes burst open as they unlocked. Would he do anything to please her?

"I've created a healing potion." As he spoke the words, he felt something unleash from his soul. "I can't go into the details of how I created it, but it heals every disease. At least, that's what I've experienced so far. It healed my bad shoulder and stopped Jerry from dying."

"Jerry knows about this potion?"

"Sure, he's my best friend."

"Who else knows about it?"

"Just me and Jerry. And a girl from work."

Lila moved into work mode as if a switch had been flipped inside her. A line etched itself into her forehead. "Will you show it to me?"

This was it. The rope had been yanked and the red handkerchief reversed directions. Would he do anything to please her?

She kissed his hand and used it to caress her cheek, closing her eyes. "You can trust me."

The limo drove through the gated community and parked outside Les's condo.

"Wait for us," Lila told the driver. "We shouldn't be more than an hour."

The two of them stood outside the door of his condo. He inserted the key into his doorknob, then stopped. He turned to Lila, letting the keys dangle from the knob. He grasped both of her arms, towering over her. He gazed deep into her eyes.

She peered back at him with eyes that gleamed certainty and desire. But what did she desire? Did she desire him? Or his healing wine?

Lila stepped forward and rested her head on his chest. "Your heart is beating fast."

"I'm scared," Les blurted out.

Lila tilted her head back. "I won't hurt you."

The conversation he'd had with Darla weighed heavy on his mind, and those were the words that broke his chains of reservation.

Inside his condo, the Tupperware sat on his kitchen counter where he had left it. He lifted the container of wine. "Here it is."

"That's it? You keep your healing potion in Tupperware?"

"It's only temporary until I find something better."

Lila's eyes widened. "This had better not be a scam, because I swear—"

"Hey, chill. It's not; trust me." He grabbed the container of wine and shot glass. Why was she questioning him when he was the one taking all the risk? "Let's go in the living room."

"Is that a shot glass?" Lila raised her brows.

"Look, it's all I had." Les sat on the couch and pushed the coffee table out of the way so Lila could watch the potion in action. He rolled up his pant leg and pulled off his bandage. The two-inch-long cut was deep, but it looked as if it had finally clotted. "You know, I have one on my elbow too. I'll change my clothes real quick so you can see my cuts better."

When Les had changed into a short-sleeved shirt and shorts for the demonstration, he sat back down on the couch and smiled. "Ready?"

Les swirled the container then opened it. "Smell it."

Lila leaned her face over the container. Her mouth dropped open for a moment. "It smells like wine. Is it wine?"

"Sort of." Les slowly poured the wine into the shot glass, careful not to waste a drop.

"How do you know how much to put in there?"

"I don't. I'm still experimenting." Les screwed the cover back on the Tupperware and sniffed the wine in the shot glass. It was invigorating. He glanced at Lila then drank the shot.

Les leaned back on the couch with his eyes closed as the warmth of the healing potion entered his bloodstream. It was the greatest feeling in the world, even better than kissing Lila.

"Oh, my gosh!" Lila pointed to his knee, her face white. "Your knee. Your cut is gone."

"Yep, I told you." Les showed her his clean elbow.

"This is unbelievable, remarkable, unexplainable—priceless."

Lila leaned over and gave him a long and passionate kiss. "You taste good. My mouth is all tingly."

Les smiled. Life was good. He was getting everything he had ever wanted.

"We have to show this to my father immediately. He'll want to test it and determine experimental dosages—how much we need to use for what ailments." Lila spoke as if her brain was in overdrive. "Do you understand what this means? We're going to be billionaires! Anything we want will be ours. Nothing will be too exotic or expensive for us."

Les wanted to feel excited with Lila, but part of him

wanted to crash through his sliding glass door and escape to a quiet place where no one could find him. Why did he feel as if he'd done something wrong?

Lila was already on the phone with her dad as Les looked out the sliding door. Why wasn't he jumping up and down, overcome with joy? Shouldn't this be the happiest moment of his life? Why did he feel empty inside?

"Hey, baby. My father wants to meet us for dinner tonight at six."

Les nodded. He'd gone this far, so he might as well talk to the man.

"That will work, Daddy. See you soon." Lila hung up the phone. "How much of this stuff do you have?" Lila's eyes no longer sparkled like emeralds. Now Les saw only deep, dark saucers of greed.

"This is all I have."

"Well, can you make more?"

"I haven't tried."

"We're going to need a lot more than just a ten-ounce container if we're going to make a billion dollars." The irritation in her tone deepened his sense of regret, and that frightened him.

She took a deep breath, her eyes glowing like a nuclear reactor. "Let's take what we have. We'll show it to my father, let him run some tests on it, and see if he can pull out the ingredients. We can start mass-producing it right away."

"I don't know. Let me think about it."

"Come on. Get changed so we can head to my house, then I can get ready. We have a lot of planning to do."

Les trudged into his bedroom and shut the door. Lila was already on the phone again. What had he done? His nerves were shot. Even after drinking the healing wine, he didn't feel right. And why did Lila think she could tell him what to do?

"Mom, I'm not going to call him. I'm not going to be that desperate girl who chases after guys. I want to be pursued." Lynn flipped over on her back on her queen-sized bed.

"It's the twenty-first century. Things are different now. It doesn't matter who chases who as long as you get married and get me some grandkids."

"I knew it! You think I'm going to end up alone for the rest of my life, don't you?"

"I think you're too picky. You always find something wrong with the men you date."

"The last guy I dated cheated on me three times! I have to go. I love you."

Lynn hung up the phone. What a wasted day, sitting around waiting for Les to call. Tomorrow she would be back at work at six in the morning and would barely find time to have a social life again.

She and Les had seemed to connect on such a deep level last night, in a way she had never connected with anyone else. Maybe her mother was right and she just needed to call him. Maybe he followed the "man law" which prohibited him from calling back for three days.

Lynn examined the cell phone in her hand. Then she rose and grabbed a nickel from the junk drawer in the kitchen. "Heads, I call him; tails, I don't."

She flipped the nickel into the air. It bounced on the floor and rolled between the refrigerator and wall. "You have got to be kidding me."

Lynn got down on her hands and knees and reached for the coin. Too far back. She took a long wooden spoon from her utensil drawer. After three attempts, she dragged the coin out.

"Heads." She turned the nickel over in her hand. "Two out of three."

She flipped the coin again and watched it bounce around on her kitchen floor. She crawled over to where it had stopped. George Washington's face stared back at her.

"All right." Lynn stood and danced around the kitchen, psyching herself up. After ten minutes of fighting it, she made the call.

Les's phone rang once, then his voicemail picked up.

Lynn punched the "end" button. Did he just roll her? She knew it! He thinks she's desperate.

She flung herself on the bed to wallow in her misery.

Elizabeth glanced in her rear-view mirror at Jerry, who gawked at her as she drove away. Tears fell from her eyes. "God, please take these feelings for Jerry away from me. The pain runs too deep. I'm sorry for not always being obedient to your voice and for not listening to the wise counsel you put around me. My soul is still tied to him. Please break this tie, please—"

Her phone rang. She took a deep breath to try to compose herself before answering. "Hi, mom."

"What's the matter? You sound like you've been crying."

"Don't get mad, but I had lunch with Jerry today." It was surely killing her mother to hold her tongue and not reprimand her. "I try to get past my feelings for him, but every time I'm around him, I want to be with him again. A few minutes ago, I even contemplated taking him back, thinking he could change for me. That this time would be different. Maybe he would stop getting high if we got serious enough."

"You know that won't happen."

"Yes, but as I was driving, I asked God to take these feelings away from me, because I know they aren't right. Why won't God just take these feelings away?" Elizabeth started to cry again.

"I wish I could give you a hug. Sometimes healing takes time. God doesn't always heal us instantly, but he always turns bad situations into good learning experiences. What do you think God is trying to tell you?"

"Not to like boys ever again." Elizabeth said in her squeaky crying voice. She paused for a moment. "I'm learning that sin hurts, and that when God's children ignore his commands, we suffer the repercussions. He disciplines the ones He loves, and discipline is not fun. I think I finally realize what it means to be unequally yoked."

"Be patient, Lizzy. God has a special man designed especially for you."

CHAPTER TWENTY-FIVE

==

"Did my phone ring?" Les strolled out of his bedroom wearing a casual gray suit jacket, white shirt, and light-colored jeans.

"Wow, don't you look hot!" Lila gave him a quick kiss on the lips and a full chest hug. Then she grabbed his hand and pulled him toward the door. "You smell good too."

"Let me grab my stuff." Les twisted his hand away from Lila. He crammed his wallet and phone into his suit pocket then grabbed his sunglasses from the counter along with the Tupperware pitcher.

Outside, the limo waited for them. Lila worked the phones, setting up meetings with various distributors. Working on Sunday. How dreary can you get?

Les stared out the window at the buildings flying by. He had made his decision without even thinking about it, and that recurring, empty feeling came back and sat in the pit of his stomach. Could Lila's dad recreate the healing wine? If he could, would he even need him anymore? Was he doing the right thing?

If Lila's dad couldn't recreate the wine, they would still need him. They didn't know about the other eleven containers. Then what?

He glanced over at Lila. She was everything he thought he wanted: beautiful, successful, career-driven, rich. She knew what she wanted out of life.

He, on the other hand, was just a factory worker who had wandered aimlessly for the last couple of years, drowning his sorrows in the bottoms of alcohol bottles. By luck or by fate, he had come across something that had changed his life: a little brown book with a section labeled "John."

Jesus was real; Les knew that. He worked a miracle just like Jesus did and was given an opportunity to change the world. But what was he doing? Selling his soul to the devil?

He looked at Lila again. Was she the devil? Les smirked to himself. Where was his mind taking him? He laid his head against the limo window. He had blown Jerry off all day. The least he could do was send him a text. He pulled out his phone.

"Who are you texting?" Lila asked.

"Jerry."

"Don't tell him what you're doing. This needs to be hush-hush."

"He's my best friend, and he already knows about the healing wine." Les raised his voice a fraction.

"That's fine, but he doesn't need to know that you're joining forces with EFIL Pharmacy to take this thing mainstream."

"What if I want him to join in?"

"You're kidding, right?" The greed in Lila's eyes gave her a hard look. "How many ways would you like to divide the pie? The fewer people involved, the better."

"He's my best friend, and I'm not going to do him like that. He's been with me through thick and thin. If we do this, he's in."

"What do you mean, 'if we do this?'"

Les turned his eyes away. "I'm not sure this is the avenue I should take."

"Look at me." Lila sidled up next to Les and held his hand. "It's okay to be scared, but I'm going to be with you every step of the way. You're on the brink of making the world a better place. We're going to help so many people. You're doing the right thing by taking this discovery public, but we need to be discreet. With something of this magnitude, people could get hurt."

Les nodded and Lila kissed him on the cheek. Maybe she was right. With her father's help, they could make the world a better place.

"Tonight's meeting is with my father and his biggest investor. Don't be nervous. You have something they want." Lila scooted to the full bar at the front of the limo. "Let me fix you a drink. Rum and Coke?"

"Heavy on the rum and light on the coke." What was he getting himself into?

Jerry climbed out of his van and slogged to his apartment. His best friend had blown him off again, probably for a woman. Jerry didn't blame him, since he had done it to Les several times. That included the time Jerry took off on a ten-day cruise with some girl he met at a night club. He hadn't told Les, but he'd made up a story for his boss, something about his grandma dying and that he needed time to grieve. Les had left twenty-three messages on his phone, wanting to know why he didn't know about the funeral.

Les was one of the few people who truly cared what happened to Jerry. His dad was a deadbeat alcoholic who'd left when he was nine.

Jerry unlocked the door to his apartment. He was alone, and thoughts of his past life threatened to make him more depressed by the second. He needed to escape. He needed to get high.

Jerry slung the clothes off the computer in the closet. He pressed a few keys then hit the control button, and out popped his superweed. He pinched off a piece of the bud and headed back into the living room, grabbing a TV tray from the corner.

He opened the tray with one hand and arranged the bud on the tray. He flipped over the couch cushion, dumping the wood chips onto the floor. He then shuffled to the kitchen and found some rolling papers and a lighter under some batteries way in the back of his junk drawer.

Jerry clicked on his stereo with his six-change CD player on random. He pulled the tray close to his body and broke the weed apart.

The excitement was gone. All he needed was something to take him out of his reality. A cloud of depression hung over Jerry's head as he rolled the marijuana into a joint.

He licked the rolling paper and set the finished product on the tray. The thought of it being a mini glow worm wasn't funny anymore.

For the first time, he realized he was becoming his mother, always running from problems, never wanting to face the root of issues. It was always easier to get high and zone out with a movie or television show. His mother taught him to ignore and escape rather than confront and face real issues of responsibility. The years of abuse had taken their toll, and she did nothing to try to break the cycle of addiction. Just get high and everything will be all right. That's what his mom always used to say.

And what about Elizabeth? He loved her more than any other woman, but he chose a drug over her. Maybe it was because he was never shown real love from a woman while he was growing up. She was right, he had severe commitment issues that stemmed from his demented relationship with his mother. Every time he and Elizabeth broke up over the past three years, he found solace in partying with Les and hooking up with whatever random chick he could pick up at a bar. The only constants in his life were Les and weed. He had no calming influence from any parental figure.

He felt alone, and a chill swept through his body. He rubbed his hands together in an attempt to keep from shivering. Was he having withdrawal?

Jerry took the joint between his forefinger and thumb and lit the end. It was the only thing that would make him feel better. As he took a drag, he remembered all the times he'd walked in on his mother getting high. Her expression was burned into his mind. She seemed relaxed and carefree, as if nothing in the world mattered. He liked her better when she was high.

Jerry smiled. The first time he got high with his mom, they ate chocolate-covered doughnuts and watched *Dumb and Dumber*. He'd laughed so hard he'd peed in his pants a little.

That was my childhood. No wonder I'm so messed up. He took a few more tokes to finish off the joint then placed it on the TV tray. He laid back on the couch, completely relaxed, watching the joint burn a little spot in the tray. He closed his eyes as the LSD started to take effect.

A soft knocking on his apartment door startled him out of his trance. He opened his eyes to a blurred reality then squeezed them shut again, trying to make them focus. Finally his vision cleared, and the knocking continued.

He got up and peered through the peep hole. Abella, the gorgeous redhead, peered back at him. He opened the door.

"May I come in, my prince?"

The prince puffed his chest out. "Where is everyone else?"

"They are awaiting your move, Master."

"You may come in, but first you must give me a kiss." The prince grabbed Abella by the elbows and yanked her in close. The redhead smiled and gave her prince a passionate kiss on the mouth.

"I've missed you." Princess Abella swung her arms around the prince's neck.

"I have also missed you, my princess. You shouldn't stay away so long next time."

"But there is so much work to be done."

The prince stepped back into his room, swinging the door shut with Abella still draped across his neck. "Soon we will establish our kingdom and be together forever."

Abella ran her hands down the side of the prince's arms and rested both her hands on his chest. She began drawing symbols on his chest with her forefinger. "When I get old, you won't replace me with someone younger and more ravishing?"

Prince Humberger clinched his jaw. "How could anyone be more ravishing than you?"

The scent of vanilla wafted from Abella as she approached her prince with her face inches from his. "I will never leave you nor forsake you."

Prince Humberger grazed her cheek and glared into her eyes. "Good, I have your loyalty. Now for my plan. Where are the others?" Prince Humberger pivoted away with his back toward Abella.

"Beezle is positioned outside the target's condo. He said he saw them leave about ten minutes ago."

257

The prince paced the room. "Which one is Beezle again?"

"The twin you choked out."

"And the other one?"

"That's Bub. He's also at the condo but only as a lookout. The others are getting ready for battle."

The prince stopped and glared at Abella. "What battle?"

Abella stood up straight. "We're going to have a big battle for control. You need to make sure you secure the weapon. That way, nothing will defeat us."

Prince Humberger put on his shoes and grabbed his keys and wallet. "Are you coming?"

"No, this a solo mission that only you can complete." Abella bowed her head low to her prince as he passed by her.

"Fine. It will be better this way. No one to screw up."

As he strutted outside, fresh air hit his nostrils. He took a deep breath and started toward his van, but the grass on both sides of the walk was moving. He reached down and ran his hand across the grass. It was as though he stirred water and made little green ripples across the lawn.

He laughed as he stood to plod toward his van. Inside, he sat behind the wheel, trying to remember what to do next. He slid the key in the ignition and accidentally hit the horn. It made him laugh, so he hit it again and laughed again.

Jerry turned the key and put the van in reverse. He backed out and drove toward the exit but forgot where he was going. He slammed the van into park and sat in the middle of the parking lot. Why was he in his van? "I am so stoned."

A pretty, young woman in running attire came jogging up to his window and made the rolling-down-the-window motion with her hand.

Jerry laughed and rolled it down. "Do I know you?"

"We met once before. What are you doing sitting in the middle of the parking lot?"

"I don't know, man, I forgot. Did we meet at a night club or something? Your face looks familiar."

She jogged around to the passenger-side door and climbed in.

Jerry leaned back in his seat checking out the pretty young runner. "What are you doing?"

"Helping you."

"I think I need help."

"Okay, focus. You're supposed to go to your friend's condo to get something, right?"

"Right. Les's, but I can't remember where he lives." Jerry's grin felt cheesy.

The woman took a deep breath. "I'll help you."

Jerry's mouth popped open as he squinted his eyes. "You know where Les lives?"

"I'm kind of like a GPS system. Let's go."

She instructed Jerry all the way to Les's condo, giving him every stop and every turn in detail, repeating herself over and over. They finally pulled into Les's condo development and into a visitors' parking spot.

"You can take it from here." She jumped out of the van and ran toward the exit.

Jerry watched her as she raced out of the development and out of sight. "Wow, what a nice lady."

He got out and stumbled around the corner to Les's condo. A dude standing right outside Les's door had a pentagram on his forehead and wore a black trench coat.

"You got the key?"

"No, I thought you had it." Jerry laughed. "Who are you, anyway?"

"I'm Beezle. Don't you remember me?"

"Vaguely. I think I bought some weed from you one time. Did that tattoo hurt? It looks like it hurt."

"Will you shut up? What's wrong with you? We're supposed to be on a mission here!"

Jerry lifted his leg and let out a loud fart. "Dude, I got you so good!"

"I can't deal with such an idiotic person. How in the world did Gretchen ever think you would be a prince?"

Jerry stopped laughing. "Did you say Gretchen?"

"She's the one who chose you to be our prince." Beezle prodded Jerry's chest with his finger.

A cold hand touched Jerry's neck. Jerry's eyes bugged as his body constricted.

"I was in the area and thought I'd stop in to see the progress." Gretchen tightened her grip on the back of Jerry's neck. He felt the veins bulging on the front of his neck.

Beezle rolled his eyes. "It's going terribly slow."

Jerry's eyes glazed over, and he entered a trance-like state.

Gretchen held her hand on his neck for a few more seconds then shook his body. "Prince Humberger, my prince, wake up!"

Prince Humberger opened his eyes and slapped Beezle across the face.

He scowled. "What was that for?"

"I didn't like the look on your face. If you look at me like that again, I'll put your head through that wall."

Gretchen grinned. "My work is done here. I will

leave you two to your jobs so I can get back to my station. We'll meet at the fortress at eighteen hundred hours." Gretchen bowed her head to the Prince.

The prince maneuvered around to the sliding glass door in the back of the condo and examined it for a second, then strutted to his van.

As he came back with a screwdriver, a frumpy, middle-aged man stopped him and stuck out his stubby little hand. "I usually don't do this since I'm a shy kind of guy, scared of people, actually. But my daughter just moved in a couple of doors down. She's about your age, and I thought I'd try to introduce her to one of the nice neighbors. My name is Charlie Blue."

"I don't shake hands with commoners. Too many diseases."

"I understand. You're one of those germaphobes." Charlie smiled.

"Listen, peasant, why don't you walk away now and go get your teeth fixed."

Charlie dropped his gaze. "Sorry to bother you."

Prince Humberger stalked past him and headed around to the back of Les's condo. Ripping through the screen with the screwdriver, he made an opening big enough for his hand, then unlocked the screen door. He swiftly removed the screws holding the door handle, flipped down the lock, and slid the door open.

He went straight to the kitchen where he found an empty milk jug. As he popped off the lid, he smelled the most beautiful, intoxicating aroma. He held his nose completely over the opening, inhaling every scent. He wandered around the corner with the milk jug still to his nose.

"What are you doing?" Beezle's' nose scrunched

up.

"Shut up! It's mine! You can't have any. I need to find it! I need to find it!" Prince Humberger ran back into the kitchen, flung open all the cabinets and drawers, and threw pots and pans everywhere. He went to the fridge and swept the whole top shelf onto the floor, smashing condiments onto the tile.

Way in the back stood four plastic containers with blue tops. He grabbed one and unscrewed the lid, drawing in the sweet aroma.

"Did you find it?" Beezle stood in the kitchen's entry, watching.

Prince Humberger slowly turned around and growled at him. "What did I tell you about shutting your mouth?"

"You can't drink that. I can't serve two masters."

Prince Humberger's anger boiled over. "You serve me. You do what I say!"

"There are two masters. I serve one and I hate the other. If you drink that, you will be serving the one I hate."

The prince stepped toward Beezle, placing the wine on the counter. Beezle backed up, pointing at him.

"You can't ride the fence. You need to choose a side. If you don't, we'll choose for you, and that will be death." Beezle hissed like a snake.

"Do you threaten me, you ungrateful swine? I am powerful. I am royalty!"

"You are weak and pitiful. The only power you have is the power we give you." Beezle sidled to the sliding glass door and slipped out.

"Run, you coward, before I destroy you." Prince Humberger lumbered back into the kitchen and picked up the wine he so badly wanted to drink, but another part of him wanted to replace the top and get out of there.

The sweet aroma touched his nose. It was too much for him to resist. He grabbed the container and chugged it. Some of it spilled down the front of his shirt as he bashed the container down on the counter.

A warm sensation ran down the top of his head and slowly worked its way to his toes. It felt as though someone had dumped warm honey on his head. His eyes went blind as a bright light like a car's headlight shined in them.

The light dimmed then, and he felt like a new person, like a dead man who had come back to life.

"Hold it right there! Slowly put your hands on your head and turn around."

Jerry's stomach dropped. He raised his hands to his head, turned around, and saw a police officer with his gun poised. "We received a phone call from one of the neighbors saying he saw some suspicious behavior going on over here. What are you doing?"

"This is my friend's condo. I came in to get something to eat," Jerry said, not even believing his own lie.

The officer moved closer. "I smell marijuana. You have the right to remain silent. . . ."

Everything moved in slow motion as the officer snapped handcuffs onto Jerry's wrists then shoved him into the car. He turned on his radio. "We have a breaking and entering suspect who smells of marijuana. Nothing was found on him, but I'm bringing him in for questioning."

CHAPTER TWENTY-SIX

"My father hates cell phones, so be sure you shut yours off." Lila slung her purse over her shoulder as she and Les followed the maitre' d to her father's booth in the five-star restaurant.

Les hadn't expected Lila's father to be the geeky professor type with a navy bow tie and glasses, white, slicked-back hair and a white beard. He looked more like George Lucas than a millionaire businessman.

Lila leaned over and kissed her dad. What a contrast. Was she adopted?

The gentlemen sitting to his right must be the wealthy investor. He could have been Lila's brother with his chiseled facial features and olive skin. Distinguished-looking in his black suit and red tie, the only aspect of his appearance that pointed to his ethnicity was the white towel wrapped around his head. Even his beard was cropped close.

Lila greeted the investor with a hand shake. "This is my friend, Lester. Lester, this is my father, Barry Fontane and Jihad Haddad."

"Nice tie," Les said as he shook Barry's hand. Barry smiled politely. "Nice—," Les paused as he shook Jihad's hand, "—towel."

Jihad squeezed Les's hand with a callous stare. *Okay, that guy might try and stab me.*

Les and Lila seated themselves.

"Lila tells me that you have come across a special formula. I've dedicated my whole life to creating a formula like yours." Lila's father paused, holding Les's gaze. "Do you really believe you have the cure for cancer?"

"As hard as it might be to believe, my discovery will cure more than cancer. It cures everything from the common cold to the last stages of AIDS."

Barry leaned back in his seat and shook his head. "You're pretty confident. I like that. What tests have you run?"

"It brought my friend out of some kind of drug overdose. It healed a women of cancerous tumors and just a few hours ago it completely healed the cuts I had on my knee and elbow."

"I saw it happen," Lila said.

Jihad raised his finger to speak. "You say this potion heals every kind of sickness and disease, but you have done only three different tests. You can't claim this is a miracle potion without more proof."

"That's why we want to give you a sample so you can run some tests." Lila set her expensive-looking handbag on the table.

Barry rubbed his beard. "That would be a start. I guess we can use some of my test subjects who have already signed waivers for experimental treatment. If this stuff works like you say it does, we have a lot to do. We need to figure out dosages and how to administer the drug."

"You drink it," Les said.

"That's it? One drink and you're cured?" Jihad reclined back into the booth. Doubt riddled his tone.

"So far, that's done the trick." Les gazed back at Jihad who took a drink from his water glass without breaking his gaze. His stare made Les's skin crawl.

Lila pulled a fountain pen from her purse. "That's why I wanted to have this meeting right away. This thing could be huge, and I wanted to get your input on long-range goals."

"But, honey, we don't even know if this stuff will work on every ailment. What about side effects? How long will the effects of the drug last?" Barry sipped from his water glass.

"For discussion's sake, let's say this stuff does everything Les says it can do." Lila pointed her pen at Jihad. "Jihad, maybe you can help me out with this. What would be the world-wide market value of a formula of this magnitude?"

Jihad rubbed his chiseled chin. "Of course, there is supply and demand. If we or Lester can produce only small amounts of this product at a time, it would be priceless. It would sell to the highest bidder."

"Let's not get too excited about the make-believe possibilities. Jihad and I have done enough real-life research to know the cure for cancer alone would be a billion-dollar discovery. The next step is getting your product into the lab." Barry leaned forward. "Do you have any with you?"

"We left it in the limo." Lila tenderly hit Les on the arm.

"You left a potentially priceless product in the car alone?" Barry scratched his beard. "I think you might want to go get it."

Les stood. "Okay, but don't you go plotting against me." He paused and gave them a smirk as everyone uncomfortably half-laughed. Les, restless, plodded toward the limo. Part of him wanted to take the wine and run, to take off and never talk to Lila or her father again. Les tapped on the window and startled the driver, who was reading the sports section of the newspaper.

He rolled down the window. "What's up, mate? What can I help you with?"

266

"I need to get something out of the back." Les climbed up into the H2 limo and saw his little plastic container sitting on the seat. He took a moment to reflect on what he was holding in his hands. All of his hopes and dreams could come true with what was inside this small container.

On his way back to the restaurant, he decided not to tell anyone about the other containers. He needed to trust these people before he gave them everything.

Standing outside the large wooden doors of the restaurant, he examined the metal hinges. Was this the door to his destiny? The moment he steps through those doors, his life will change. He won't be a nobody anymore. His name will be written on the greatest discovery of all time. He will have instant celebrity status overnight. People will soon know who Lester John is.

So why did he have such an uneasiness in the pit of his stomach?

He needed some comfort, needed to hear a familiar voice. Les reached for his cell and turned it on. He dialed Jerry's number.

"There you are. We're waiting on you." Lila had both hands on her hips, tapping her foot. "Who are you on the phone with?"

"My mom, just checking in with her."

Lila gave him the hush sign with her finger and stepped back inside.

Jerry's voicemail picked up, and Les cursed. "Hey, Jer, sorry we haven't been in touch the last couple of days or so, but I have some real exciting news. Call me."

###

Alone, isolated, and surprisingly cold in his four-by-four jail cell, Jerry sat on the solid concrete bench that doubled as his bed. The small, rectangular window on the cell door was foggy and scratched. He could barely see out of it.

What had he done? Had he broken into Les's condo to steal food? It was as if he was separated from his body at times, like he became a different person, not knowing what that other person inside of him was thinking or doing.

I hate what I've become. I push everyone away because of my desire to get high. I just want to escape from reality and my problems. I'm going to end up like my mother, in an endless cycle of promiscuity, never engaging long enough to form any kind of lasting bond. Retreating back to a substance makes me believe everything in my life is great and disguises the truth with silly laughter.

Something spoke inside of him. *Laughing doesn't mean you're happy.*

"Laughing doesn't mean you're happy." Jerry repeated the phrase out loud over and over. *What makes me happy? I mean, what truly makes me happy? Am I happy when I'm at work? Not really, I'm mostly bored, daydreaming about the weekend.*

For a moment, Jerry tried to recall different things that made him happy. Les made him happy. He always had a good time hanging with Les. But most of the time, they were drunk. Was his relationship with Les built on false laughter?

Elizabeth always brought a smile to his face. When he made her laugh, was he happy?

Marijuana? Did that make him happy? He always felt like he was in a good mood after smoking. But how could something make him happy if it ends up pushing away the people who made him happy? Especially Elizabeth.

"What am I doing with my life? Wow, jail kind of makes you go crazy. There's nothing to do in here but think."

A voice came through his intercom. "We've made several attempts to contact the homeowner, a Lester John, and have left him a message. If he's willing to come and drop the charges, we'll let you out. If not, you'll be spending the night with us, unless you know someone who would post a five-hundred-dollar bail."

Where was Les? "Come on, man. I don't know how much longer I can take it in here." Jerry stood to look through the skinny, rectangular window. Just another row of gray cells.

Maybe he should call Elizabeth. He could pay her back the five hundred.

But would she come? Yeah, she would come; she loved him, right?

The graffiti on the wall above the toilet caught his attention. *Dirk was here.*

Jerry stared at those four letters that spelled out his dad's name. A wave of hopelessness overwhelmed him. It felt as though someone punched him in the gut.

"I hate you. I hate you," he yelled at the wall. "Look at me! I'm messed up, and you did it to me. Years of telling me I wouldn't grow up to be anything. That I would end up like my mother, a burnout. I could've finished college. I'm smart enough!"

Tears fell from his eyes. He slammed his fist into the etching on the wall. "You taught me to run away! Deadbeat scumbag."

Jerry sat on the concrete bed with his knees curled

up to his chest, rocking back and forth. As his anger started to settle, Jerry cried out, "I don't want to end up like him. I don't want to end up like either of my parents. Someone help me not end up like them. Someone, please."

He wiped his eyes with his sleeve and took a deep breath to compose himself. He stood and hit the intercom button. "I'm ready to make my call."

###

Les handed the plastic container to Professor Barry.

"What is this, Tupperware? You're keeping possibly the most powerful healing solution in the world in a Tupperware container?" Barry laughed.

Les's face heated. "It's better than what I had it in before."

"What did—never mind. I don't want to know. Let's not talk business anymore until after dinner." Barry raised his wine glass.

Les settled in to enjoy a five-course meal of all different kinds of foods he had never heard of, each complimenting the others, and all tasting delicious. After the meal, Barry pulled his briefcase out from under the table. He took out some documents and laid them on the table in front of Les.

What was this about? Les bit his thumb nail. Lila rubbed his arm, presumably to comfort him. *Whose side is she on?*

"These are all the docs we need you to sign. There's a lot of legal jargon, but basically the first few pages give us permission to test your product in our lab. The section beginning on page five talks about testing your products on animals then on humans."

270

"How do you test on animals?" Les asked.

Barry smiled. "We inject them with a disease and try and get rid of it before they die."

"Sounds cruel to me."

"Well, we use mostly mice, not monkeys or anything." Barry turned the pages. "On page ten here, it says that neither you nor EFIL will be held liable for any deaths that may occur during the trial studies."

"Deaths?" What was he getting into? Les massaged his forehead.

"It's standard," Lila said, as if any kind of death was standard.

"Look now at page fourteen. This is where it states that you will receive fifteen percent of all annual revenues from the sale of your product."

"Fifteen percent? I'm not signing that."

Barry reclined. "Once you sign this product over to us, we will pull the ingredients out and, we hope, mass produce. You won't have to lift a finger. Jihad will front all of the capital we need for marketing, advertising, and to run the tests. I will do all the studies, and Lila will contact drug companies across the world, setting up meetings and selling them on our product. All you have to do is sit back and collect a check."

"Yes, but without my product, you have nothing."

Jihad gave him an I-know-better-than-you smile. "You have no clue how much time, energy, and money goes into producing something like this. We're also providing you with the most important feature: safety."

"What do I need safety for?" Probably from them.

"Think about it. You have a healing potion that can cure people of any kind of disease or sickness. A lot of powerful, desperate people would be willing to hunt you

271

down, break into your house, and kill you for what you have." Jihad's face looked stone-cold.

Les dropped his gaze. What had he gotten into? He should never have told Lila. . . .

"It's business. We want to help as many people as we can with this, but we need to be realistic, and we need to be safe. It's going to cost a lot to do what we want to do with your product, but we need full control over the manufacturing and marketing. That's why we're giving you this deal." She rubbed his back in what he was sure she meant to be soothing, comforting motions. In reality, it made him more anxious. "You sign your name on the dotted line, and you get fifteen percent of a company that's going to make billions. Think about it. What's fifteen percent of ten billion? One hundred and fifty million dollars. Think you can live on that?"

"I'll take a night to sleep on it and look over the documents."

"Absolutely. Why don't we meet for lunch tomorrow?" Barry said.

"I can do that." Les's nervousness subsided a fraction.

"If your product works like you say it does, we're going to change the world." Barry stood with him.

Jihad slid him a squinty-eyed smile that sent Les's uneasiness back to the forefront.

Barry took care of the bill, then the four of them strode outside. Barry pulled Lila to the side and whispered in her ear. She nodded then gave him a hug.

As Les and Lila pulled away in the limo, she turned

to him with a too-innocent face. "What did you think of my father?"

"He reminded me of George Lucas."

Lila laughed. "Are you wondering why we don't look anything alike?"

"I didn't see much resemblance."

"My mom is full Aramean, and my real dad died when I was a baby. Soon after that, my mom met Barry, and he's been my father ever since. He's a fair man."

"I don't want to sound money-hungry or anything, because I'm not, but I was shocked by the fifteen percent."

"A lot goes into something like this, but you're good hands." She kissed his cheek. "Where should we tell the driver to take us?"

"Do you feel sober enough to drive?"

Lila ran her fingers through her hair. "Not really."

"I'm fine, so I'd like to pick up my car and send your limo driver home."

They pulled up to the Max Bistro and climbed down out of the H2 limo. The driver rolled down his window and pointed to Les. "No worries, mate."

Les nodded. "No worries."

They strolled toward Les's car. "Do you want me to take you home?"

"I was hoping I could come home with you."

Les paused for a second, taking in Lila's gorgeous figure. How could he say no? The Civic pulled out of the parking lot and headed for Les's condo.

"Did you enjoy the food?" She flipped down his visor to touch up her make-up.

"I'm surprised how good duck liver can be."

She laughed. "I try not to ask the waiter what they're serving me. Sometimes it's better not to know."

He down-shifted as he drove up to his parking spot. A van that looked like Jerry's sat next to Les's spot. "Wonder what he's doing here."

Les got out and jogged over to the driver-side window. "This is his van, all right. I can tell by the fast-food wrappers."

They started back toward his building when Martha, the lady who lived across the hall, stopped him. "Are you okay?"

"Fine. Why?"

"You haven't heard? Someone broke into your condo today."

Les ran to his front door. He unlocked both the bottom lock and the deadbolt. Inside, the first thing he saw was the open container of wine sitting on the counter. A queasy feeling sank into his stomach. Then he noticed his pots and pans and broken condiments all over his kitchen floor.

Martha and Lila rushed in. "Who would do such a thing?" Lila asked.

"They arrested some man they found in your condo, drinking some juice or something. They said they think he was high on drugs." Martha said.

Les stepped over the pots and pans. "How did he get in?"

"They said he broke in through the back door."

He glanced at the door and the torn screen hanging from the frame. "Did he take anything?"

"I don't know. Maybe you should call the station."

When Martha left, Les grabbed the lid to the wine container and screwed it back on.

"It's already started." Lila folded her arms. "Someone broke in here looking for your healing potion."

Les kicked one his pots. "Not that many people know."

"Name all the people who know about this healing tonic."

"There's Jerry, Susie, the guy I met at Super Mart and his wife, but they don't know where I live. Just Susie and Jerry do."

"Do you think it could have been one of Susie's friends? Or what about Jerry?"

"Jerry? Why would he do something like this?"

"This is powerful stuff. He knows its potential, and he wanted it so he could sell it himself." Lila held the wine container up to the light.

"You know what?" Les bent down to pick up his non-stick skillet from the floor. "I don't even care right now. I just want to clean up this stuff and get out of here."

"I'll help you."

Lila gathered the pots and pans while Les threw the broken condiment jars into the trash. They made a trip to the dumpster then mopped the floor, making the kitchen look good as new.

"All right, I need to make a call to the police department." Les turned his phone back on. He saw that he had two missed calls from a number that he didn't recognize. When he listened to his voicemail, he found out the calls were from the police department, letting him know they had a man in custody for breaking and entering.

Les dialed the number and reached the officer in charge. "My name is Lester John. You have someone in custody for breaking into my condo?"

"That's right. Do you want to press charges? His name is Jeremiah Humberger."

Les felt queasy again. Jerry's betrayal burned inside

of him. "You've got to be kidding. No, I don't want to press charges."

"You'll have to come down here and fill out some paperwork if you want the charges dropped. Otherwise, we have to hold him for twenty-four hours."

Les paced the condo. "Do I have to see him?"

"There's no rule that says you have to see him."

"I'm on my way." He hung up. How could this be happening? "Unbelievable. It was Jerry. That's why his van is outside. I think I'm going to throw up."

She pulled him close for a hug. "Let's just go sign the papers to get him out of jail and be done with him."

"Be done with him? He's my best friend."

She snorted. "I don't know too many best friends who break into someone's house, trash their kitchen, and try to steal their most valuable possession."

Les turned his face. He didn't want to talk about it. Jerry's betrayal hurt too bad. "This makes my decision a lot easier. Jihad was right. If my friends are breaking into my house trying to steal the potion, what would a stranger be willing to do?"

Lila nodded. "You can stay with me tonight."

"Let me get a bag together." Les darted into his room and grabbed a rolling suitcase and a gym bag. He packed clothes and other essentials in the suitcase, then he took the two Tupperware containers from under his bed and crammed them into the gym bag. He needed to keep this stuff as close as possible. He left one container out.

"Why didn't you tell me you had all this potion?"

"Honestly, I didn't trust you."

Lila crossed her arms. "Have I ever done anything to lead you to believe you can't trust me?"

"How can you fully trust someone you've known

only a couple of days?"

Without a word, Lila stormed out of the condo and slammed the door.

Les closed his eyes as he gripped his duffle bag with his right hand.

Do you know what you're doing, Les? A voice spoke from inside of him.

"No, I don't." He dropped his bag, and with his eyes still closed, he drew deep breaths like he used to do before a race. He took air deep into his lungs through his nose then slowly let it out through his mouth. He felt like he did on the starting block at his first freshman collegiate swim meet—nervous but confident that he was better than anyone else on those blocks, heart pumping fast, mind clear and focused as he crouched, waiting for the gun. He had one objective, and that was to win by as much as possible. When he touched the water, it was as if he glided through air with no resistance.

It was liberating. It was freeing. It was the only time in his life that everything seemed right. No freshman ever swam as fast in the one hundred free in that pool. Lester visualized himself coming up to the wall to look at his time—

"Hello? I've been waiting outside for you for, like, five minutes. What are you doing?" The door slammed shut, and Lila's words brought Les out of his dream-like state. He opened his eyes. So much for that fleeting sensation of freedom.

CHAPTER TWENTY-SEVEN

==

Jerry gripped the telephone. His nerves stood on end. "Please answer, please answer," he said after every number he pressed. He got a ring, then another. He held his breath as the tones rang hollow in his ear.

"Hello?"

"Elizabeth, it's me, Jerry."

"Where are you calling from?"

"Promise me you're not going to freak out. I'm in jail."

The phone went silent for a moment. "So what do you want me to do? Come down and get you?"

"That would be great except for one thing. I need five hundred dollars for bail."

"I don't have five hundred dollars. All the banks are closed, and it's Sunday."

"I guess I'll be spending the night then."

"I'm sorry, but maybe this is what you need to wake you up."

"What I need? How do you know what I need?" Jerry gripped the phone tight.

"Look, Jerry, I love you, but I don't need to take this from you. I don't even care what you did to get yourself put in there. I just know that I've decided to separate myself from you until you want to change. I'm not talking about changing for me or because you're lonely and depressed and want me back. I'm talking about a complete mind-set transformation, and the only way you can get that is from God. You need to ask him to help you, because no one else can. I love you and I'll be praying for you."

Jerry was silent for a moment. "I don't want to end up like my parents, but I don't think I can change the course of my future."

"I'm done feeling sorry for you. Your pity party will get you nowhere. You need to go to God."

"You have thirty seconds." The officer standing a few feet from Jerry, monitoring his phone call, pointed to his watch.

Jerry leaned his body against the wall.

"Use this time to think about what you want out of life. What does your future look like? I promise to be there if you decide to change, but if not, I can't do it anymore. It's not fair to me to have my emotions sucked back into you. You need Jesus, Jerry. You need Jesus."

"Time's up." The officer hung up the phone, grinning. "Looks like you'll be staying with us tonight."

"Do you smell something?" Jerry sniffed the air.

"I don't smell anything." The officer gave Jerry a curious look.

"I'm pretty sure I do. I know what it is: bacon. I smell bacon! Oink, oink, oink."

The officer yanked Jerry by the arm and shoved him toward his cell. "Shut up, you little punk! Why don't you get a haircut?"

"'Why don't you get a haircut?' That's your big comeback?" Jerry laughed while the officer removed the cuffs.

When the cell door slammed shut behind Jerry, he immediately felt alone again. Elizabeth, the only person besides Les whom Jerry thought would always stand by him, had totally rejected him. She'd said he needed Jesus, needed to go to God. What did she mean by that? And if Jerry were to go to God, how would he do that?

He fixed his focus on a crack in the floor. If only he were an ant, he could crawl through that crack and escape to freedom. Maybe Elizabeth was right, that he needed some kind of spiritual enlightenment in his life. Where did he see himself in the future? Jerry sat on the concrete bench, fixated on the ceiling.

If I could convince Les to sell his healing potion, my future would be incredible.

He jumped up clapping his hands together. "That's what I need to do, convince Les to go into business with me, selling the healing potion."

A smile spread across his face. He sat back down on the concrete bench. He didn't need God. He needed money, lots of it. Maybe this healing potion was his way out of a terrible, unfulfilling life.

Keys rattled the lock of his cell. The officer opened the door. "You're free to go. The homeowner dropped all charges."

"Yes! I knew Les would come through for me."

Jerry signed a couple of forms, and within minutes, he bounded into the parking lot. "Les? Where are you?"

Jerry zigzagged through the parking lot, looking for Les's car, but he couldn't find it anywhere.

He meandered back into the police station and approached the sergeant at the desk. "Excuse me, but where is the guy who dropped the charges?"

"He left about fifteen minutes ago. Looks like you're walking home, bud."

Jerry turned and walked outside. Alone again. "Why does this keep happening to me?" It was going to take him at least two hours to walk home or to Les's condo to his van.

He decided he should get his van. He had no money,

no phone, only keys. Jerry kicked a rock as he slugged down the road with his hands in his pockets. It would be dark in less than an hour, and the temperature was supposed to drop into the forties. His arms felt chilled already, so he picked up his pace. With each step, his bitterness and resentment grew. Hate had already infiltrated his mind at the irony of finding his dad's name etched into the cell wall. This was his mother's fault for introducing him to drugs. Elizabeth had left him to rot in jail, and Les? Well, he understood why Les probably didn't like him right now. A cloud of darkness formed over Jerry's head as he continued his bitter journey of hate.

Les shifted his Civic into neutral as they came to a stoplight. "I feel bad leaving him there."

Lila's mouth dropped open. "Are you demented? He broke into your house and tried to steal from you."

"I should have at least given him a chance to explain. I hope he got a ride home." They pulled into Lila's driveway. A black Lexus LS 600 HL sat parked across the street, and Lila's dad was at the wheel. "What's he doing here?"

"I called and told him you were ready to sign the papers and make a deal."

Les swallowed the lump in his throat.

Barry got out of the car and strode over to them. He patted Les on the back. "I heard it's already begun. We're going to take good care of you, Lester, good care of you."

The three of them filed into Lila's town home. Lila led the way as they climbed the stairs to the second story into Lila's dining room. Les plopped his bag down on the long, cherry table.

"So, is this everything?" Barry pointed to Les's bag.

Les nodded. "It's all there."

"Let's take a look." The professor leaned over and unzipped the bag. He peered inside, lips pressed together, mind visibly working. "This should be enough until we learn how to manufacture it."

Les got that sick feeling in his stomach again.

"Let's sign the documents in here." Barry flipped his briefcase on the table.

Les sat down but at this point, he felt like a cow being led into a butcher shop. He read all the pages and nodded as if he knew exactly what they meant, but the jargon was like a foreign language to him. He picked up Barry's pen from the table. Signing page after page of this document felt like a cross between buying your first home and making a deal with the devil.

Les's last autograph brought a big gratified smile to Barry's face. "Let's go change the world."

Les smiled half-heartedly and rubbed his eyes.

Barry grabbed the bag of healing potion. "Wish I could stay, but I have a lot of work to do. I'm taking these over to the lab right away. You kids have a good night."

As Lila walked Barry to the door, Les studied a picture on the dining room wall. It was a large black-and-white wall photo of Marilyn Monroe, and she was laughing. Under her photo, a caption read, "I don't want to be rich, I just want to be loved."

Did Lila love him? How could she? They had known each other for only a couple of days. Did she even like him? Sometimes he wondered by the way she talked to him. Was she using him? *Maybe I just need to be loved.*

"You thinking about cheating on me with Marilyn?"

Lila had a certain tease in her voice.

"She was beautiful, wasn't she? Do you think she's really laughing in that picture? Or do you think she could possibly have been having the worst day of her life and made herself laugh for the camera?"

"What kind of question is that?"

Les shifted close to the image. "I don't think she's happy in this picture. Look, her head is tilted back, and her mouth is fully opened. How many people do you know who naturally laugh that way? She's totally acting."

"Are you going to stand there and ruin my picture?" Lila put her hands on her hips. "I love that picture of her."

Les pointed at the words on the picture. "What about this phrase down here at the bottom? 'I don't want to be rich, I just want to be loved.'" He turned to face Lila with the dining room table between them. "If you had to chose right now, love or money, which would you chose?"

Lila stood speechless, seemingly revolted by his words. Her eyes squinted and her top lip and cheeks elevated.

"Come on, right now, which one?" Les raised his voice.

"I chose money." She stomped out of the room.

"I knew it!" Les chased after her. He grabbed her by the arm and turned her to face him. "If I was nothing more than a factory worker making twelve dollars an hour for the rest of my life, would you love me?"

Lila jerked away and started up the stairs. Les ran after her and grabbed her by the arm again. He glared into her eyes. "Would you love me?"

"Stop holding my arm like that! How can I answer such a question after knowing you for two days?"

"That's not my point. If I wasn't on the brink of

becoming a multi-millionaire, would there ever be a chance for us?"

"Like I said, it's been only two days. Why are you acting so crazy?"

Les's eyes bulged as he pressed his hands on the sides of his head. "My brain is on overload. I need to be alone, and I need to think. I need to get out of here."

She stomped up the stairs. "Lock the door on your way out."

Les ran down the stairs and out to his car. He jammed it in reverse and took off down the road, squealing his tires.

His mind was playing tricks. Did it matter if Lila wasn't in love with him after only two days? What would he chose, love or money? Did he just sign a gift from God over to the devil? "Oh, God."

He was having a nervous breakdown. What had he done? He needed to stop and think.

Les whipped the Civic into the empty parking lot of an old hardware store. He slammed the car in park and closed his eyes. He took a few deep breaths.

"Jesus, I know you're real. I know you are somehow listening to me somewhere. Give me the holy force, God. I need your holy force!"

Les struggled to remember something Jesus said in the book of John. All he could remember was John 14:14: "You may ask me for anything in my name, and I will do it."

"Jesus, help me calm down." Les took a deep breath. "Jesus, somehow tell me what I should do next." Les sat in his car in silence. He picked up his phone and dialed Lynn's number.

When she answered, Les cleared his throat. "I know

it's late, but can I come over?"

"Are you okay?" Her voice sounded tired.

"Yeah, I just need to talk to you. I'm about twenty minutes away."

"See you in twenty."

CHAPTER TWENTY-EIGHT

===

As Jerry trudged along the dark road, his insides ran cold, and his head was hot with anger. For two hours he had walked alone in the dark, freezing his butt off, with only his own thoughts to keep him entertained.

He punched in Les's code for the walking path into the condo development. The streetlights cast weird shadows on the parked cars and the landscaping.

As Jerry passed the first building on his right, he felt as though someone was watching him. He spun around and looked behind him but saw nothing but a few parked cars and a stop sign.

Jerry continued past the second building. Footsteps sounded about fifty feet behind him. He stopped and the footsteps got louder. He turned and looked again. The footsteps stopped. No one was there.

He did another scan of the first and second buildings. Nothing. He picked up his pace and spotted his van up on the left. The footsteps quickened with each step he took.

He made a break for his van, running as fast as he could. When he got there, the driver's side door was locked. He reached in his pocket for his keys but dropped them on the ground.

The footsteps came closer. He didn't want to look back. He picked up the keys and kept his focus on them, trying to get the right one in the van door.

As he turned the key, the footsteps stopped. A piercing scream shot through his brain. He pressed his hands over his ears. What was the sound, and who made it?

Jerry stumbled around the parking lot, disoriented and needing to get away from that sound. The screams got louder. They were coming from inside his brain, piercing his every thought. With each passing second, another voice was added to the choir of screams.

He dropped to his knees, screaming. Not a football-game scream. This sound held the intensity of a man caught in a torture chamber. The more he screamed, the more he could drown out the sounds in his head.

He screeched louder and louder. Martha ran out of her home, cautiously keeping a safe distance. Other people joined her, standing about twenty feet from him, all watching in silence, their shock permeating the air. They looked as if they were paralyzed by fear.

Corliss, a muscular, copper-skinned man from Jerry's department at work, approached him. The ex-college linebacker stood three feet from Jerry with a puzzled look on his face. He squatted down, peering into Jerry's eyes. Jerry went silent, so Corliss looked back at the crowd gave them a thumbs up.

Jerry dropped his hands from his ears and sat on the ground with his legs underneath him and his head facing down, focused at the ground. He smelled his own sweaty odor of funk.

Corliss jerked Jerry's shoulder. "Hey, you okay, man?"

Jerry slowly raised his head. His hair dripped sweat. *He's come to hurt you. He's trying to destroy you. He wants to take your kingdom.*

With one quick and powerful motion, Jerry grabbed Corliss's arm and bent it backwards, breaking his arm at the elbow.

Corliss fell backward, grabbing his arm. Jerry rose

and kicked Corliss straight in the mouth, breaking several of his teeth. Jerry held his gaze on each person in the crowd. "If any of you call the police, I will cut your head off and stick it on the front gate." His voice was deep, raspy, unhuman.

The crowd stood motionless as if gripped by fear. Corliss writhed in pain on the ground.

Jerry ran to his van and sped out of the complex. His body was cold inside, but he was dripping wet with sweat. His muscles shivered with spasms.

He held the steering wheel with both hands, drifting in and out of consciousness. Something was driving his van, and it wasn't him. The van went up on two wheels as it made the left turn into his apartment complex.

As he hit the brakes with both feet, the van slammed into the curb and came to a stop. He turned the motor off and sat in the parking spot in front of his apartment. He felt helpless, as if all self-control had left him. He felt dragged toward his apartment, stopping several times to try to gauge his surroundings, but he could not.

In the hallway, he rattled his keys in the door, and it opened. As he walked into his apartment, the familiar smell of stale marijuana hit his nostrils and brought comfort to his tortured spirit. He hustled to his closet, climbed the chair to his superweed, and hit some keys then the control button.

Within moments, he was breaking down the bud on a television tray. His memory was spotty. Several times, he blacked out for a few seconds and then came back, but when he came back, he was doing something else.

Jerry licked the ends of the joint and allocated it on the tray. Although he was alone, he felt the physical presence of several other people in the room. He squinted, but it didn't help.

He closed his eyes again, and when he opened them, he was halfway through smoking his joint. As he took deep tokes into his lungs and let the smoke filter down into his belly, he started to see dark images standing around the room. They were like shadows moving through his apartment. His body was too numb to feel any emotion. He took his last drag, set the roach on the tray, and closed his eyes again.

"I can't believe you waged our hopes on this pathetic moron!"

Jerry jolted out of his seat with his eyes wide open, knocking over the TV tray. Who said that?

Then he heard more voices, and nine vaguely familiar people appeared.

"Where have you been?" Nasty-looking Gretchen screamed from behind the sofa.

Jerry's eyes amplified twice the normal size as the large Native American man stood right in front of him. The man's breath smelled like a bellowing smokestack of sulfur. He didn't say a word but continued to stare into Jerry's eyes.

All of a sudden, he picked Jerry up by the throat and threw him down violently onto the floor in the middle of the others. The nine stood around Jerry while the African warrior kicked him in the gut and screamed. "You feeble piece of scum."

He knocked the wind out of Jerry. Jerry writhed on the ground, trying to catch his breath.

Gretchen then came up behind him and yanked a clump of hair out of his head. "What a pitiful excuse for a man."

Jerry yelled, holding his head as a woman in a purple robe kicked him square in the mouth with her pointy shoe. His blood dripped from his mouth onto the cream-colored carpet.

What was happening? Had this gang come to kill him? If so, he would at least give them a fight.

He then closed his eyes -and sprang to his feet as he launched his own assault of fist and elbows, swinging and kicking wildly into the air. He braced himself to feel the impact of flesh, but he was hitting nothing. He stopped to catch his breath and open his eyes.

The nine stood around him, gazing at him with devilish grins. Their eyes were black pits of emptiness. The twin with the pentagram on his forehead spit on Jerry. A green goo covered his chest.

Gross. Jerry touched it with his hand. He felt a piece of hard metal strike the back of his head, and he went crashing to the floor.

Was this real? The pain certainly was. He tasted his own blood, dripping down the back of his throat. Jerry lay motionless on the floor, his head throbbing. If he played dead, maybe they would go away and leave him alone.

The Arian-supremacy dude grabbed him by the hair and stood him up against the wall. The pain was so excruciating that Jerry faded in and out of consciousness. The man slammed Jerry against the wall to keep him awake. "You failed us! You stale piece of rubbish!"

He pulled a knife out of his pocket and held it to Jerry's throat.

The cold piece of steel pressed against Jerry's skin. He shut his eyes as a part of him wished the man would split open his neck, ending his suffering.

"Does anyone have any reason why we should keep this useless piece of trash alive? All in favor of slicing his throat, say 'aye.'"

Amid a chorus of "ayes," the beautiful redhead stepped out from the circle. "Wait! We can still use him."

Jerry wrenched his left eye open to view the women speaking. *Abella.*

"Shut up, wench! Slit his throat already." Saliva dripping from his chin, Beezle pointed his finger at Jerry.

"Listen to me. He is still our only chance of getting the healing potion. There is no other way." The redhead gazed at each one in the circle. "We control his mind now. We need to keep him sedated and under watch."

"Abella," Jerry whispered. But no one paid attention.

"He's too unpredictable, not to mention spineless." The African warrior spit on Jerry's foot.

"We can't eliminate our biggest asset. He is still valuable. Today's circumstances have bred new hatred inside him. They brought up a lot of old wounds and new hurts that we can use against him. He is now completely isolated and alone. No outside influence can penetrate the wall we've built around him. He is certainly no prince, but he can be our pawn. Once we have established a new host, we can sacrifice the pawn." The redhead back-pedaled to her place in the circle.

The Arian-supremacy dude lowered his knife and sheathed it then punched Jerry in the chest.

I am a sacrificial pawn? Jerry's head withered as he fainted. Seemingly moments later, he was brought back. His head pounded and now his chest was stinging.

Gretchen stepped out of the circle. "She's right. At this point, he's more useful to us alive then dead. Abella, I station you on surveillance. Don't let him out of your sight. Keep him alone in the apartment as much as possible. Jezatra, you will be in charge of keeping him sedated and under our control at all times."

The drunken woman in purple nodded.

"Take him to his bed. Fill his mind with all kinds of sin, especially the deadly ones. The rest of us will do some scouting to see if we can set up a situation. Beezle, you have guard duty. If anyone comes by other than Les, get rid of them, especially his friend Elizabeth. She's bad news and has the potential to unravel all our hard work. May the one and only true prince of this world be exalted, and may all of us receive the honor we deserve."

All nine then dispersed to their assignments.

Les pulled into Lynn's driveway and shut off his lights. He sat there in the dark for a moment, his focus on the little house.

What am I doing here? I need to get out of here rather than involve another person. This could be dangerous. The more people involved, the more people who can get hurt.

He started up his car again and turned on his lights then sat a few moments with his hand resting on the stick shift. What should he do? "Help me, Jesus."

Lynn stalked out of her house, waving at Les, her brows drawn together.

At the sight of her, a sense of peace covered him and made him forget all his thoughts. He turned off the ignition and got out of the car.

Lynn studied his face. "Are you okay? You sounded nervous on the phone."

Les swung his arms around Lynn, engulfing her. He squeezed her tight, locking his arms around her. He had missed her. Even the watermelon scent of her hair brought comfort. Lynn reached back and pulled his arms off her.

"Let's go inside. It's chilly out here." She led him by the hand into the house. "Can I get you anything to drink?"

He eased himself onto the living room couch. "I could use a nice glass of water."

Lynn brought a tall glass of ice water to Les and sat next to him on the couch, watching him drink almost the whole glass in one single gulp. "Would you like some more?"

"No, thanks." He turned and looked her in the eyes. "Can I trust you?"

Her silence and stiffened back weren't what he was looking for. He set the empty glass on the coffee table and angled closer, hoping to close the gap that remained in their relationship. "I need to know that whatever I tell you is going to stay between you and me."

Her face paled. "Les, you're starting to scare me a little."

"Look, I haven't gone and killed anybody or anything. I got myself involved in something that is top secret, and I need to know that I can trust you." He paused, looking down at her tiny hand. He laid his hand over it. "I need to know, or I have to leave."

At the doubt in her eyes, Les pulled his hand back. He needed her. His head warmed, and the room felt as if it was moving. Would she want to get involved with his mess, or would she ask him to leave? His mind flip-flopped between his need for her help and his desire to keep her safe from the strangeness that had become his world, his life. "I understand if you want me to leave. I won't be mad. I want you to know that I asked Jesus to help me, and when

I turned on my phone, I had a missed call from you. I took it as a sign from God that I should call you."

Lynn's eyes turned liquid. He watched her fear and anxiety melt away. "Tell me."

Thank you. Les let out a deep breath. "Do you remember when we read John yesterday, and it talked about Jesus performing his first miracle, turning water into wine? Well, I stayed up all night one night and decided that I would try to do the same thing. Somewhere in John it says that we will be able to do greater works than he did. I figured that instead of trying to do something greater, I'll do something he did, and why not start from the beginning?"

Lynn nodded as if this craziness made sense to her, so Les told her how he had turned the water to wine. "That's not the best part. An incredible feeling comes over your body as if you're wrapped in a cocoon of love. Your whole body gets all warm and fuzzy"

"No way!" Lynn's mouth dropped open.

"Not only that, my shoulder has been in constant pain for years since my car accident. The doctors told me that I would never be able to raise my arm above my shoulder again." Les raised both his arms straight up into the air and laughed. "It's a healing potion."

Lynn covered her mouth with her hand, lowering her gaze to the floor. "Okay, so? Why are you so freaked out?"

"Here's the bad part. I got involved with Lila and her father's company. I sold the rights to my healing wine to them for fifteen percent of all annual revenues."

"All of it?"

Les looked away. "Not all of it. I kept one container."

"I don't get it. Why do you feel bad about selling it? Lila's dad will use it to help a lot of people."

"I can't explain the feeling I got when I signed those papers. I felt sick inside, like something was telling me to stop. I felt as if I was signing a deal with the devil."

Lynn tilted her head. "Don't think you're being overly dramatic?"

Les clamped his hands in front of his mouth in a praying motion. "I should have told you about this the other day when I was here. Remember when we were talking about what Jesus would do if he were alive today—going to the children's hospitals and healing the sick children? I believe God gave me that chance with this healing potion, and I blew it. I chose to make money with it instead." Les's legs felt restless, and he stood and paced the room.

Lynn pivoted to face him. "Can you ask for it back?"

"I just finished signing a bunch of legal documents that basically gave away all my rights to the healing potion." He clasped both hands on top of his head.

"You still have some left. You can use the rest to heal children and sick people."

Les stopped pacing and faced her. "Yeah, but I would still feel like I was doing something wrong. I sold out! I'm a traitor! On the ride over here, the story about Judas kept coming to my mind. He sold out Jesus for thirty pieces of silver. I feel like I just sold out Jesus. It's wrong to do only a small portion of what he wants me to do." Les knelt down at Lynn's feet, his vision blurred by his tears of regret. "Don't you see? Jesus gave me a gift, and I sold it for money."

His head dropped with shame, and Lynn leaned forward and held his head in her lap. He began to weep.

295

The *Rocky* theme song blared out, and he yanked the phone from his pocket. Lila. He hit "ignore" and threw his phone down along with his body. He lay on the floor, facing the ceiling. "What should I do now?"

"Why don't we ask Jesus? He's the one who gave you the gift."

"Have you ever heard the voice of God?"

"I don't think so, but I know that he spoke through Mr. Allen, so it's possible. Do you want to try?" She lay next to Les on the floor.

Les turned to her and grabbed her hand. "I don't know how to talk to Jesus, but he's the one with the power, so I guess we should ask him."

The phone rang again. Les crawled over to it and saw that it was Lila again. He hit "ignore" and turned his phone to silent. He lay back down next to Lynn. "Did Mr. Allen tell you anything special about God's voice, maybe what it sounded like?"

"No, why don't you say what you said when you turned water into wine?"

"Good idea. Now if I could only remember. We need to connect ourselves with the holy force. We need to believe that God will talk to us, and he will."

Les took a deep breath before he began his request. "God's son Jesus, I know that through you the holy force is at work, because I've seen it with my own eyes and felt it in my own body."

Tears ran down the sides of his face. "I'm sorry, Jesus, for selling your gift that you gave me, but I need your help. I need direction. I need to know what I should do."

Lynn's body trembled next to him. "I can feel him. God is real. He's all around me."

The book of *Lester*

A white, puffy cloud formed in front of them until it encircled them both. It was as though they were in a dream land, lying in the middle of a cloud, floating in the sky, feeling the complete comfort of God.

Then it was gone. Les's upper body shot up. "Whoa! Did you feel that? It felt like we were floating in a cloud."

"I have goose bumps all over my body. That was unbelievable! I have never in my life experienced such peace and comfort. God is real. God is so real!"

Les's phone vibrated. He picked it up. "Lila."

"Maybe you should answer it."

Les looked at her to make sure she was being serious, then he answered the phone.

"What are you trying to pull?" Lila screamed into the phone. "My father just did some preliminary tests on your so-called healing potion. It's nothing more than a low-grade cooking wine. So where is the real stuff, Les? We had a deal! I want the stuff that I saw heal your leg."

Les laughed into the phone. Was Jesus answering him already?

"Stop it! We had a deal. I want the real stuff, or we'll take you to court."

For once, she didn't have the upper hand. Les laughed again into the phone. "I gave you the real healing potion. That's the same stuff that I used to heal the cut on my knee, a lady's cancerous tumors, and my friend Jerry."

"Liar! That's impossible! What you gave us is cooking wine. Cooking wine can't heal anything." Lila went quiet for a few seconds. "I'm sorry it didn't work out between you and me. You're a smart guy, and I think you did the old switch-a-roo on us when you realized you were getting only fifteen percent."

297

Her voice turned small and quiet. "Listen, I can respect that. You got us. You want to play hard ball, so let's play. What do you want?"

Les hesitated. His healing potion was nothing more than cooking wine? That didn't make any sense.

"Are you still there? I'm asking what you want. Let me make it clear. You can have anything, and when I say anything, I mean anything. I'm willing to do whatever it takes to get this deal done."

"Give me a minute." Les put the phone down, resting it against his leg, and looked at Lynn. "They think it's cooking wine. What should I do?"

Lynn whispered, "Ask for it back."

Les nodded. "This is what I want. I want my cooking wine back."

"Well, you're not getting it back. You already signed that crap over to us. Besides, my father already destroyed it in a fit of rage."

"What? How could you do that?"

"What do you care? It's a bunch of old cooking wine that you probably bought at Super Mart."

Les hung up the phone. He felt the blood drain from his face. "They destroyed it."

"All of it?"

"All of it. Her father ran tests on it, and it came back as nothing more than a low-grade cooking wine. They think I was playing hard ball with them to get a better deal"

"Are you sure you gave them the right containers?"

"It's not like I have cooking wine sitting around my house."

"At least you saved that one container."

Les stood. "I know what I gave them. It was the healing potion. I know it. I used it on myself right before we left. It healed my leg and arm right in front of Lila."

"Could it have gone bad?"

"I left the stuff I used in the car. It was unusually warm." Les paced the living room. "Wait a minute. That container is still in my car!"

"Did anyone else have access to your healing potion?"

Les stopped pacing "Jerry. He broke into my house before I got the rest of the healing potion. They said that he was drinking some kind of juice when they caught him. I wonder if Jerry switched all the healing potion with cooking wine."

"Jerry broke into your house?"

He gave her the details. "My old friend might have just saved the day. I'm going over there and get the wine. Grab a jacket. We have a healing potion to get."

CHAPTER TWENTY-NINE

==

Both Abella and Jezatra whispered into Jerry's ears, influencing his mind so they could control his actions.

Stop it. Go away. Leave me alone. Jerry's mind was entrapped. Somehow the women had disabled his ability to send messages to his body. It was as if they had unplugged that area of his brain.

"Lester has been spotted pulling into the complex." Beezle stood at the bedroom door, glaring at the two women. "Get your tongue out of his ear. Get focused!"

In an instant, Beezle composed himself. "Here's the intelligence we've received. There is a possibility that Les has a container of the potion with him in his car. Gretchen's source saw him bring it with him after they left the restaurant. We need to flush out the container. And, by the way, make sure the host looks normal. Don't blow it. If you need to reveal, then reveal. This is where we make our stand."

As Beezle hurried out of the apartment, the two women propped Jerry up to a seated position. Then they pushed him up so he was standing. Both women climbed inside of his body. His legs were a little wobbly at first as the women became adapted to their new human host.

"Make sure his eyes are open," Abella said.

"I know! What do you think this is, my first rodeo?" Jezatra threw Jerry's arms up in disgust. "Wench, you do your job and I'll do mine. I'll work his body movements and his eyes and you work his brain and speech. You've been around him the most, so make sure you do a good voice."

300

"Make sure he doesn't fall down. I feel like I'm inside a wet noodle." Abella snapped back.

"I hate you. I usually work alone. I hate sharing the glory. You think that because you're young and pretty, everything revolves around you. If I wasn't assigned to work with you, I'd gouge out your eyes with my nails. Do your job so we don't have to look at each other anymore." Jezatra took Jerry for a few practice laps around the bedroom so she could get used to his motor skills. Soon she had him walking semi-normally.

Beezle ran back into the apartment. "We have a slight problem."

Both women looked at him through Jerry's eyes.

"He brought some woman with him. It doesn't look like Elizabeth, so I think we're okay. Just improvise. I'll be in the bathroom."

A knock sounded at the door. Jerry limped into the living room and to the entry. Abella cleared Jerry's throat. "Coming." His voice sounded as if he had a sore throat. He unlocked each of the locks and opened the door.

"Hey, buddy, what's going on?" Jerry stuttered a little, but his voice sounded almost normal to him.

"What's wrong with you? Your eyes are all bugged out, and your face looks lopsided." Les frowned at him in a way he'd never seen before. "How high are you? Your pupils are dilated so much, I can't see the blue in your eyes."

Lynn stood close behind Les, peering around him at Jerry. "Are you okay? You look sick."

"Why would I be sick?"

"Because you look totally trashed, dude."

"Me? No, don't touch the stuff."

"Dude, you are acting so weird right now."

"You're weird, dude." Jerry turned his back to Les and Lynn and limped his way into the living room. Lynn was still standing behind Les as if she was afraid to come out from behind his protection.

Les slid into the living room with Lynn close behind him. "What have you been doing? What's up with that huge hole in your wall?"

"Well, I got to hang out in jail for a couple of hours. Then I had a nice, cold, two-hour walk in the dark. That was blast." Jerry could feel the bones in his face shifting.

"Maybe I shouldn't have left you there, but you did break into my house. I'm worried about you, bro. Look at yourself. You don't usually hang around in dirty clothes, but you've got red stains all over your shirt. You need to get off the weed, man, or whatever you're smoking. That stuff is making you go insane."

Jerry stood there with his arms crossed in front of his chest, not blinking, staring back at Les.

Les shifted his weight, his eyes cutting to the right. "Why did you break into my condo today?"

"Do you have any of the healing potion with you?" Jerry licked his lips.

"Dude, you are weirding me out."

"I think we should go." Lynn tugged on Les's shirt.

"No, I need to help him. I can't leave him like this."

"Do you have any potion with you?" Jerry rubbed his hands together and hunched his back over.

"Actually, I do. Let me go get it."

"I'm coming with you." Lynn followed Les out the door. "He's wasted."

Jerry stumbled to the bathroom, and Beezle grabbed the front of his shirt and pulled Jerry's face within inches of his own. "Here's the plan. Get the container from Les no matter what. Whatever you do, don't let Jerry drink it. It will kill both of you instantly. Grab the potion, run into the bedroom, and lock the door."

"That's it? That's the plan?" Abella screeched.

"Gretchen hasn't come up with anything better. Just get the potion, and we'll scare them off or something."

The apartment door opened then slammed shut. "Jerry, where are you?"

Jerry came limping out like the hunchback of Notre Dame. "Quit yelling."

"Why are you limping?" Les's brows drew together in a frown. "Why don't you sit down on the couch? I'll bring you a glass of healing wine."

Jerry froze for a moment then followed them into the kitchen. Les had placed the container on the kitchen counter, and Lynn stood by it, watching Jerry with a keen eye.

He stood in the kitchen entryway, staring at the clear plastic container with its red liquid inside.

"Dude, go sit down. We've got this."

Jerry bolted for the container, but Lynn stepped in his way. Jerry bulled over her, crashing them both to the ground.

Les grabbed Jerry by the back of his shirt. "What are you doing?"

From her place on the floor, Lynn kicked Jerry in the stomach.

"You whore!"

Les wrenched his old friend into a head lock, but instead of fighting to pull Les's arm off, Jerry dug his nails into the fronts of Les's arms, opening deep cuts. Blood poured out of Les's forearms, and he tore them away. "What is the matter with you?"

303

Jerry turned around to face Les, standing toe-to-toe.

"You have no idea who you are messing with!" Jerry had the chilling voice of a woman. He drove both fists simultaneously into Les's chest.

Les flew back against the wall as Jerry turned to grab the potion. Lynn was now standing in the kitchen, analyzing Jerry as she held the plastic container in her arm like a football.

Abella laughed from inside of Jerry. With a grin, he strutted closer to Lynn. Then he felt his face contort into all different shapes.

Lynn raised her head and stood tall, holding the container under her right arm.

Jerry now stood a few feet from her, smiling. "I'm going to take that from you. Then I'm going to take something else from you."

Lynn slapped him across the face. "In Jesus' name, come out!"

Jerry's eyes rolled into the back of his head, then they rolled back again. He smiled and started to reach for Lynn's arm.

She slapped him across the face again and yelled. "In Jesus' name, come out!"

A high-pitched female voice screamed from within Jerry as he covered his ears.

"In Jesus' name, come out!"

The next scream dropped Jerry to his knees. Les pulled himself to his feet and stood behind him.

"Go away and leave me alone. I just want to be left alone. I am begging you to leave me alone." Jerry banged his head against the kitchen floor.

Les bent over Jerry and allocated both hands on his back. Lynn placed both her hands on his head, and they said together, "In Jesus' name, come out!"

Jerry immediately felt as if someone had taken all the air out of the room. He gasped for breath as Abella and Jezara stepped out of him. Both women stared at Les and Lynn with their hate-filled eyes as if trying to burn them.

Les reached for the wine. "Let's give him the potion now."

A sound like thunder erupted from the bathroom. "Leave this place! You are not welcome!"

Les and Lynn both stopped as if frozen with fear.

"You are not welcome! You need to leave, or something terrible will happen to you."

"Holy force, be with me now." Les thundered toward the bathroom. "I've got to see what that noise is."

As soon as he entered the room, he felt a dark presence hovering about. It was like walking through a room full of cobwebs. The bathroom door was closed, but the light was on. He slowly turned the knob and swung the door open.

A man with a tattooed forehead lay on the floor in a fetal position, crying. Les jumped back. Who was this freak?

"I'm so scared." The man curled up on the floor sniffled like a baby.

Les kept his distance. "Scared of what?"

"My master is going to be very displeased when he finds out we've failed."

Lynn screamed, and the sound of it tore through the maudlin scene in front of him. Les raced back into the kitchen to see two women holding knives to Lynn's and

Jerry's throats. "Who are you?"

"We are allowed in here." The redhead inched her knife closer to Jerry's throat who laid blacked out on the kitchen floor.

"No, you're not! Not anymore." Les crept toward them.

"If you take one more step, I will slice your pretty little girlfriend's throat." The woman in purple slurred her words as if exhausted.

"No, you won't, because you don't belong here. By the Holy force of Jesus, get out!" Les barreled over to the door and opened it. "I command you to leave, now!"

Both women clinched their jaws, dropped their knives, and stormed out of the apartment.

"You too weird guy in the bathroom, by the Holy force of Jesus, get out!"

The weird-looking guy with the tattoo on his forehead scampered out the door. Les slammed it shut and let out a huge breath as he bent over with his hands on his knees.

Lynn stood there, eyes wide and motionless, with tears rolling down her face. "That was so scary. First Jerry, then those women coming out of nowhere. I didn't even hear them come in. But what was strange is through everything, I felt protected."

"It was the holy force working all around us." Les wiped the sweat from his forehead.

"Don't be intimidated, have no fear, for the Lord is with us." Lynn gazed up at Les.

Les smiled back at her. "Let's get my friend well again." He filled a regular-sized glass to about the halfway point. "That should be enough."

Les clutched the front of Jerry's shirt, raising his

upper body. "Can you hold his head for me?"

Jerry was still out cold, but his body trembled, and now he was foaming at the mouth. Lynn secured the back of his head, and Les dribbled in the wine. It dripped out of the corner of Jerry's mouth as Lynn lowered his head back onto the vinyl floor.

They waited about forty-five seconds. "Does it usually take this long to work?" Lynn asked.

"It usually works immediately. Let's give him some more." He gathered Jerry in his arms and held out the half-filled glass.

A small pecking noise sounded at the bottom of the door.

"What's that?" Les laid Jerry on the floor and scooted over to the door. The tapping sound came from the bottom of the door again.

"What if it's those weird people, trying to trick you?"

Les turned the knob. A large, black bird stared back at him and screeched, flapping its wings. Les jolted back, slammed the door, and locked it with the chain. He then rushed to Jerry, picking up the glass of healing wine on the way.

"What was that?"

"Some dumb bird." The black bird tapped on the door again. "Man, I hate that noise. Lean his head up." Lynn propped up his head so Les could trickle the wine into Jerry's mouth. The tapping sounded again.

"I want to go out there and kick that stupid thing." Les finished pouring the last drop into Jerry.

"Why isn't it working? Are you sure that's the right stuff? Is he even breathing?" Lynn leaned her face down with her cheek next to Jerry's mouth. "I don't think he's breathing."

She pressed the first three fingers of her right hand onto the side of his neck. "He doesn't have a pulse. Call 911!"

The bird outside screeched louder than ever. Les grabbed his phone to call for an ambulance. As he waited for the phone to respond, he stalked to the door. "That's it. I'm going to kill that stupid thing."

He unlocked the chain and swung open the door, ready to punt that stupid bird across the hall.

"Lester." A tall, muscular, blond man with white sunglasses stepped to the door.

Les yelled and flung shut the door, but the blond man easily held it open with one arm.

"Who are you?" Les still pushed on the door.

"I've come to help your friend."

"How did you know we needed help? He's not breathing, and I was calling the ambulance."

"I heard the commotion from where I was standing, and I knew someone needed help. May I?" The man pointed to the inside of the apartment. Les turned and looked at Lynn, but she was busy pumping Jerry's chest with her two clasped hands.

"Come in."

The man stepped inside, his all-white jacket, pants, and v-neck t-shirt gleaming. The only thing of color was his belt. It looked as though it was made of pure turquoise.

"Les!" Lynn yelled. "How soon will the ambulance get here? I need help!"

The blond man took off his glasses. His eyes matched his belt. As Lynn continued chest compressions, he knelt over Jerry as if he was going to perform mouth-to-mouth. He pinched Jerry's noise and tilted his head back, opening his mouth. He then took a deep breath and blew air into Jerry's mouth.

"You're not doing it right. You need to put your mouth on his."

The young man did the same thing again, only this time Jerry's chest started to move up and down. The young man stood, put his glasses back on, and peered at Les. "Don't be intimidated, have no fear, for the Lord is with you."

He then ambled out the door and closed it behind him. Les bounded over to the door to see where the young man in white was going. He was nowhere in sight.

Les looked across the hall, and there was the black bird, lying dead on Mr. Allen's door mat.

"Help me! Please Help me! I'm burning!"

Les ran back inside. Lynn was holding Jerry in her arms as he screamed for help.

"Wake up, Jerry. Wake up!" Les filled a glass with water and threw it in Jerry's face.

Jerry lay still, then he slowly opened his eyes and wiped his face. "I just had the worst dream. I was falling into a dark pit filled with prison cells and coming from those cells where piercing screams of hopelessness. There was no light anywhere. I just kept falling and falling. Then my insides started to burn like I was on fire from the inside out, and then all of sudden I woke up. Hey, why am I all wet?"

CHAPTER THIRTY

==

Les set the glass on the counter and held out his hand to Jerry. Jerry grasped it and Les pulled him to his feet. "I'll help you get some clothes and an overnight bag together, because you're spending the night with me."

"I've got to get going too. It's been a crazy night, and I have to be at work tomorrow by six." Lynn stood and placed the wine glass on the counter.

"I'll walk you to your car." Les held out his hand. They strolled to Lynn's car. She leaned up against the driver's side door, looking up at Les with her beautiful eyes.

"Sorry for all for the craziness." Les brushed a loose piece of hair from her eyes.

"I needed some excitement in my life."

"Just think, this is only day two of our relationship." Lynn's eyebrows perked. "Relationship?"

Les broke eye contact as he grinned. "I like you." He paused for a second. "Okay, I like you a lot."

"I like you a lot too."

"Well, thanks for everything." Les opened his arms, and Lynn moved into his embrace. They stood there in each other's arms. Les didn't want to let go. "I'll call you tomorrow. I have to get back to Jerry."

She snatched Les's hand as he backed away. Their eyes embraced for a few moments longer as Les deliberately released his grip. At that moment, he knew she would be in his life forever.

When Les got back into the apartment, Jerry was sitting on the bed, staring at the floor like a little kid scolded and told to sit in time out.

"Hey, man, what's up?" Les flopped on the bed next to him.

"Hell is real." Jerry's eyes burned. "It started like that recurring dream I have about falling, but this time I was dropping into a never-ending pit of darkness. As I was cascading down, I faintly saw thousands of prison cells built into the sides of the pit. The bars covered the cells, but when you looked in them, you could see nothing but total darkness. The screeching of human voices singed my ear hairs and made up a choir of torment. Then in the background was this low, eerie grinding sound. Kind of like this constant grind of gears as my nerves were thrown into a scorching hot tub of oil, frying the inside of my skin."

Jerry stood and grabbed Les by the arms. "You need to help me stay away from that place."

Les wrapped his arm around Jerry. "Ask Jesus to become your master. You can do it any time you want." Les patted Jerry on the back and bounced up off the bed.

Jerry seized Les by the shirt and held it tight, looking like a frightened child who had just seen a ghost. "You can't leave me until I know I won't ever see that place again."

Les swallowed hard as he gazed in the eyes of his desperate friend. "Okay, Jer." He gripped Jerry's shoulders and slid his eyes shut. "Say whatever you want to Jesus. He is always listening. Close your eyes and say whatever is on your heart."

"Jesus." Jerry exhaled. "Jesus, I need your help. I need you to save me from that empty pit of hell. I don't want to go back there. Help me to not go back to drugs and the things that are burning my soul. I want you to have my soul so you can show me the way I am supposed to live."

311

Jerry hesitated. "The end."

Les opened his eyes. He was looking at a new person.

Jerry popped open his eyes. "I am going to be a better friend. I promise."

"I love you, man." Les said, half-jokingly giving Jerry a hug.

"You're such a dork, but I love you too." Jerry patted Les's back.

"This is awesome, man! We have new start." Les bobbed his head. Jerry joined in on the bobbing.

"Not to change the subject or anything, but I just remembered what I wanted to ask you. Did you take the healing wine out of the containers in my condo?"

Jerry scrunched his eyebrows. "Not that I can remember, but everything is splotchy. My mind is all over the place right now. Look around if you want."

Les looked under Jerry's bed and in his closet. He went into the kitchen and looked in the refrigerator and the cupboards. Nothing.

Jerry entered the kitchen, carrying his bag. "I'm remembering now that I wanted to steal the healing potion, because I wanted you to sell it. But that's all I remember. Why, is something wrong?"

"This stuff didn't work on you." Les picked up the plastic container. "I think it's gone bad."

Jerry grabbed the container from Les and smelled it. "Doesn't smell bad."

Les took it back and smelled it himself. He was right. It still smelled wonderful. He sealed the container back up. "Let's go."

"Wait a minute. What happened to your arms?"

"Nothing. I'm all right."

"Do you at least want some bandages? The cuts look pretty deep." Jerry got some bandages from his bathroom. He wrapped Les's arms, and the two of them walked toward Les's car. *Jerry really has changed.*

"Hey, are you going to work tomorrow?" Les unlocked the car doors.

"I'm going to call in and take some time for myself. I might even read the Bible and clean up my apartment."

"I need to go in tomorrow and talk to Ms. Copeland. I want to give her back her Gideon's Bible. Plus I need to put in my two-week notice."

Jerry's eyes brightened. "You're quitting?"

"Everything that happened to me the past week has made me realize that I was created for more than just being mediocre. When I got into that accident, I thought my life was over. But God was trying to get my attention. He gives and takes away. I believe that he has given me a second chance."

"Me, too."

"You want to follow me home? I might have to work tomorrow."

Les started to drive toward his condo with Jerry behind him. It was good to have his best friend back and have everything right between them again. They had a new lease on life.

He took a quick peek at his phone. He had nine missed calls, all from Lila. He flipped his phone back down on the passenger seat and turned on the radio. How did he feel about not being a millionaire? What was he going to say to Ms. Copeland tomorrow? What was he going to do

313

for a career? What happened to the healing wine? All these questions revolved in his head, but he didn't have answers for any of them.

The two vehicles pulled into his condo development right before the gate. A man stepped out from the dark wooded area surrounding the development. He planted himself right in the middle of the road in front of Les's car.

Les squinted. Who was it? As he rolled closer, he saw it was Charlie, moseying around to the driver's side door, waving his hands. Les rolled down his window. "Charlie, what are you doing here?"

"I'm here to warn you and your friend. This place is crawling with cops looking to arrest him for assault and battery. He broke a man's arm and knocked out his two front teeth earlier today. The police are just now putting together that the man who assaulted this guy is the same one who broke into your condo."

Les banged his steering wheel with the palm of his hand. "What should we do?"

"He needs to go back home and turn himself over to the police tomorrow."

"What? No, he doesn't have to do that."

Charlie pointed his stubby finger at him. "Listen carefully. God has his own plans for Jerry. Don't try to interfere with that."

Les looked away, into the wooded area. Wasn't there a better way? "What should I tell Jerry?"

"The truth."

Les put his car in park and left it running. He and Charlie made their way back to Jerry's van.

Jerry rolled down his window. "What's the matter? The gate broke?"

"Jer, this is Charlie, a friend of mine. He says a

bunch of cops in there are waiting to arrest you for assaulting some guy. They say you broke his arm and knocked his teeth in."

"What? No way!" Jerry flung his body against the bucket seat.

"You need to chill, Jer. Do you remember coming to my condo to get your van?"

"I do, but after that, everything else is kind of foggy."

Les held onto the side of the van as he peeked his head inside. "Look, why don't you head back home? I'll go in, check it out, and give you a call if it's safe, all right?"

"Fine, but I think this is messed up."

Les got back into his car with Charlie. "What are you doing here, anyway? Is your wife okay?"

"Bonnie is fine, thanks for asking. My daughter lives over here. I was visiting her today and saw Jerry at your condo. But that's not important. I have a message for you."

"A message? From whom?"

"From God."

Les raised both of his hands with his palms out. "What do you mean? Why would God send me a message?"

"Are you going to question everything I say? After all you've gone through, do you still think it's shocking that God could send you a message?" Charlie slapped his own forehead. "Look, we don't have a lot of time, so don't talk; just listen. Lila's dad is going to send over a bunch of his thugs to kidnap you. They're going to tear your condo apart in search of the healing wine. All of the wine has been contaminated except for the one in the freezer. The cops hanging around will hold off the thugs for a little while, but what you need to do is get the container to this man."

Charlie handed him a slip of paper. "Here is his phone number. Call him when you leave the complex, and he'll give you directions where to meet him from there. Do you understand?"

"Then what?"

"He'll tell you what to do next. You can let me out here."

Charlie climbed out and disappeared into the wooded area. Les slowly drove through the condo development. Charlie was right. There were cop cars everywhere. He parked his car and was swarmed by police officers.

"Excuse me, sir, but do you live here?" An officer shined his flashlight into the car.

"Yes, I do."

What's your name, and what condo do you live in?"

"Lester John, and I live in this building, number fourteen."

"Do you know a Jerry Humberger?"

Les swallowed as a voice whispered in his head. *Don't lie.* "He broke into my condo earlier today."

The officer nodded. "Thank you. That's all."

As the police officers walked away, Lester hurried to his condo and unlocked the door. He opened the freezer and grabbed the frozen wine. He snatched his backpack from the dining room table, placed the container into the bag, and was out the door within seconds. Looking around the complex, he thought he looked a little suspicious with a backpack, so he kept his head down and looked at the ground. He drew in a few deep breaths through his nose. His bottom lip quivered as he exhaled.

Les got into his car and exited the complex, then he

pulled his car over to the side and dialed the number on the card that Charlie had given him.

A deep, distorted male voice answered the phone. "Take a right out of the complex drive. Go exactly two miles and wait for me behind the discount bread store. Make sure you're parked in the back, between the loading dock and the Blunder Bread truck. Roll your passenger-side window all the way down. Leave the product on the seat and shut off your car engine. We will not approach your car until you have shut off the engine. We are going to give you a package in trade for the product. Do not open the package until you are in a safe, lighted area. Do not go back to your home tonight. It's not safe."

When the man hung up, Les sat for a moment with his heart beating fast. He put his car in first gear, hit the reset button on his odometer, and skidded out. What had he gotten himself into? Why was he trusting some weird guy he met at Super Mart?

Les kept an eye on the odometer as he got closer. Charlie was right about the police looking for Jerry. He was probably also right about Lila's dad sending thugs to his house. The only thing left for him to do was to trust.

He pulled into the discount bread store and drove his car around to the back where the gate with a chain-link fence stood open. He saw the Blunder Bread truck and parked his car between the truck and loading dock.

Les took a deep breath as he rolled down his passenger-side window and turned off his ignition. This was ridiculous. The way he was parked, sitting here in the dark, he couldn't escape.

What was he thinking? What if Lila's dad had paid Charlie to get him out of his condo and away from the authorities so they could quietly take care of him with no witnesses?

A dark shadow moved behind his car. Les clutched his chest. A man dressed in black slipped around the bread truck and approached the car. He reached in the window, grabbed the wine, and threw a package on the floor of the car. Then he disappeared back behind the truck.

Les sat there for a few seconds, gazing at the package on the floor of his car. His heart beat fast, and adrenaline coursed through his veins.

He started the car and backed out of the parking spot as he pulled out, his heart rate slowed to normal. *Now what? Am I some kind of fugitive who has to hide out in a hotel?*

His hands felt dirty as though he'd just completed some kind of black-market drug deal. The hotel next to his work would be the best option for the night.

He needed to talk to Jerry. He scrolled down to his friend's name and hit the dial button. The call went straight to voicemail. "Where is he?"

CHAPTER THIRTY-ONE

===

The night was cool and crisp as Jerry lay on the top of his van, gazing into the heavens. He'd parked only a few miles from Les's condo, behind a mom-and-pop grocery store. The sky was clear, filled with thousands of stars scattered about. It had been years since he had sat outside and admired the sky.

What did the future hold for him? If Les's friend was right and he had assaulted some man, he was looking at prison time. Five, ten, maybe even twenty years depending on what he was convicted of.

Tears poured down the sides of his face. "God, I can't go to prison. Please, God, I'd rather die than spend the next twenty years behind bars."

A shooting star arced across the sky. Jerry watched it disappear into the atmosphere. What were his options? He could run. He could get into his van, drive as far as he could, and start a new life learning about God.

Another option was to confess and beg forgiveness from the man he had assaulted. Maybe he would drop the charges. Maybe he wouldn't. Was he willing to take the risk?

Raindrops started to pelt him as a single cloud blew across the sky. Jerry sat up. "If I run, I'll become the very thing I hate. I need to find out what hospital this guy is in and make everything right."

In his excitement, Jerry slipped on the wet roof and fell backward, landing neck first on the pavement. Jerry stood next to his van then looked down at himself getting smaller and smaller as he was sucked up into the sky.

All of a sudden, he was walking in a meadow of the greenest grass and most luscious rolling hills he had ever seen. Each blade was perfect in shape and color. He reached down to touch it, and it made a sound like a guitar string. He laughed each time he ran his hand over the grass. It had its own different-sounding melody, perfect in every form.

He looked up and saw a man running toward him with a huge smile on his face. He looked familiar, but where had he seen him before? He raced across the meadow like a cheetah, never breaking his big smile.

The man slowed to a trot when he was about ten feet from Jerry. He was a handsome man, with all his features perfectly proportioned to his face. His skin was perfectly smooth without a spot or wrinkle.

Jerry was sure he had never met this man before, but there was something familiar about him. The handsome man strode over to Jerry and wrapped his arms around him. An overwhelming feeling of love came over him.

"Welcome home." The man pulled away and gazed at Jerry. His eyes were not a color Jerry had ever seen before, but they were the most beautiful thing he had ever seen. "Home?"

"This is your new home. Nice to see you again, Jerry."

"How do you know my name?"

"I used to be your neighbor. I was called Eugene on earth, but you used to call me Old Man Al."

Jerry laughed. "I knew I recognized you!"

"Let's take a walk. Someone wants to meet you."

They walked through the grassy meadow together. "So I get a new name?"

"That's not all you get."

When they reached the top of the hill and the massive gates of heaven, Jerry's mouth dropped wide open.

Eugene laughed as he slapped his leg. "They all have the same reaction." He shook his head and smiled. "Just wait. It only gets better."

Les slid the card into the hotel door and waited for the little green light. He turned the handle and walked in. His backpack was slung over his shoulder, and the package rested inside. He placed it on the bed.

What a teeter-totter of emotion this week had been. In just a few hours, he would have to thank Ms. Copeland for giving him that little brown book and a week off. Then he would try to explain to her how God's son, Jesus, changed his life forever. Even though he had no clue what he was going to do with his life, he knew he wasn't satisfied with his current situation.

"I was created for more than mediocrity." Les paused, sat on the bed, and put on his best Yoda voice. "The force is strong with this one, yes."

Lester glanced at the alarm clock on the stand. Two twenty-three. He grabbed the backpack and pulled it open.

The package looked like an old shoe box wrapped in yellow manila envelope paper and heavily taped. After several minutes of struggling with the tape, he tore off the wrapping paper and lifted the top. Sitting in the box was a large stack of one-hundred-dollar bills with a hand-written note strapped around it with a rubber band.

The rubber bands quickly came off as Les examined the stack of money. How much was in there? He deposited the money back into the shoebox and opened the letter.

"'For I will restore health unto thee, and I will heal thee of thy wounds,' Jeremiah 30:17."

He read the second line. "'And I will restore to you the years that the locust hath eaten, saith the Lord,' Joel 2:25."

That was it. Two lines from two different guys. What did all of this mean? The Lord would restore what the locust had eaten?

Les could barely keep his eyes open. He stored the package on the floor next to his bed, set the alarm clock, and laid his head down.

EPILOGUE

==

    The smell of chlorine burned Les's nostrils as he gazed up into the crowded stands to see his mother and beautiful, pregnant wife. He caught their attention and waved. His mother and Lynn waved back.

    He had never felt better in his life. His body had once again become a six-foot-five work of art, molded to skim through the water as if he had fins.

    He took in everything from the huge banner proclaiming the Olympic Trials to the freshly inked tattoo above his heart: a black Celtic cross with a red fish symbol.

    This was it. All the hard work, sacrifice, and dedication came down to this one moment and a few seconds in the water. His adrenaline pulsed through his veins as he stood ready to explode into the water.

    He stepped to the block. "Don't be intimidated, have no fear, the Lord is with you."

    The gun fired and they were off. Les cut through the water like a dolphin coasting through the ocean, leading his pod. His turn was fluid and flawless as he launched himself toward the other wall.

    He couldn't see anyone in his peripherals. This was his moment to put the accelerator down. Water whooshed by his ears.

    Come on Les, go faster, faster. You can go faster. You can do it. You're almost there.

    His long index finger grazed the wall. The buzzer beeped. He lifted his head to see the time.

    Six forty-two?

It's just the beginning. . .

About the author

Andrew Thurber is passionate about seeing people transform their lives through Christ and helping them realize God has given them a dream that matches all of their talents and deepest desires. Andrew and his wife Dawn along with their son Jude will be moving to Denver Colorado in March 2012 to start and pastor Passionate Life Church.

For more information about Andrew and Passionate Life Church you can go to **AndrewThurber.com**

Books in the works

-Perfect Will to the Promise Land
(Non-fiction inspirational)

-Book of Lester part 2 "The chess piece"
(Fiction Supernatural Thriller)

-Jumping Jude (Fiction Suspense)

Dreams can be shattered or restored with one choice. We serve a God of the second, third, and fourth chances. No matter how far away you are from your dreams God can bring them back to life.

Don't ever give up.

The book of *Lester*